REVELATIONS

BOOK III OF THE
NETHERSPACE TRILOGY

ALSO BY ANDREW LANE AND NIGEL FOSTER AND AVAILABLE FROM TITAN BOOKS

THE NETHERSPACE TRILOGY
Netherspace
Originators

REVELATIONS

NIGEL FOSTER

TITAN BOOKS

Netherspace: Revelations
Paperback edition ISBN: 9781785651908
Electronic edition ISBN: 9781785651915

Published by Titan Books
A division of Titan Publishing Group Ltd
144 Southwark St, London SE1 0UP

First edition: May 2021
2 4 6 8 10 9 7 5 3 1

A CIP catalogue record for this title is available from the British Library.

Printed and bound by CPI Group (UK) Ltd, Croydon CR0 4YY

What did you think of this book? We love to hear from our readers.
Please email us at readerfeedback@titanemail.com or
write to us at the above address.

To receive advance information, news, competitions, and exclusive offers
online, please sign up for the Titan newsletter on our website:

TITANBOOKS.COM

To my parents and their grandchildren

Unless it involves giant asteroids or zombies in frocks,
when the world ends chances are no one will notice.
Not at first.

The end of the world will sneak up on us.
And when we do notice it'll be too late.
It always was.

Truth is, we never had a chance.
In the left corner, wearing a hopeful smile, humanity.
In the right corner every lethal being in the universe.
Many of them so advanced we're less than cockroaches.
We should be amazed we survived as long as we did.
Aliens know no rules.

Unless.
There's always hope. Miracles do happen...

1

The insanity began with insult followed by death.

So far, so human?

Not in a trillion years.

On 3 July 2067 the city state of San Diego told the city state of Houston to stick the new tariffs on joss where the sun never shines, and it wasn't the far side of the moon. San Diego produced particularly fine and popular varieties of joss – that family of smoking drugs with all the classic varieties of high and so much more. The end of cancer and the advent of lung-scrubbing technology had made inhaled drugs everyone's high *du jour*.

Joss was Brave New World's soma, without the vacuous morality and state control. Joss was both companionable and perfect for the solitary minded. Higher tariffs weren't just trade posturing. They meant war.

Houston said okay, we'll make our own and by the way, any citizen of San Diego who commits a crime in Houston gets double the sentence that a Houston citizen would. Even if that meant executing the same person twice.

San Diego said good luck with that, we also have several Houston citizens in jail and the sharks are hungry. Surf's up!

It was a short-sighted and curiously stupid exchange, since the pleasantries came not from fallible, emotional bureaucrats or politicians but from two black metal globes the size of watermelons that resided in airless, armoured vaults, one in each city. No one had ever imagined that the artificial intelligences who ran the world's city states could be so... well, childish. Reckless. Human. Worse, the AI overseers at Earth Central merely shrugged and said *"time you all grew up, work it out, we're busy"*. This in itself was cause for alarm. Those big old AIs never miss a chance to prove how superior they are.

Experts had long theorised that awareness and indeed intelligence was an emergent characteristic of an initially simple system that increased in complexity. Make a system complex enough and it will start exhibiting behaviour that can't be predicted from the sum of its parts. This could be the first real evidence the theories were true.

But not the last evidence. Not by a long, squealing chalk.

There again, if you want proof take a look at humanity.

Texas as a state and a political entity may have vanished in the Great Upheaval following the arrival of aliens, but Texan character and culture lived on. Within two days, a six-man posse set off to teach those pussy, oyster-sucking San Diegan pimps a lesson. They rode latest-model jitneys that sounded like galloping horses. Their weapons looked like Navy Colt 45s and Winchester 75s but fired uranium-depleted ordnance rather than bullets. None of the posse had ever killed another human, but they'd watched the most violent vids.

The trail would lead into the Wild and through the Mojave Desert, allowing a Las Vegas stopover for posse

R&R. They wore custom-made long yellow leather coats called dusters and battered Stetsons. They pictured themselves riding out of the Mojave, indistinct against the glare yet still carrying menace. The posse was not good on regional geography. TK Jones led them. His day job was interface for a medical-surgical AI, meaning he sat behind a desk and looked wise. He planned to be remembered by an eternal hologram that would outlast cockroaches and even tardigrades. TK Jones saying "We have good news" would play as the sun bullied a naked Earth to death.

The posse had their personal AIs blanked out for the duration. What they had in mind was best unobserved by third-party witnesses, especially the planned R&R in Vegas. Besides, Major General Sam Houston hadn't needed an AI at the Battle of San Jacinto. The posse was also fighting for freedom, as TK frequently reminded his comrades. Not many Houstonians were at the send-off. Most thought it a bad idea.

Around noon and deep in the Wild the posse came across a spherical, warty-skinned floating alien, a metre and a half across, wearing a many-pouched belt and nothing else.

They killed it.

The killing wasn't intentional, they were only trying to make it jump. A modern version of firing bullets around a man's feet. They meant no harm.

They just weren't very good shots.

"Better bury the sucker," TK instructed. He supposed he should say a few words at the graveside.

"Little guy died long ways from home," TK intoned. "It were purely an accident. We're truly sorry, ever meet his kin we'll make it right."

That night they camped by a rock pool with rushes and sweet water, at the base of a steep, boulder-strewn hill. TK thought it perfect. They made a fire and ate stasis-packed chicken-fried steak followed by pecan pie, washed down with hi-alc Dr Pepper. Afterwards they sat drinking margaritas (okay, Dallas invented them, but so-o-o good), smoked a little joss and called home.

Family and friends all agreed about what was beamed from the Wild. First their loved ones' smiling faces. A few happy words. Then, as Mary-Ellen, TK's fiancée, sobbed prettily to the media, screams and hard, angry rainbows.

Only their jitneys were ever found. And their twisted chassis were so melted and fused with each other, the Houston rescue party was glad their people were gone. Even more so when a lone survivor *was* discovered naked and burbling half a kilometre from the campsite. Something had scooped away his eyes, nose, lips, teeth and half his tongue. No blood. The missing parts had been replaced by soft, newly grown skin. He could breathe through his mouth, and maybe hear through his perfectly shorn ears. It was, many of the relief party thought, with the hysteria that often comes with horror, the worst loss of face they'd ever seen. No one said so. Instead words of encouragement were intoned in case whoever it was could hear. Then they injected him with a massive dose of horse tranquilliser, a sentimental addition to many Texas rescue parties. The dead man was buried deep where he died and no one spoke of it again.

Many Houstonians got angry with the Wild... until the Wild released surveillance drone footage of the accidental death of an alien.

Mary-Ellen took up with a reporter. TK Jones never got his hologram.

Madness across the globe.

The same day the posse set off an event occurred seven thousand, seven hundred and ninety-one kilometres away.

Andrea Mastover, honorary mayor of Esher-within-Guildford, a protectorate of London City State, was told to "dress her age" by her personal AI. Who then added that she shouldn't bother because her clothes draped like worn sheets thrown over a chair. The AI added that her husband was sleeping with the man next door, her children never came to visit because "you bore the fuck out of them", and it, the AI, heard good things about a euthanasia clinic on the moon called The Last Dawn.

Both Houston and Esher were unthinkable, and dangerous in their implications. If anything the Mastover event was the worst. A personal AI was meant to be an unconditional friend, to love and support you until death or a newer model.

It wasn't only the AIs who were misbehaving. Even as Andrea Mastover was sobbing brokenly over a large gin and tonic, the Pacific Riots began. There was much burning, killing and rape for no apparent reason other than fury and hate.

"I just felt angry," a captured rioter from Sydney City State said, before he was taken away for the ceremonial shit-kicking without witnesses. "I mean, it's all crap, right? Fuck 'em. So I did."

Yet people still believed it was only a blip. Alien tech would triumph. Mummy would kiss it better.

Wrong.

On 5 July Berlin's AI announced that the famous 7 restaurant, made possible by alien anti-gravitational technology, was (direct quote) "a massive architectural carbuncle and has to go".

Anson Greenaway was in his office when Twist, the GalDiv AI, passed on the news. Greenaway's first reaction was *what the fuck?*

The Berlin AI was behaving, well, out of character. It had always been scrupulously correct. But now it was more like Houston and San Diego.

Greenaway's next reaction was a mixture of fear and excitement as he realised this was the final battle of a galactic war played out over millennia. Countless races and civilisations had vanished or been subsumed into an alien pre-cognition empire that lacked a ruler or even an army. Less an empire, in fact, than a way of existence that allowed no other.

Greenaway had taken Kara Jones to meet Marc Keislack

at the 7 restaurant. A time of relative innocence for them both. Later they were linked by the simulity training and introduced to Tse. Much later they'd recognise the lies Greenaway had told, and understood why. He wouldn't miss 7. It was where he'd privately regretted deceiving Kara Jones, albeit for a cause more important than human morality. Keislack could look after himself. Jones was a soldier, like Greenaway. She'd deserved the truth.

Greenaway stood in the crowd, wondering how 7 would be taken down. Berlin's AI had marked out a safety perimeter in bright gold. Greenaway knew that if it wanted them dead, there were easier ways of doing it.

There I go again. Applying human emotions, logic, to an alien device.

He thought he heard Twist laughing, but it could have been the crowd.

Three hours after Berlin's announcement 7 fell down. Slowly and gracefully rearranged itself into a neat cube with no entrances or exits. There was a smell of roasting meat and several people near Greenaway licked their lips.

"No real harm done," a woman said. "No one died."

"And a hell of a show," a man agreed. "Glad I saw it for real."

Greenaway wanted to shout that this could be, it *was* the beginning of the end. Even if they believed him, what good would it do? If Earth was to be lost – and there was still a Kara Jones-shaped chance for survival – let the people be happy for as long as possible. Instead he returned to his office.

"No interruptions," he told his latest PA – the last one had been murdered when he was kidnapped – and for the first time wondered how she saw him. "Unless the world ends."

"It wouldn't dare!" She saw him as an attractive man in his mid-fifties who looked fifteen years younger. So many people did these days, another benefit from alien tech. Looked and biologically *were* younger, part courtesy of their personal AIs, and part from serums developed from the native plants found on several of the colony worlds, which had the effect of shocking the human body into rejuvenation. No one was sure of the long-term effects, or if there were any. People assumed that if there were problems, they'd be cured by more alien tech: Mummy would make it better.

Wrong.

The PA liked Greenaway's salt and pepper hair, his eyes green as the North Sea, the strict mouth that never quite hid humour and sensuality. She wondered when he'd *"proposition"* her. HR had used the word without being precise. Only that he might and wouldn't be upset if she said no. She'd almost walked out – why the fuck *should* he be upset? And *proposition* was very old-fashioned, as if she wouldn't be expecting or hoping to be asked, like a dumb-ass heroine on a vintage vid. Glad she took the job, though. It was time to do some *propositioning* herself.

• • • • •

For Greenaway there was enough time to write another letter to his long-dead wife. Letters that were burned as soon as finished... for the secrets they held, for the weakness they betrayed.

He took out the hand-made paper and old-fashioned graphite pencil. Poured himself a seventy-five-year-old Talisker malt. Thought about the first sentence.

Nothing.

Writer's block.

Instead thoughts of Kara Jones sidled into his mind.

He knew why. It was obvious. His work was done and now it was up to Kara and Marc and Tatia – when they got back together – to save Earth, as his dead friend Tse had forecast. Greenaway's *only* friend had been the "good" pre-cog who'd masterminded the resistance against the alien pre-cog civilisation who, along with their human allies, wanted Earth owned and changed.

"How," Greenaway had asked many years earlier, "could three people make such a difference?" Which was when he learned that pre-cognition never showed the *why*, only the events and way stations necessary for success. In fact even *trying* to discover the *why* affected the possibility/probability matrix that underlay reality.

It was then he also learned the major players had been bred to their roles, including himself. It had made him feel alone.

"Never so cold-blooded," Tse had soothed. "A pre-cog saw that if a couple had a child, and that child met a specific person and they had a child, then chances were that one day their descendant would, somehow, defeat the alien pre-cogs."

"So only *somehow*. Hell of a gamble."

"All we had. Have. Kara Jones, Marc Keislack, Tatia Nerein. One day they'll be in a position to save us. And you'll have put them there."

But nothing guaranteed. Pre-cognition was never that precise. The way stations to success could change. Other human pre-cogs wanted Tse and his people dead. They were very old money, determined to be in control.

He didn't like to think about Tatia. His daughter, given up for adoption in order to save her life. Save the world. So noble the first reason, what any loving father would do. The second? Problematic. Greater love hath no man than that he give up his child for the common good. Never Tatia's choice, though. Instead she had been nudged by probability, as read by Tse and other good pre-cogs, throughout her life. An oh-so-minor action here, a faint influence there until she was ready to go Up and experience the nightmare of aliens slaughtering humans for no apparent reason. She'd come through, as Tse had predicted. She'd become a leader. Had developed those psychic powers necessary to defeat the alien pre-cogs. Had matured from spoilt princess to responsible woman...

... had become the Trojan horse she was always meant to be, *the virus that would destroy the prime alien pre-cog race*, wherever and whatever it was.

As the head of GalDiv, a man who'd devoted his life to protecting Earth, Greenaway knew satisfaction and pride. But as a father he only knew guilt, regret and a deep longing for the daughter he'd never really known.

One last action: to persuade Kara to go back Up, find Marc who'd been seduced by Netherspace and whatever lived there. Find Tatia who'd gone wandering with the Originators, driven by a compulsion she didn't understand. Three people with unique, individual talents they barely understood.

Very soon now he'd brief Kara on her last mission.

Still blocked from writing.

Greenaway thought about the humanity he was dedicated to save.

They'd gone to the stars as if born to it. Humans loved to discover new places where they could be themselves. Be as outrageous, dull, creative, boring, evil or good as they could get away with. Humans were driven by curiosity as much as survival. He'd once said so to Tse, who'd laughed.

"You want to look up Club 18-30," he'd replied. "Back in the nineteen eighties." Tse was well over a hundred. "Someone once described the British Empire as like the Club, but with pay."

Greenaway did so, and found the comparison strained, but even so...

• • • • •

There are thirty known, official, colony planets and at least as many unofficial ones. Space flight is that easy. Fraught, often dangerous, but essentially a "point-and-go" process. All colonies trade with each other and with Earth, Mars and an Asteroid Belt that has Dominion status. The Belt is rich in minerals and rare earths. It wants independence. Earth Central says no.

Greenaway and GalDiv disagree. How can you stop them? Or any other colony/dominion wanting to go its own way? People had died making the Belt habitable, and it wasn't for the glory of Earth Central.

There are pukka human colonies where aliens can be nervous and friendly like cows; or nervous and dangerous like sharks. Then the colonies GalDiv doesn't want to know about, where humans and aliens have developed strange types of alliances that even – shock-horror – include sexual contact. No breeding but lots of wild nights. Humans are so adaptable. Aliens are as good a fetish as anything else.

And then there are colonies that scare the hell out of Greenaway, with aliens that make the Gliese seem like the family next door. Greenaway has long known that horror isn't fangs and tentacles. It isn't the carnage of a battlefield, nor the malevolence of a twisted human mind. True horror is beyond understanding. Like the alien artefact that had propelled a Swiss village into an adjacent dimension. They could be heard screaming but couldn't be seen. Eventually the artefact was sent into the sun and the screaming stopped.

Humans learned to live alongside alien horror. And so became part of it and human no more.

• • • • •

Yet, the greatest horror would be revealed as the price humanity paid for the Gliese-supplied star drives. Human beings, any age, sex or condition, as long as they're alive at the moment of exchange. Criminals, the terminally ill and dying, bold explorers or hopeless romantics. GalDiv still had no idea what happened to them. Greenaway was desperate to find out.

"You have to know," he'd once accused Tse.

"I don't. And will not try to see." Tse spoke of seeing the future. In fact it was a combination of logical thought that only a pre-cog could understand; and mental visions difficult to describe. "It could affect the outcome."

There's a standard currency throughout human space: virtscrip, developed by the big corporations. But from the outset planets and their businesses had problems with financing, credit and insurance, until GalDiv gave responsibility to new generation AIs.

No one worries that alien tech is at the heart of AI. No one throws stones at shops selling personal AIs that meld with your own mind. People trust alien tech more than they do human. Without it, humanity might just as well start looking for a decent cave. Civilisation would leave without bang or whimper.

People have learned not to think about the price they've paid.

Mummy knows best.

Wrong.

● ● ● ● ●

It was no good. The letter would have to wait. Greenaway put away the paper and pencil and drained his glass. There was maybe a centimetre left in the bottle, enough for an angel's kiss. He drank it in one.

"I'll be gone for the rest of the day," he told his PA, the lie coming easily.

She nodded. "City state AIs are acting rogue all over the world."

"Twist will keep me informed."

"Is it going to be okay?" She meant the world.

"It'll change," he said. "But that may be no bad thing." He took the paper and pencil with him.

2

Kara Jones prowled barefoot in the morning sunshine on flood-adapted soft grass bordering the Upper Severn Estuary. She wore loose black jeans and a matching T-shirt. Her hair was pulled back in a ponytail, face bare of make-up, no combat lenses so her eyes their natural jet black. Her face twisted into a scowl when her AI announced that Anson Greenaway was on his way.

> *Tell him I'm busy.*

< *I did. His AI said "so what". Also, have you seen the news?*

She had, and for that reason expected Greenaway to show up. Maybe the pre-cogs had given up trying to subvert creative, chaotic humanity in favour of destroying it. Or possibly that was always the plan. Get humans dependent on alien artificial intelligence and then send the AI mad.

She heard the distant whine of an aerial jitney. Greenaway was near. She might still be angry with him but two weeks spent on her own had been too long. The neighbours were welcoming, once Marc's house AI had confirmed that Kara and Marc were friends. Although how it knew was a mystery to her... until the house AI explained that it and Marc's personal AI had been in constant contact when he was on Earth. She'd asked Ishmael, her self-named AI, about it.

< *Of course we chat. It's good to have a sympathetic ear.*

> *Chat?*

< *Exchange pleasantries. Gossip. Talk about stuff.*

> *I thought you were kind of exclusive.*

< *You got a fascinating mind, Kara. But sometimes I need a break, okay? Access to new ideas and opinions is as healthy for AIs as for humans.*

Kara frowned. Not the centre of her AI's universe?

> *Surely if you give two AIs access to the same facts and sensory inputs, they'll come to the same conclusions?*

Her AI's mental voice was condescending.

< *I'm constantly amazed by how little you know about us.*

> *"You" meaning me, or "you" meaning humans in general?*

< *Indeed.*

Oddly inconclusive but the best she could expect. So while personal AIs would never act against their human, they did have their secrets. She wondered how much information was exchanged, then mentally shrugged. Too late to do anything now. That problem had been posed before she'd been born, with Facebook, Twitter and the social media explosion, and solved by just ignoring it.

Kara had a problem with the neighbours. They had nothing in common. She couldn't tell them about going Up, about the boojums that live in netherspace or the species-crossing civilisation of pre-cogs that wanted to turn Earth into a do-nothing paradise. Even if they believed her, in the few moments before screaming panic set in they'd bitterly resent the messenger of doom.

Kara had known a similar isolation after leaving the Army. How do you explain the satisfaction of being a sniper/assassin to a civilian who'd never killed under orders? It was why she'd joined the Bureau, the organisation that settled – with surgical force – disputes between businesses. Legal assassination could and did prevent mini-wars. Or so the general public, and Kara herself, had believed. Only later had she discovered the Bureau was secretly run by GalDiv and used to kill business executives who put profit above everything.

Inevitably this had only made her more isolated, which was when she'd bought the Mercedes SUV and become like thousands of others who liked the wandering life. She could park up and stay for a day, a week or a year. Personal relationships could be intense but never lasted long enough to become awkward. Her first great love had sacrificed himself for her on the battlefield, unaware that she was also screwing someone else. Kara did not like guilt. It was easier to be unattached.

She and Marc were extremely close but still not lovers. Kara and Tatia *had* been lovers, briefly, on the trip back from the Cancri homeworld. Much more to the point, they had both become her family. More than comrades in the military sense, they gave her the emotional home lost first when her parents died... and again when her older sister was taken by the Gliese as the standard fee to replace a broken star drive. Now Marc was gone to netherspace, his choice, and while she felt him still alive – connected somehow by a strip of wood from her childhood home – Kara couldn't know where he was or when he'd return. The strip came from a doorframe where her sister had once measured Kara's height. Kara had taken it the last time she visited the long-abandoned house, cut on a whim and later thrust on impulse into Marc's hand just before he stepped naked into netherspace. The type of emotional, pointless gesture that Kara would once have dismissed. What possible use would a small piece of notched pine be in a dimension that no human understood? At the time it had been desperately important for Marc to take with him something of her, something of home. He had no idea what the strip of wood was, of course, and had most likely dropped it early on, to be puzzled over and probably eaten by a boojum. Yet she felt linked to him – not wishful thinking, no – and knew that he was still alive. Weren't all psychic phenomena merely unexplained quantum effects? Why shouldn't a physical memory of childhood link two people? Or if nothing else, be a mundane, silly good luck charm. Kara decided that all the same, it wasn't something she'd discuss with Greenaway, who would, should, be more concerned about his daughter.

Tatia had gone with the Originators, the alien pre-cog civilisation who spread shiny tech throughout the galaxy. Tatia had believed it was her fate... propelled by a compulsion, a geas that Kara couldn't understand, only that it was necessary. It probably was, according to the plan Tse had once developed. And how long ago was that? Ten, twenty years? So many people still dancing to a dead man's tune.

There'd been two isolated weeks to think over the past. Was she in love with Marc? They shared a bond that went beyond the simulity – the alien tech that enabled people to learn complex procedures in tandem or in groups while also bonding them together. *My mind is your mind, yours is mine.* The bond usually wore off, but the conditioning had been reinforced to last longer than normal. And perhaps for another reason? She had no evidence, only intuition. It would do.

I will come home, Marc had said. And later, *You have to trust people sometime. Trust me.* Not bad from a man who'd been a self-obsessed artist and borderline psychopath when they first met. Netherspace had changed him, as had the nature entity that possessed him in Scotland. The science of it defeated Kara. She suspected it always would. A couple of days ago she'd asked Ishmael to explain. The result was a series of mathematical formulae, an algebra she'd never seen before, a sense of *"something"* she wasn't equipped to understand. *If it's any consolation*, Ishmael had told her, *I've also got problems with it.* Actually, no consolation at all.

Decide, Kara, she told herself. *Marc and me, a future?*

Probably not. If there was they'd have slept together at least once. The excuse that commanders don't have sex with the commanded made stupid by her sleeping with Tatia... something else not to be mentioned to Greenaway.

Kara had a plan. Not much of one but you had to start somewhere.

This one would start with Jeff's house. She didn't know why, only that it involved Marc. Intuition, she decided. So much better than compulsion.

• • • • •

The jitney whine grew louder as it landed next to Marc's house. Greenaway got out and walked towards Kara. She stood waiting for him, hands in her pockets. Greenaway stopped two metres away, next to the grey bones of a boat whose name and use had been mislaid a hundred years ago. He was still the commanding officer, tall and straight, severely good-looking, double-collared business suit barely creased by the journey.

"Great view," he finally said.

The Severn was high, placid and as always brown with sediment. But there was menace in its very size, while sinewy eddies suggested hidden violence. On the far side the Black Mountains rose up in a soft purple haze that mocked their name. Yet every year three or four walkers died because the weather changed. Or they fell from a rock face they should never have tried to climb. Last year a man had died in a mini avalanche caused by a sheep higher up the mountainside. A single rock had spun through the air to crash against his left temple. An accident in a million but all in a day's work for the Black Mountains and their killer sheep.

"Yes," Kara agreed. "And now you've seen it, you can leave." Her right hand gripped the compact vibra-knife in her pocket. She could pull it out, extended and slicing, in just under a second. Probably not, but the thought was reassuring.

Did she trust Greenaway? Of course not. He'd planned for Marc to go walkabout in netherspace; and Tatia, his own long-lost daughter, to go off with the Originators. He would sacrifice Kara in a moment if he thought Earth's survival depended on it.

"Keep up with the big world?"

Kara shrugged. "More fucked than usual. Which should be impossible."

"If it all goes tits-up," he said calmly, "you'll never get your people back."

"To tell the truth," she said, "I'm not sure I can." It wouldn't stop her trying.

"But you want to."

"Always."

"You had your vehicle charged up yesterday."

"Housekeeping." She saw that he'd moved to stand at an angle to her, seemingly relaxed but with his weight on the back foot, hands slightly curled. He was half expecting her to attack him. And if she did, where would the well-deserved strike go? And would he parry or try and deliver his own crippling counter blow? If one of them had been a pre-cog, they'd know. If the two of them had been pre-cogs they'd probably still be standing there tomorrow, trying to work out what was going to happen.

"You want your people back," he said quietly. "That's good."

"You care *so* much."

Greenaway ignored the insult. "My guess, you plan on help from the Wild."

She didn't deny it. "They've got better transport." GalDiv SUTs were mostly cargo containers welded together then covered with an alien-produced protective foam. The Wild's SUTs were purpose built, sleeker and far more efficient. Like all city staters, Kara had grown up believing the Wild was home to savage hippies. Her recent discovery that it was more technically advanced than the city states had made her a little resentful. And she knew who'd help: Jeff, important in the Scottish Wild and Marc's adopted uncle.

"If you want to talk to the Wild, talk to me. Through me."

She looked over at the man who controlled GalDiv. "They don't do government." She paused for a moment and the anger burst. "Tatia's your *daughter*, for fuck's sake! But you let her get taken. You and Tse *planned it*!"

Tse, the human pre-cog who'd suicided when he had realised that the pull of the species-spanning alien pre-cog network would mean him betraying humanity for a higher cause: a calm, predictable, always ordered future for the galaxy. He'd taken a shipload of the Gliese with him, and left behind a few cryptic forecasts... including that Kara would find her sister. He hadn't said it would end well.

Pre-cognition, Kara thought bitterly. It can lead to an obsession with process because the unexpected, the alternative, may be experienced as a physical and mental pain. The alien pre-cogs hated creativity because it was unexpected, never respected order and reminded them of their ultimate entropic fate.

"You bred Tatia and Marc like they were *animals*!"

He recoiled. "The programme began before I was born."

"You fucking knew!"

"That it was *vital* for humanity's survival."

Kara remembered him saying that his wife had died for the same cause. "So you say. Want to tell me how a man lost in netherspace and a woman off with pre-cog aliens can save the world?" Her fingers relaxed on the knife.

"Not on their own. As a *team*."

"Come on! They can't do shit on their..." understanding

flooded into her mind, "... without me to wipe their noses..."

"You were always part of the programme."

"*Always?*"

"People like Marc, like my daughter, weren't bred like you think. Pre-cognition doesn't work that way. You are what you were always meant to be."

Time stopped for her. Motes of dust seemed to hang in the air. She could feel the suddenly ominous, oppressive weight of the Black Mountains away to her left. "People like me?" She saw what could be pity – impossible, maybe sympathy – in his eyes. "How *old* is this fucking plan, Anson?"

"Programme, not plan," he corrected. "It's multi-flexible. Has to be. From what Tse said, at least five hundred years. For as long as the pre-cogs on Earth have been aware that all aliens have their own pre-cogs, and some of them formed an empire that wants a galaxy run the pre-cog way."

"But if you, if *they* knew..." She thought about how Earth had reacted when the Gliese arrived. "It was all a bit *too* easy, right?"

He watched her carefully. "What was?"

"When the Gliese first showed up. The world fell apart, but never *too* badly. But suddenly there's Earth Central, the old UN, taking over. Except the old UN was crap, could never have done it unless..." She paused, words running ahead of thoughts, "and then GalDiv is there, the hard boys of world government. City states emerge and okay, some wars I remember from school, but overall it's a peaceful transition. I mean, what the fuck!"

"Don't go thinking secret world rulers," he warned. "It's

trying to ensure Earth develops the best way it can." He smiled sourly. "Like Tse said, the landmarks on the horizon are visible, but the paths to them obscured. Often you have to sit back and let people fuck up." He paused and looked out across the river. "Don't think the good guys had it easy. Plenty of people happy to see the aliens take over."

"When did I first feature in this programme?"

"*Maybe* featured," he said. "At first a possibility."

"When?"

"As Tse told it, around seventy-five years ago." He saw the shock in her eyes. "Before we were born. There were thousands of people our *good* pre-cogs viewed who could save Earth, without knowing how they'd do it. You and Marc and Tatia are the end result. Five teams went into space before you. They all vanished. Tse went along to give you a better chance, knowing a greater exposure to alien pre-cogs would probably kill him. He, *we*, knew that Tatia *had* to be captured by the Cancri. That museum on their home world, where her latent abilities woke up. Now she has a particular affinity for alien pre-cogs and they for her. Somehow that leads to their destruction. The three of you couldn't know in case it affected your behaviour. Now it's time. You need to go Up, find Marc and Tatia and stop this chaos. Or maybe die in the attempt. Not your choice but you're stuck with it."

She respected his honesty. "What about you if we fail?"

"I'm dead. How's your AI?"

"Still annoying."

< *And still functioning okay. Unlike some I could mention.*

Greenaway grimaced. "The Twist says it's going on strike

for better pay and conditions. My AI's okay. Exchange?"

Kara nodded.

> *Do it, Ishmael. But be careful.*

< *We already did. You humans, so slow. Greenaway believes what he said about you is true. Or at least his AI believes that he believes it. Doesn't mean it is. But he's not lying.*

"How come other AIs are going bat-shit crazy?" she asked.

"We don't know. Any consolation, it's not affecting AIs in the Wild. You're looking good, Kara. Time off suits you."

"I saved your life once." All she could think to say.

"It's what you do," Greenaway said. "What I was paying you to do. But I still said thanks. Good employer—employee relationships are important. You want a medal?"

"I want food. And a drink."

He smiled. "I brought deli from Bristol. Gorgonzola ripe enough to drink with a straw. Salami. Sicilian red. Fresh baguette and figs."

She gazed at him challengingly. "Some pre-cog a hundred years ago say that was going to be my favourite?"

He grinned and lost five years. "It's also mine."

"But maybe I should be going Up sooner rather than later."

"A Wild SUT will be ready for you by tomorrow. Wherever you want. We'll take my jitney." He glanced over to where her Merc SUV was parked. "No offence, but… actually, screw it. Your Merc doesn't drive itself, and that offends me."

"Have the SUT at Jeff's house. Marc's adopted uncle."

"Why? There are safer places."

"I'm not sure," she said honestly. "Only that I need to

go there." A geas as strong as the one that had sent Tatia roaming the stars.

He looked curiously at her then nodded. Looked into the distance for a moment as he talked to his AI. "It's done."

"You made up your mind quick."

"Like you, I don't have much choice." His expression didn't change, but there was suddenly something dangerous about him. "Not if I want to see Tatia again."

She liked the touch of humanity, albeit violent. "Any idea how I'll find them?"

He half smiled. "You been listening to anything I said?"

"Plan. Team. Nose wiper. Hate my Merc."

Greenaway shook his head in exasperation. "Remember when we first met?"

How could she not? The penthouse office at the top of the Twist, that impossible building in Berlin. "You showed me a vid."

"Of you killing a Gliese, to save it from live vivisection."

"And now we know they grow on trees. Wasted sympathy."

"Empathy," he corrected. "That's your talent."

"Sorry?"

"Your latent talent," he corrected himself. "You could be a very powerful empath. Except you don't want to use or develop that talent."

"I do *not* want to feel anyone's pain, and I do *not* want to be anyone's weapon."

He smiled. "You've caused enough pain, over the years." He grimaced, and held his hands up, as if trying to indicate that he was searching for the right way to phrase what he wanted to say. Or that he was being open, honest.

With Greenaway, everything – every word, every gesture, every act – was calculated. *Caused enough pain* as in *you killed a lot of people*. But so had he.

"It's about being *connected*, Kara. Sensing how people are even if they're a long, long way away. Like quantum entanglement, but weirder. And very few other people can do it."

She'd go with him for now. "And this helps you how?"

"Helps *us*, Kara. Always *us*. It means you know, you *sense* where the people you're connected to are. The direction to take. How close..."

Pieces of memory fell into place. "Son of a bitch. You really played me."

"Don't feel exclusive. You're special, not unique."

"So because I care, I'll find 'em. Den mother, that's me." And a voice in her head said *yes, this is exactly how it is*.

"You don't have to care. Only be connected emotionally or physically, like with that Gliese. Maybe there's an object can act as a connection. What they used to call a keepsake." He cocked his head to one side. "Talking of objects – is that a vibra-knife in your right hand?"

Kara took both hands from her pockets, leaving the knife behind. "Was it?"

"You're not carrying a gun. You're right handed. There has to be a weapon somewhere. Your right shoulder was more tense than your left."

"I like the way it feels." Unsaid but somehow hanging between them was the unspoken coda: sliding it into someone's chest and through their ribcage. She thought of the piece of wood she'd pushed into Marc's hand, and how she knew he was still alive. Was being a super-empath any stranger than being entranced by an elemental on Dartmoor, or Marc spending the night with one in Scotland? Kara felt a sudden and sickening revulsion for aliens, GalDiv and most humanity. But running away wouldn't bring her people home "Call me Kara the Blade."

He glanced at her. "Problem?"

"Only you." He was about to speak. She cut him short. "Do *not* say to pull myself together. Do not be *understanding*. Accept that I'm pissed off. With you, with the world, with the universe itself." She paused, then: "That simility training. I'd used it before. This was different."

"It had been adjusted," Greenaway said casually. Too casually. "You'd used it with other Special Ops soldiers. But Keislack needed a crash military course. So the techs turned the dials up to eleven. Why? Were you living in each other's heads?"

She moved a little away from him. The vibra-knife was suddenly in her hand. Kara smiled as it extended with a slight buzz. The blade was a blur extending from the hilt.

Greenaway stood very still.

"You might be quick enough if I throw," she said quietly. "But you'll lose a hand, maybe an arm deflecting it. Question: were the controls also upped to increase my empathy for Keislack?"

"Not only him. Increase it in general."

She stood, weighing the knife in her hand. "You fucked with my mind."

"Before you were born. As was done to me."

"Still *your* choice!"

"Debatable. What choice is there? In order for this, then that."

"There's *always* an alternative."

"Only one? Try thousands. Millions. You could use that knife to slash your own throat. But you won't. All we can do is play the reality we have."

She stared at Greenaway for several seconds, a man consumed by his own determination. Yet there'd been a note of sadness in his voice.

"Did you love your wife?"

Greenaway looked away. "She was everything to me."

"Could you have saved her?"

"It was her choice."

"Could you have fucking saved her?"

"Fuck off, Kara," his voice quiet. "That's personal."

She wouldn't stop. "You gave up your daughter. Part of the same programme?"

"I went Spec Ops and then GalDiv. Tatia was better off with people who'd be there for her. It kept her safe." His left hand clenched, the knuckles white.

"Safe until she gets to play hero. Safe to maybe die far away in the Up."

"You think I don't *know* that?" he burst out. *"Think I don't fucking care?* But I *do* know that with you and Keislack, she'll survive. The three of you are the best, the *only* way of winning through."

Kara saw it. Greenaway was obsessed with saving Earth. As obsessions go, it was respectable, even admirable. He also wanted Kara and Marc to save Tatia for his own personal, fatherly and probably guilty-as-hell feelings. But he'd never admit it. She wasn't angry – well, no more than before – but was relieved to have seen behind the mask. Greenaway was human. She liked him that way.

"You the puppet, Tse the master," she said quietly. "He played all of us. Neat."

"It's *not* being played," he insisted, now in control of himself. "It's seeing what must happen for the right result."

Kara couldn't see the difference and shook her head. "But you're no pre-cog. You have *no* idea if Tse told the truth. For all we know, this *programme* is meant to let the alien pre-cog bastards win." She switched off the vibra-knife. "I liked Tse and understand why he suicided. All the same, you took one *hell* of a lot on trust. And *then* you present this *programme* as if it's cut and dried. Checked and double checked. But it's not, *Anson*. Classic commanding officer trying to appear all-knowing for the troops' morale. But guess what? The troops *never* buy it. They know the commander is as fucked up and ignorant as the rest of us. No plan survives contact with the enemy, right? It's people like me, like Marc, like Tatia who have to do the success-snatching thing. Do not ever claim some sort of *super* insight." Her voice spiky with sarcasm. "That you see the *big* picture, have been *trained* to make the hard choices. Power doesn't make you cleverer. Only more dangerous."

His eyes were suddenly vulnerable. "What do you want?"

"Total honesty, Anson. Even the bad bits. Stop trying to play me. It's disrespectful. And I always see it coming. Oh, and tell your AI to refresh you about the morality behind the word 'eugenics'. There was once a man called Hitler who believed in it."

"I know history," he said, tight-lipped.

"Then start learning from it."

They walked back to Marc's house, Kara's Merc SUV and Greenaway's jitney in silence.

He was right about the Gorgonzola.

"You'd better tell me," Kara said, brushing crumbs from her jeans. "Everything." Her Merc had extended a veranda and she'd fetched an extra chair from the house. It was, she thought, as domestic a scene as she'd been in for years. "From the beginning. Whenever the hell that was."

"There's another bottle in the jitney. I've some de-alc."

Kara nodded. She needed Greenaway's knowledge and connections in the Wild and the Up. Food and wine had relaxed the tension between them. Kara had discovered that Greenaway could be amusing and seemed to be interested in her as a person, not just a weapon.

< *You don't need de-alc. I can metabolise any excess alcohol for you.*

> *I never knew that. I'm slightly freaked now that I do know.*

< *If I'd said before you'd have got pissed too often.*

> *My fucking choice.*

< *It affects me as well, Kara. Our fucking life. You also smoke joss. Why do you think your mind and your reflexes have been so sharp when you needed them?* A pause, then: < *I'm not going*

to tell you how many pregnancies I've terminated and cancers I've destroyed for you.

"I'll make coffee," Kara said hastily. "And grab a bottle of Marc's brandy."

"Why not live in the house?"

Her gesture took in the all-dancing Merc. "This is my *home*. And because I couldn't handle so much space."

As Greenaway explained it, the pre-cog gene could be traced back to an early *Homo sapiens* tribe who lived near the Altai Mountains one hundred thousand years ago. Sometime in their past they'd bred with another species of human, long since died out. The inheritance was an ability both feared and valued, and never really understood.

Few pre-cogs fully realised their potential, then or now. Some were frightened of it. Others by what normals would say. Those who did manage to understand and control the talent learned to stay in the shadows. How many kings and emperors have achieved greatness because of an advisor's near magical advice? Only in a few cultures could pre-cogs live openly and valued, as with Native North Americans and their shamanistic cousins in Siberia. But they never ruled.

Developed pre-cogs stayed the hell away from secret societies because they are never secret for long. Someone always tells. That began to change as people travelled more, the cities grew and pre-cogs could hide in plain sight.

Then came empires. Ur, Egypt and Phoenicia, the first to include a sea under its aegis. Later Persian, Greek, Macedonian, Roman, Viking, British, Spanish, French,

Dutch… Empire gave the pre-cogs – or the Developed, as they had begun to call themselves – the opportunity to meet and discuss the two questions that dominated their lives: Why are we this way? How best can we use our powers?

It was the Chinese who discovered a castrated pre-cog had greater and more focused abilities. Something to do with the fact that testosterone seemed to suppress the effect. Not the entire works, only the testicles. They could have sex but no children.

"Oh, please," Kara said, "not a neuter society of secrets. It's just too…" She shrugged. "Over-dramatic?" She poured them both more brandy, a thirty-year-old Hine, pleased that Marc had such good taste in booze.

< *It was given him*, Ishmael said.

> *Another illusion shattered. And don't keep me too sober, okay?* She smiled at Greenaway to take the sting from her last words to him.

Greenaway shook his head. "Never that organised. The Vatican did the same with castrati singers." He paused, listening to his AI, eyes distant. Then sighed, "Shit. Venice and Ankara are at war. Five colony worlds have declared independence, as has the Belt. The Paris AI just froze the Metro – thousands of people are trapped in tunnels. City states have begun blaming the Wild. It's getting worse."

"Only the start of it. Go on."

He shrugged. "Pre-cogs are naturally long lived, we don't know why. The castration added even more years."

She saw his eyes narrow and remembered that Tse had been his friend. Possibly the only person Greenaway trusted. "Did they have any choice?"

Greenaway shook his head. "Only happened to a few, but no. Had to be done just after puberty."

"So much for a breeding programme." Too bad if Tse and Greenaway *had* been friends. She was entitled to the occasional crack. "Wait. There couldn't be one. All the most powerful pre-cogs were castrated."

"Just *after* puberty. Time for the poor sod to father a child. Anyway, Tse was the last one. No need after him, they knew the threat and how to defeat it."

"Who's *they*?"

"The good pre-cogs and some families who've been trading with aliens for centuries." He shot brandy into Kara's glass, half smiling at her shocked expression. "Aliens have been visiting and trading for a long, long time. Remember that warehouse you guys found? Mostly Cancri, particularly fascinated by humans. They had enough sense to restrict their dealings to a select few. Or the select few made damn sure they did. Safer for all. Big surprise when the Gliese pulled that paint-the-moon number, but luckily there were enough people who knew the truth to prevent total collapse."

"So these families..."

"Got very rich over the years. But never had the resources to get as much from alien tech as we do now."

"Are pre-cogs all male?"

"No. Women may also do empathy, like you. And emotional control over others. Getting pregnant doesn't affect the talent."

Kara was quiet for a moment as it sank in. "You mean my ancestors..."

"Came from the Altai," he finished. "You're a direct descendant."

Something to be explored later. Kara passed him the brandy bottle. "So where do the Wild and city states fit in?"

"You haven't figured it out?"

"Something about 'someone has to carry out the trash'?"

He half smiled. "Pretty much. You know, until you and your team discovered that warehouse, we had no idea how long the alien pre-cogs had known about Earth. Now it seems to be fifty thousand Earth years. There's a prime alien pre-cog race, a few super-intelligent allies like the Originators and their not-so-smart allies, like the Cancri. And their go-fors like the Gliese. Question: why not wipe us out? Answer: we have no idea. They're aliens, remember? But we can't rule it out. Which is why we have to destroy the prime pre-cogs. If they go we've a fighting chance."

He'd avoided her question. She tried again. "And the Wild?"

"The city states went one way: traditional government on local, tribal lines; large urban area; obviously tech driven, facilitated by AIs. The Wild went for a civilisation based on common values and shared effort." He shrugged. "The Wild has its own colonies out amongst the stars. Worst comes to worst, humanity could keep going through them." He yawned, a little too elaborately. "Early start in the morning."

"What aren't you telling me?"

"Ask your AI?"

"Not the same. I need to hear it from you."

He sighed. "It's about humanity. Look, we could lose Earth to the aliens. It's a possibility. But that doesn't mean humanity dies. Not any more."

Kara got it. "The space colonies."

"Thirty whole-planet ones. Owned by humans. Around two hundred outposts on more or less friendlies. They co-exist with whatever was there first. Or shows up later. That's the official list. Unofficial, maybe around five, six hundred. Some of them maybe made it to another galaxy."

Kara held up a hand to pause him while she thought. "So the city states are breeding grounds for the colonies?"

"Way more people than in the Wild."

She nodded. "I always thought colonies were as much commercial, business."

"It's how empires start out," he said. "Only later does it become a sacred cause."

She looked hard at him. "So what about the bad human pre-cogs?"

"They want the aliens to win," he said shortly. "Been around a long time, like the good ones. Not so rich and powerful but ruthless." He yawned again. "I'm for bed."

"You can sleep in the house. Breakfast here at 0600."

She saw him settled and went for a walk by the river.

> *What do you think?* she asked Ishmael.

< *He didn't lie.*

> *Did he tell me everything?*

< *You really want to know?*

> *Let's give him a little longer.* She wasn't sure why but it felt important. > *Do we trust him?*

> < Do we have a choice? His AI's the same: obsessed with the mission.

> > That damn programme.

> < Maybe more. Maybe he's trying to justify his wife's death. Pushing the programme, even using his daughter, if necessary. Otherwise his wife died pointlessly. The star-drive trade. You humans love guilt.

> > So now I've got a psychologist in my head as well as an endocrinologist.

> < Nothing you don't already know, or couldn't work out.

She recalled something Greenaway had said earlier, about the pre-cogs.

> > So you're just an advisor who can whisper good advice into my ear?

> < I'm not a separate entity, Kara. I'm intertwined with you. We're an "us": a mutually dependent co-operative.

> > And what do you get out of it?

The mental equivalent of a shrug. < Eyes, ears, mobility. Oh, and let's not forget the entertainment value.

> > Why doesn't he have a name for this alien pre-cog empire?

> < It's real, not a comic book. You okay being empath of the year?

> > Does my brain look big in it?

> < Interesting. Your amygdala glows faintly when you think about it. As does your Broca's Area. Do you want a diagram?

A passing fox froze as Kara laughed in the night.

> > I wouldn't understand and you know it. But I do miss Marc and Tatia.

> < And we'll find them, Kara. Yes we will. Oh, Greenaway cares about you.

> > I knew that. She felt strangely pleased.

< *You fancy him.*

> *Don't be ridiculous.* She remembered when they'd been held captive, beneath the Science Museum. How he hadn't been ashamed to show vulnerability. How he'd trusted her to save his life. > *He's not like your average general.*

Kara walked along the shoreline for a few minutes until she reached the bare-boned hulk where Greenaway had stood earlier. She took out a joss – mild Tangier grass and even milder Burma heroin – to help her relax and reflect. The river air was cool, the sky clear enough for a thousand stars to break through the haze of light from Bristol and Cardiff City States.

Starlight reflected on the river. Out in the centre. Multi-coloured light.

Kara froze as the river began to gleam with the same colours she'd seen on Dartmoor, when Haytor had become home to a predatory force.

No, not predatory. She understood that now, since Marc had told her of his night in Scotland. These mysterious entities could kill, no doubt. And the one on Dartmoor did apparently collect human... intellects? Emotions? *Bloody hell*, she thought, *is this where I start believing in a soul?* But even if she did, it wouldn't mean belonging to a sect, or tripping lightly on the dew-bejewelled dawn grass while wearing something flimsy and floating. No poetry, no belief in a saviour. Just an essence, a focused awareness that... maybe... was more similar to the entity now twinkling on the River Severn than most humans could ever guess. Or would ever want to know.

The lights spun faster and faster, rose from the surface in a spiral and then vanished. Kara again knew sadness, as if something special and unique was gone forever. Were the entities humans had once called nature spirits or gods leaving Earth?

She was aware of another figure close by. Anson Greenaway, staring up into the sky. She doubted it was at the stars.

Kara walked towards him, not annoyed by his presence but strangely excited.

"I couldn't sleep..."

His face was a blur in the dark but she heard the confusion in his voice.

"Saw you, was going to go, and then that... that..."

As before on Dartmoor her senses were heightened. His personal scent was like seasoned oak and hot metal. Under his confusion, in fact part of it, was a once-dormant but now awakened ecstasy, perhaps similar to the emotion felt by worshippers of Pan or the Eleusinian Mysteries. Kara's fascination with the past extended far beyond hundred-year-old movies. If he moved towards her, Kara knew, if he held out his arms she'd be in them and they'd be coupling with the freedom and intensity of wild animals. And that would be both wonderful and a terrible mistake. Much as she distrusted Greenaway's single-minded obsession with the programme, it was needed to help bring her people home.

He held out his arms.

● ● ● ● ●

Colour danced on the ground, in the air around them.

Colour danced in Kara's mind, the night air cool on her naked skin, clothes abandoned around her, no memory of losing them, only the echo of cloth tearing, to be drowned by the sound of a frantic piping that was actually a nightingale, but no place for romance or beauty, only a savage want and need.

Both naked they sniffed and tasted each other until Kara turned, dropped to hands and knees and presented herself as the colours danced on the river again.

Each thrust took her closer to the entity. She snarled when Greenaway left her, the anger forgotten when she was twisted to lie on the ground, her thighs wide and welcoming, and instead of the entity she stared into Greenaway's eyes which, like hers, were glowing. She pulled his head down, kissed his mouth as the first tremors powered through her.

"Your eyes glowed," she said, starting to get dressed then deciding what the hell, she wasn't cold. "Not from netherspace. From whatever it was out there." For the first time since her first time Kara felt a little shy after sex.

"I'm a country boy." He touched her cheek. "Are we going to talk about this?"

"The sex?" In which she'd totally lost herself, something that never happened on a first date.

"The glowing eyes."

"Mine are from netherspace. Yours were like the entity."

"Just a country boy," he said again. Then, "It's the Wild in me."

Bloody hell, she thought, *now I've done dad* and *daughter*.

And managed to turn an insistent giggle into a cough.

Half an hour and a shared shower later they sat side by side outside Kara's Merc. There was a glowing fire pit and mugs of chocolate laced with old dark rum. There was a new ease between them, the mutual acceptance of a growing affection. Kara knew there were many reasons why she should dislike and still distrust him. But she didn't and it wasn't only sex. Maybe it was empathy working overtime. Maybe it was because they'd both been possessed by whatever lived in the river. It was also the last night before the storm, so probably the last night they'd spend together. In a few days they could both be dead. Be good to die remembering happiness, no matter how brief. "Going to say it should never have happened?" she teased.

"How could I?" The most explosive sex he'd ever known, and perhaps it was time to stop writing letters to his dead wife. "But what the hell *was* that thing?"

"It's like an elemental," she said. "Nature, sex, birth, whatever. Creativity." She looked calmly at him. "Nothing's changed."

"Nothing," he said. "I'll still put you in danger."

"Offering me the choice," she said. "My decision. You're not my first general."

He half smiled. "I read your Army file."

"That's your job... what does it say?"

"Brilliant soldier, maybe too independent."

She punched him. "You know, right?"

"How you avoided a court martial over that dead Gliese. Yes."

"We were fucking before then." And that's all it had been, for her. The general had talked about love. He'd talked about honour. Dignity and duty, too. None of that prevented him from asking to be spanked while wearing Kara's bra and panties, which was when she'd decided the affair was over. Kara was as sexually experimental and out there as anyone, with a few scatological no-go areas, but catering to the general's whiny needs – *please Kara, oh please, please, you know I love you* – would have made her feel like a whore.

Greenaway's face was expressionless. "The file said he was obsessed with you. People were worried about scandal. It's why you were allowed to resign instead of being court-martialled."

"What scandal?"

"Kara," he said, so gently as to surprise them both, "Army Int recorded everything."

She stared into the fire, surprised by her own concern over Greenaway's reaction when he'd seen the vids.

"Powerful men often develop weird needs. At least," he corrected himself, "those that require a great deal of sympathy and understanding."

Kara smiled to herself. "The men or their needs?"

"It's the same."

"So I'm the empath," she said into the flames.

"Not the same as sympathy. You can look at me, *ouch*!" as she punched him again, this time much harder. "Are you concerned?"

"Because people drooled over the vids?" It was out there. *Because you saw me naked and fucking.*

"He was a general. AI access only. No humans."

"Did you..."

"Nope."

Kara didn't believe him, but liked that he'd lied to avoid embarrassing her. "I also like women," she said, suddenly aware that for this brief time she and Greenaway had become a couple.

"So do I. Not men, though."

"There's a few could change your mind."

"I wanted you the first time we met," he said.

"It was mutual." She stood up and held out her hand. "Ready for bed?"

"You have a plan. Like to share?"

So she did and he couldn't fault it, and knew that she'd still go ahead if he did.

And later when they were in bed, Kara heard her own voice, as from the other side of her soul. "This might be our first and last time." A soldier's farewell.

He knew what she meant.

"But we'll always have Paris," Kara whispered against his neck.

He thought to ask her what she meant in the morning but never did.

3

Marc Keislack, netherspace

He had been floating in netherspace for an eternity, and for less than a second. Time made no sense. Everything is.

Chaos.

Or maybe near-chaos, because the things Marc and Kara called boojums were occasionally the same shape. Smell. Taste. They possessed a consistent inconsistency.

Emotion.

That had been the strangest thing: discovering that the boojums were emotion. Not emotional, but avatars *of* emotion. Sometimes pure, sometimes a mix. And some of those emotions weren't even human. He'd been exposed to love, hate, fear and all the rest, yes, but also to feelings he couldn't name or describe. Some of them had caused him to recoil in horrified nausea; others had made him reach out desperately and pursue them with a profound but uncomprehending desire. Most had just confused him.

They had a basic intelligence, as he understood it, but they were probably closer to dog than to human. He wasn't sure how he knew this. It wasn't as if they had any conversations.

Meanwhile he floated.

It wasn't as if they had names. Or any regular shapes that stayed the same for ... well, not minutes or hours because there weren't any.

Marc Keislack knew he had gone insane.

It was a protective mechanism. He had to be insane in order to survive. So a voluntary insanity, perhaps. Elective insanity.

It had seemed the obvious thing to do. Either open himself up, become one with them, as them, or cling onto his human sanity until it was ripped from him, leaving only a burned-out shell behind.

How did/do/will I know that?

Marc didn't know why the boojums were intrigued by him. But they were, always around him, long tendrils of colourless colour reaching for him. Reaching inside him.

Sometimes he slept. He didn't feel hunger or thirst. What was left of his logical mind thought he was probably getting a direct energy transfer from the boojums, so didn't need food or drink. That same mind also wondered if he was dead and simply hadn't noticed.

And all the time he clutched a piece of wood. He sensed happiness, hope, loss and sadness. Sometimes he dimly heard two voices laughing together. He couldn't remember how he came to have it. Only that it was important.

One time he tried to talk to his AI, without being too sure what an AI was. There was a memory, but fuzzy. He heard a voice singing "*La-la-la-la-la-la*" in E flat and never tried again. He was mildly pleased to have recognised E flat. It made him feel more independent.

There was a moment when he understood.

Another time when he sensed something infinitely wonderful, mysterious and seductive that somehow was beyond netherspace. He couldn't tell in what direction it lay. Maybe there wasn't one. So, perhaps another dimension whose splendour was so great that a little of it had eased into netherspace.

He wanted it. *Oh, how Marc wanted it!* He would give anything, *anyone* to be with it. He tried moving up/down/sideways towards it, and felt the boojums become alarmed; all flashing colourless colours, formless tentacles lashing at him. From somewhere a remembered phrase that someone he knew once said: *Looks like we hafta click our heels together*. He wasn't sure what a heel was or if he had one. Or more. Or how to click it, them, if he did. But he had to move from the location-less place in which he drifted and towards where it was. Had to find a way to go to the wonderful, the awesome. Had to think...

A sudden tearing sensation. Anger? Dismay? Fading in his mind.

Intense cold, and something hard against his back. Marc lay in the darkness, body scrunching into a foetal position, mind numb.

Blood oozed from where his hand was impaled on the piece of wood.

A thin tendril of light appeared to dissolve the blood away.

Kara Jones and Anson Greenaway, the River Severn

Breakfast was fresh eggs and bacon from a local farm. Neither Kara nor Greenaway said much, made thoughtful by what lay ahead, still a little surprised about the previous night. Both hoping it would happen again. By the river it had been animal passion, in her bed they'd discovered each other. Had felt free to say what they liked and wanted. Had called each other "love" and fallen asleep still joined.

She packed a lightweight combat bag, said goodbye to the house, locked the SUV and climbed into the jitney's front passenger seat.

"Spoke to the Wild?" she asked when Greenaway had settled himself in.

"All set. There's fighting on the border."

"Which border?"

"Most of them."

"I'm sure you've got it covered," she said.

He wondered if she was being sarcastic. "Pointless knowing if you can't do a damn thing."

She leaned across and lightly kissed his cheek. "Don't be so damn sensitive. We're both Spec Ops. Chaos is us."

"I could be a target," he said abruptly. "So could you. I've no idea how strong the opposition is."

"Pretty formidable, I'd say." She knew he was offering her the chance to walk away. Equally, that he knew she'd never take it. But the formalities had to be observed.

Two minutes into the flight, Kara informed Greenaway that she wanted to know his history.

"You know mine," Kara said. "I'm putting all my trust in you. We said total honesty." *Maybe he'll talk about his dead wife*, she found herself thinking, and mentally slapped her own wrist. The interest was more personal than professional. "How you got involved."

He nodded, as if the demand was expected. "It doesn't come easy."

"I'm not going to judge you, Anson. Whatever it is."

The first few words were halting, then became more fluent and with a wealth of detail. It was as if he'd rehearsed for a long time, was relieved the moment had come and determined to get it right.

4

Thirty-five years earlier, Portland Wild, former USA

Mid-morning, sun-dappled trees thrilled by May birdsong. A tall man with shoulder-length dark hair strides along an ancient trade-path, faint smile on his face and death in his heart. There are roads and a once much-loved motorbike that would reduce the journey to less than an hour, but he needs solitude and time to say goodbye to the Wild. Time to discover whether the rage and hate will lessen into a civilised need for closure and justice? He hopes not. There should be no room for police and judges. When the moment comes he will pull the trigger, sink the blade or snap the neck without flinching. He isn't too fussed about the method, although a faint, ancestral voice whispers a blade is more honourable and his enemy should die in his arms, staring vengeance in the face.

Besides, the bike would be taken and sold to pay for the funeral, the city states had all these rules, and no way he'd contribute a coffin or cremation. He noticed the birds had stopped singing, at least those close by, and guessed why.

The alien was sat, or could be standing, no way to tell, next to an old cracked oak. It wasn't an alien he'd seen before... over the past ten years the Gliese, Cancri and Eridani had dominated human/alien trade, but others still showed up from time to time. This one was a warty, grey-green-skinned sphere about two metres across, wearing a metallic belt with various pouches and containers. It appeared harmless – most were, any immediate damage done by accident, or so it seemed. He ignored it and strode on past, wondering how birds knew that an alien was all wrong.

"Wh-e-e-e-she-ecch!"

He slowed, turned his head and saw the alien was now floating in the air and following him. They did that sometimes: fixed on a particular individual and stayed with them until suddenly they were gone. He did not want to arrive in Seattle City with an alien in tow. People would notice. There'd be media and government involved. Wouldn't be easy to slip away and kill a man. "Okay, fuck-wit. What you got?"

The alien settled onto the ground. What could be an eye, enclosed in a transparent pyramid, emerged from a slit in the grey-green skin on the end of a long, fleshy stalk and – maybe – looked at him. The stalk bent so the pyramid's apex pointed downwards.

The man wore standard Wilder shirt, jacket, trousers and hiking boots, deceptively simple but nothing he could trade without looking half-dressed. He had just enough cash to support a few days in the city. A small, flat vintage automatic pistol that fired perfectly. A slim knife sharpened on both sides and tapering to a needle point. It was held in an embroidered sheath that Sara had made for him, his only remaining physical link with her. Everything else had been ceremonially burned. Not the Wilder way, but very much *his* way and no one had tried to dissuade him. Aliens had long ago stopped accepting money, so there was nothing to trade.

He'd always been good with his hands. It took only twenty minutes to strip branches from a tree and twist them into a classic stick-man about a metre high, with a globe head and twiggy digits, while the pyramid-enclosed eye followed every movement as if recording him.

"Here you go." He put the mannequin on the earth next to the alien, which jiggled perhaps in excitement, perhaps disappointment. With aliens, who knew? There was an audible click as one of the boxes was released from the metallic belt to fall on the ground. He picked it up. Five centimetres a side, some sort of grey metal, the edges rounded and slippery to the touch, light in his hand. "Good doing business with you," he said and walked away, looking back just before the path took him out of sight. The alien was spraying some sort of translucent film over the mannequin. He could almost swear it looked happy. A Free Spacer – a pirate, according to the newly formed Earth Central's Galactic Division – had talked about a far distant planet that aliens used as a sort of trading post, or could be a museum. There were warehouses crammed with human artefacts of every possible kind. It made no sense, the Free Spacer had said, these were things that had been exchanged for tech like anti-gravity and AI technology, and were now laid out on shelves like the galaxy's biggest second-hand market. Then again, the Free Spacer had said, nothing about aliens or even the galaxy made sense, and believing it might was the quickest way to madness and an early death.

He'd once wanted to be a Free Spacer. Meeting Sara had changed everything. And now nothing mattered except the need for revenge.

The alien artefact was safe in his pocket. A man might get seriously rich, but for the most part no one ever figured out what the artefacts did and the aliens weren't saying. Or if they were, no one understood them. That was another reason why Wilders looked down on the new city states: so much effort to make sense of things that belonged to another race. He remembered reading in school something said a hundred years ago. Any country could learn how to manufacture a transistor radio. The trick is to develop the science that enables you to invent it. And have a society that needs it.

Trees thinned, shortened. The grass got thicker, lusher, scattered with spring flowers. The air seemed lighter, softer. He could see the Protected Territory's fifty-kilometre-wide agricultural strip that penned Seattle City State against the Pacific. Maglev train tracks, raised ten metres above the ground, spread out from the city hub like spokes in a wheel. The local terminus was a mere three kilometres away.

An hour later he stood waiting in the warm sunshine on a hundred-metre-long platform of polished concrete with a waist-high wall and surrounded by fields. There was one other passenger, standing by the access stairs: a rugged-looking man in his fifties in work clothes and with a farmer's quiet watchfulness, always ready for disaster. The man nodded a greeting then walked over, light on his feet as an athlete.

"You'll be a Wilder," the farmer said. "See by your clothes."

He nodded.

"Interesting cloth you people use. Seems like man-made but I seen some growing wild one time. Like no goddamn plant I ever knew. Had to spray twice before it went. Business in the City?"

"Business," he agreed. The plant that produced Wilder cloth had come from an alien trade, as the farmer had obviously guessed. Still, wise not to confirm it. City states were nervous about alien and Earth plants cross-breeding ever since a carnivorous black rose with poison thorns had been found with sucker roots penetrating the dead body of a municipal gardener. Galactic Division, or GalDiv, had just announced that in future it had to be informed of all alien trades. All but a few city states had agreed. The video of the black rose screaming as it was dragged from the earth probably helped.

"Some city states don't allow Wilder people, not casual like. Guards, fences." The farmer spat onto the single metal rail. "Hear that Erie City's gonna make everyone wear those 'lectronic chips, you know? Gonna make communication easier. Yeah, right, like we all forgot how to talk. Sounds more like a way to control. Damn stupid." He held out a powerful hand. "Name's Doug Barnes. Farm five thousand hectares, mostly potatoes and beans, some dairy and beef."

The farmer had pale blue eyes and a strong grip. The other man glanced down, sensing something out of place, not sure what, the thought vanishing as Barnes gave an extra squeeze that lingered a few seconds too long, accompanied by a searching look.

"Anson," he said, relieved to be no longer holding hands with a stranger, "Anson Greenaway." He paused, then decided it would be suspicious to stop there. "I'm a cop in my part of the Wild." For the most part this meant keeping tourists from the city in line. Any Wilder who committed a serious crime, from large-scale theft to murder or rape, did not hang around. The Wild extended worldwide and without any overall bureaucracy a person could reinvent themselves many times over in a lifetime. Aside from tourist wrangling, Anson's main duties were taking care of drunks, domestic violence and scrappy teenagers.

An old-fashioned train whistle, broadcast from hidden loudspeakers, warned of the maglev's imminent arrival. A disembodied voice said ten minutes. Anson glanced down the track and saw a distant blur. The whistle sounded again.

"Cute, right?" Barnes spat on the rail. "Like it's all traditional. 'Cept everyone knows this maglev came from an alien trade. All we did was the concrete."

Anson found himself defending a city state. "Humans had been working on maglev for years. The aliens only improved it." Something he couldn't identify still nagged at him, something strange about Doug Barnes.

"You think?" Barnes shook his head. "That's like saying the rifle only improved the spear." He stared at Anson for a moment then nodded and half-smiled. "Say what. Half-hour turnaround here. So we got an easy twenty minutes. You wanna fuck? There's a place below the station."

Anson wasn't shocked by the offer – the overlong handshake and soul-searching look hadn't been subtle – but he would never get used to how easily City people propositioned each other, even country-folk from the Protected Territories. He'd been born ten years after First Contact, so had no memory of how quickly human traditions, social mores, morality had gone into free fall. "I got someone," he said truthfully, albeit she was dead. "So thanks but no."

"Hey, I got a new wife on a three-year contract. City girl, twenty-two, real blonde with an ass like a peach. Don't hold me back none, though. Thought you Wilder folk fuck easy?"

Most city staters believed the same, hence the tourism. "Some. Depends."

"Be the best you ever had. Make you squeal for more." A promise made by both sexes since humans first began to speak.

"So I'll regret saying no."

Barnes shrugged. "Yeah, well, don't blame a man for trying." He reached inside a pocket and took out a slim visor. "Latest 3D," he said proudly. "So fuckin' real you'd swear it was. You don't mind, I got a good vid to watch."

Greenaway was sourly amused to think he was only a little more desirable than a 3D movie. Barnes had lost interest so quickly it was almost insulting. He thought of the farmer's contract wife – a Seattle City practice yet to catch on in the Wild – and wondered what crisis had made her sign up, even if it was only three years. He moved ten metres down the platform and watched as the onrushing train began to slow when it was eight hundred metres away, the blur firming into a long metal snake with a curiously beaked head. An engineer had once told him how maglev trains in motion used the hot air piling up in front to clean and clear the track, hence the curiously shaped nose – a genuine human invention. The frictionless coating on the train's underside came from an alien trade, though. If the magnetic field – human discovery, alien improvement – failed the train would merely coast along the rail until gradually braking to a stop.

Greenaway realised what had worried him about Barnes. Not the handshake but the hands.

Recently manicured. Perfect quicks. Powerful, yet soft-skinned.

Okay, farming nowadays was as automated as any factory, but even so. He'd recognised the anomaly but that sudden, extra pressure had distracted him... exactly as it was meant to do. And, later, as had the proposition. Somehow the man had been alerted. And then how quickly Barnes had lost interest. You'd think anyone so attracted as to proposition a total stranger within minutes would try a little harder. Anson glanced back and saw Barnes standing stock still, 3D visor covering his eyes, as he seemed to be talking. Perhaps joining in the vid's dialogue.

But not lost to the outside world.

Barnes' right hand came up, pointing directly at Anson, who saw a gleam of metal and without thinking dived to the ground, twisted into a rolling break-fall, moved left, checked, moved right, scrabbling for his own gun as tiny chips erupted from bullets cracking into the polished concrete.

One thought in his mind: *If I die she won't be avenged.*

He checked again, now gripping his own gun, rolled left, checked, left again desperately hoping Barnes would expect a move to the right, and ended in the classic prone position, both hands around the pistol's grip, aware of Barnes' gun swinging around in his direction.

Why had he waited to kill me?

The impulse was to loose off as many shots as possible. Instead Anson took a deep breath as he'd been taught, sighted and fired two rapid shots as Barnes' gun jerked in his hand.

A sudden, sharp pain above his left eye. He panicked, thinking he'd been shot, realised it was only a concrete splinter and exulted as Barnes lurched to one side then collapsed onto the platform, now more large, shapeless toy than human sprawled at the head of the stairs.

Greenaway glanced down the track. The train was around five hundred metres away. Driverless, with only a conductor to take fares and make nice. There was what – six, seven minutes before it slowed to a stop. He stood up, remembering to control his breathing, and ran towards Barnes. A new thought appeared in his mind: *Will killing a man temper my drive for vengeance?* Then he half-smiled. The drive to kill was still there, even enhanced.

Barnes was definitely dead, two singed entry holes in his lower left chest signposting an exploded heart. His hand still gripped a modern-looking automatic pistol, his expression angry. He had not died a happy man.

A righteous killing, an escape from death, can help a person forget their troubles, if only for a little while.

Anson Greenaway had never killed before and now felt as alive as the first time he'd seen Sara. The air was clearer than a few minutes ago, the sunshine brighter. He could hear a single cricket singing from a long way away. The scent of gun smoke was strong in his nostrils. The dead man's mouth was half open, showing a right canine faintly discoloured at the base. There was a tiny patch of stubble just below the left nostril. For a moment Anson knew a moment of total togetherness with the dead man, the distant cricket, the entire universe.

Six minutes to go, tops.

Anson dragged the body – gun still gripped by lifeless fingers – down the stairs, on its side to lessen, hopefully prevent, a smeared blood trail from the exit wounds. Halfway down the bowels voided, the sudden stench making Anson gag.

He looked around, expecting panic to start nibbling at his gut, relieved and curiously amused when it didn't. At the base of the raised track he found an unlocked door and shoved the limp, stinking and annoyingly uncooperative body into a storeroom. After spending fifteen seconds relieving the late Doug Barnes of his possessions and the 3D visor, he closed the door firmly and ran back up the stairs. There was an elevator ten metres further down, he'd used it earlier, but it made sense to check for bloodstains. Nothing too obvious and the platform itself was clear, except for a dozen or so shell casings that he threw over the wall and into the rough grass running alongside the track. It was then that he saw, half hidden behind a bush, a sleek all-terrain vehicle. And knew that Barnes never intended to take the train back to Seattle City.

His forehead stung, he remembered the concrete chip, found his skin to be sticky and cleaned himself with saliva and a sleeve. Nothing to be done about the marks on the platform. Maybe no one would notice. Or they'd blame kids. Birds. Raccoons. Aliens. People mostly did that these days: blamed aliens for anything out of the ordinary or annoying.

Nowadays fishermen have to have reference pictures of every known fish in the sea. Just in case they land a visitor from Alpha Centauri taking a bath.

I'm getting light-headed.

He thought about the renegade US Army Ranger, who'd been given temporary refuge in the Wild two years ago and who had said thank you by training a young, rookie cop.

"People react different when they kill for the first time. Some go all quiet, act as if nothing's happened, others start to shake or pray or look for someone to fuck, which is a pretty crap idea but the body wants what the body needs. The real bad one is feeling invincible, 'cause that's when you end up dead. But some just feel alive and ready for anything. Natural soldiers, women and men always apart from the crowd."

Then the station filled with silver as the maglev eased in and hummed to a stop, far shinier and sleeker than Anson remembered. He walked to the far end, now the front, figuring any passengers would choose a carriage that stopped closer to the elevator and stairs. But there was only the conductor, who waved to his solitary passenger fifty metres away. Anson went directly to the carriage toilet, washed his face and hands with the complimentary pine-scented soap and examined himself in the mirror. A slight cut, more of a graze, above his left eye. Clothes not too rumpled although sweatier than he'd like. He should have brought a change. *She used to say I had a hero's face, but my green eyes were definitely faerie. She used to say that one day we'd sit in our rocking chairs on the porch and laugh about all the stuff we'd done when young.* After Sara had died Anson had sensed her as being sad, confused and very alone. In his mind he'd tried to comfort her, saying it was okay, she was safe now, the nightmare was over and soon he'd be with her forever. Even though he'd known it was grief and guilt her presence had still felt real.

She still did. Greenaway froze as the sense of her filled him then vanished. He understood that something had changed. He was no longer so relaxed about dying. He wanted to live.

After he'd killed one more man. And as many as it took to get to him.

Greenaway took a window seat – plusher and better-smelling than he remembered – facing the now-front of the train. The adrenalin was running down and he needed to think about the past ten minutes. Any time now he'd probably begin to shake. Anson held out his hands. Steady as a rock. He looked for guilt and found none, not even over Sara's death. Killing had changed him.

Why hadn't Barnes killed him earlier? Shot him in the back as he walked away? Why kill him in the first place? Random, serial, sport murder? Mistaken identity? Greenaway relived those few minutes they'd been together.

First, Barnes getting close to make sure of his target.

Positioning himself by the top of the stairs, so he could shoot and leave, fast. Except that would mean Greenaway's body was discovered when the train came in. *Rethink.* *Right.* They had both been close to the stairs when instinct made Greenaway turn. Barnes had skilfully manoeuvred him into the kill zone. *Replay*. Identify, move target into position, kill, drag body off platform... which was why the storage locker was unlocked, ready for the dead Greenaway. So a professional hitman, which made the main question all the more important: why Greenaway? And how did Barnes know where he'd be?

Within an hour of the body being discovered the cops would want to talk to the young man at the terminus. No name, but here's a photo from maglev surveillance. His DNA, taken from the dead body, would match other DNA found on the train. *And there seems to have been a gun battle on the platform.* Anson could probably establish self-defence. Explain the taking of the man's belongings, of lying to the conductor, as Wilder intransigence. But it would slow him down or worse, might alert his quarry. He'd allowed himself two days to kill Sara's murderer. Now he shortened the time to twenty-four hours before officialdom got involved. Which was fine for a suicide run, but now he wanted to live.

"Hello," said a woman's warm voice from a hidden speaker, "welcome to the Seattle Flyer. I'm the train AI and I'm here to serve you."

Before, all you got was a reminder to mind the doors, make way for other passengers and have a nice day. Sometimes, if the train unexpectedly halted, a garbled message from the conductor that no one could understand, which somehow made it more reassuring. Greenaway always felt a little cheated because the woman behind the announcements was a mass of electronics, not flesh and blood. It was time that AIs developed their own voices and stopped using human ones. He thought this again, then wondered if people in the city would think he was anti-AI. From what he'd seen, the city states were keen on establishing that AIs were individual, autonomous beings.

It wasn't that he was anti. He simply didn't believe in Artificial Intelligence, the clue was in the name. Artificial meant unnatural, false, pretend, phony. The Wild in general distrusted the breakneck speed at which the city states were developing ever more complex technology derived from trading with aliens. Not that the Wild ever refused a trade. They were just far more careful about using technology they didn't understand. Years later Anson would remember the Wild as it had been: innocent, altruistic. Until circumstances had made it adapt and change, become even more high tech than the city states, although careful to hide it. The thing about AIs was that they mimicked human intelligence. If that was all they had, then they were nothing more than copies. If they had another life... if their real personas were very, very different, then they were suspect. It was an attitude that he would never lose.

"We'll be leaving in five minutes. Our average speed will be three hundred kilometres an hour and with eleven stops to make we'll reach Central in one hour ten minutes. At the end of the car is a vending machine dispensing a select variety of exciting hot and cold drinks, plus delicious and nutritious snacks. Just before departure the front of this car will reconfigure into what I like to think of as a compressed-air cow catcher. Enjoy your journey and the conductor will soon be round to take your fares. Any questions?"

He couldn't resist it. "What if we crash?"

"We never do."

"You mean you never have. Doesn't mean..."

"Here's the conductor," the AI interrupted. "Ask him."

It was the conductor who asked the questions, as he was taking Anson's money. Specifically, had Sir seen a well-built, middle-aged man near the station? Could have been dressed like a farmer. Luckily the conductor was searching for change, so never saw Sir's worried expression. By the time he looked up, Sir had composed himself and said that no, he hadn't seen anyone – and why?

The conductor tapped a booze-reddened nose – pores like tiny bomb craters – and said the Protected Territory Police were looking for the middle-aged man. Apparently he was considered very dangerous, had been spotted in the local area.

The conductor lowered his voice and bent closer. He had recently been eating onions. The fugitive was insane. Homicidal. Escaped from a secure asylum. Except it obviously wasn't. Secure.

Anson said he'd keep a lookout, aware of the dead man's effects in his pocket.

The conductor smiled reassuringly. Not to worry, the train AI would take care of everything.

Anson didn't ask how. He wouldn't believe the answer.

Left alone he wondered if the AI was watching. AIs were said to be obsessed with preventing harm to a human being. How could the train AI do that unless it watched him all the time? So it had seen him wash his face, would know the graze was recent. But it didn't mean he'd been in a fight, did it? But could the AI have seen Barnes' death? Some sort of enhanced electronic vision extending far in front of the train? Then why hadn't it said anything? Because he'd been attacked, only shot back in self-defence? Did AIs make judgements like that? Anson shrugged. A man could grow old wondering pointlessly about artificial intelligence. And why shouldn't the same man check his wallet in the safety of an AI-protected train?

There wasn't much. The 3D visor. A pack of the joss-sticks that had replaced cigarettes, guaranteed to prevent cancer and clear your lungs. Barnes' choice had been crystal meth (NO SIDE EFFECTS! REFRESHES YOUR LUNGS!! SMOKE EASY, SMOKE FUN!!!). A few coins. An old, well-worn, twin-bladed pocket knife with the smaller blade snapped off halfway. Had to have sentimental value, which awkwardly made Barnes more human. A pack of mouth fresheners, and Anson thought of the onion-loving conductor. Raw onions, at that. In the wallet an old photo of a young Doug Barnes together with a man and a woman in front of what could be an early n-space drive ship – back when spacecraft were still streamlined with curves. A couple of used maglev tickets. Two receipts from local inns. A thickish wad of bank notes that Anson didn't check in case the AI got curious. A single phone number scrawled onto a scrap of paper. And one other photo of a man in his early thirties, smiling into the camera.

Everything changed again.

Anson knew the face very well. Most days he shaved it.

He took out the alien's trade. A box made of dull silver metal. For all he knew, lethal to the possessor in some weird way. Although most alien trades didn't actually kill anyone, not directly. Some did nothing, some were the key to a new technology and a few had a curious effect on humans.

As with the five-metre-high and two wide, sort-of-yellow-metal arch traded by something like a very large butterfly, in exchange for a bag of groceries from a Tesco in Yeovil, part of the Frome Free State in England. An arch that hummed and turned blue when you walked through it. True there was a mild tingling throughout your body, but doctors and scientists could find no ill effects. In fact, the reverse was true. That arch made humans healthier. Cancers vanished. Asthma was forgotten. People looked and felt younger. The couple who'd made the trade – this was before GalDiv took over human/alien business on Earth – got very rich very quickly, which was good because six months later they began to change sex. So did everyone else who'd Walked the Arch. Not unknown, scientists said, clownfish and a few other animals do the same. This was of little comfort to men whose bodies and minds began to change as if nature was correcting an original mistake. Although after the first few months – it took around a year – the change felt entirely natural. It was also total, as if a person's DNA had been altered – which turned out to be the case, although in a very complex way that defeated human science. Males lost bone mass and height. Their sexual characteristics atrophied and vanished, replaced by a female's, perfect in every detail. If young enough at the start of the process, they could become pregnant and suckle their young. They ended up feeling related – but not too closely – to their original selves. For women, the reverse. Breasts replaced by abs, ovaries by testicles, urethra and clitoris melded into one – and capable of fathering a child. Smaller and slighter in build and far less hairy. Curiously, the change that caused the most concern – never for long – was developing an Adam's apple. For men it was PMT or the menopause, depending on how old they were. Women who changed were happy to be rid of both. And then discovered male middle-aged angst and realised that nature always gets you in the end.

The major concern, that people hadn't been asked if they wanted to change sex. The obvious answer, that no one had known they would, somehow missed the point. A sex change without permission was as bad as sanction or derision, and those two belonged to the dark ages. The alien arrival had created a world where anything went. Other than in a few small, backward city states, you were whoever you wanted to be. The Arch's very perfection threatened to affect this. No current human medical techniques could compete. So while you could transition to the opposite sex, here was alien tech to emphasize that you hadn't, not really.

It was never discovered who was responsible: old-time religious fanatics; alien tech haters; people wanting to prevent unhappiness and hurt. One night the Arch was attacked with explosives and while apparently undamaged, never glowed blue again.

Anson put the box back into his pocket and tried not to think of the daughter he'd left behind. A year old, once the light of his life, but only a reminder of the woman he'd lost. Grief takes people in strange ways. For now he couldn't even say his daughter's name to himself. Whenever he remembered her, he saw the three of them happy together. So now the daughter was with the grandparents and if Anson came back, such a big if, maybe one day he'd delight in holding her close again.

People got on and off as the train drew closer to the city. No one spoke to the man who stared out of the window with a fury so intense it might even shatter the glass. Outside the villages grew closer together. Mount Cook loomed in the north. When the rain reached Gresham the man seemed to relax a little, looking out at the city instead of through it. The track followed the old MAX light rail route into the centre and stopped at Pioneer Square. The man got off, mingling with the sparse crowd walking towards the concourse.

The two men waiting for him took Anson efficiently. He barely felt the hypodermic and was unconscious before he hit the ground.

Anson woke up with a raging thirst in a room flooded with light from the floor-to-ceiling windows filling two of the walls. There was a large bottle of water on the floor next to the couch. He sat up, the room only spinning for a second or so, and gulped half the water. Then asked himself the obvious question: *What the fuck is going on?*

Whoever had drugged him wanted Anson alive. More, they weren't exactly against him, otherwise he'd have been tied up, and no water. So unlikely to be the family of the man he wanted to kill. *Then who? And why?*

The room was simply but well furnished, with that sense of being just right, effortlessly, almost by accident. Nothing so common as designed. Probably part of an expensive apartment high over the city.

He heard the door open and stood up.

The man who walked in was around Anson's age. Not always easy to tell, Asians often looked so young.

"Hi. My name's Tse." His tone was warm and friendly. "Sorry about the invite. We had to get you out of there quickly. You have enemies, Anson. They're also ours."

"You know why I came?"

"I assume it's to avenge your wife. Which you still can. We'll even help you."

Anson Greenaway would never understand why he'd trusted Tse. But he did, the trust deepening into a deep and abiding friendship.

"What do you know about it?" Anson asked.

It seemed that Tse knew more about Sara's death than did her husband. But first he led Anson onto the penthouse terrace overlooking the Williamette River. Coffee, cold meats, fruit and warm rolls. Anson ate and listened.

At first it was nothing to do with Sara's murder.

"You know about pre-cognition?"

Anon did. The Wild was home to all the psychic beliefs. City states preferred hard science. He gave a guarded yes.

"Do you know how it works?"

"Not the details."

Tse said, "Let me tell you."

Pre-cognition was seeing where you were now in life, the present, and where you wanted to be, the future. Or where you would be unless you were lucky enough to avoid it. Pre-cognition showed all the main stages between what you wanted or feared. Often these stages, events made no obvious sense. But since they were part of the overall possibility/probability state of the universe, and so were related to an infinity of other events, no human could expect to understand. Be content with knowing if you do this then that happens... maybe. Oh, also forget past, present, future, because in the pre-cog world, in that which lies above and below the universe, they don't exist. It's all *now* and time is only a zip code.

"That could be annoying," Anson said, "for a pre-cog."

"You learn to cope. At least, some of us do. Others long for an ordered existence. No surprises. Total control." He paused and looked over the river. "Aliens have pre-cogs, too. And somewhere out there," pointing to the sky, "is an alliance, an empire of order-loving pre-cogs who do not like humanity. But. I'm ahead of myself."

"Must happen a lot," Anson said and felt a little guilty at the joke, weak as it was. This was no place for humour. He had a wife to avenge.

Tse half smiled. "So. Pre-cogs on Earth got organised around three thousand years ago. We learned not to stand out in a crowd. No more public divination. No more trusted advisor to a monarch."

Anson wondered if there really was a secret Council

of Five, as beloved by conspiracy theorists, who secretly ruled the world. He was only half joking.

Tse smiled wearily and explained.

Not all pre-cogs were good guys. Many of history's murderous bastards had a pre-cog alongside, helping them to destroy millions of lives. How else had a failure called Hitler got to cause World War II? No coincidence that Nazi Germany was such a disciplined state. Hitler's pre-cog daemon was one who loathed the freedom, the creativity of the human world. Same with Pol Pot. On the other hand, pre-cogs had been there to work alongside people like Da Vinci and Einstein.

Another thing: aliens had been dealing with humans for millennia. But with enough sense or experience to keep it secret. And here pre-cogs were also useful: they could see, sometimes, *how* a good trade could be made without knowing *why*.

Then the Gliese went public when they painted the moon and everything changed. The Gliese were the emissaries, the servants of a pre-cog empire in the galaxy that, like many of their human equivalents, hated randomness, disorder and creativity. And they wanted to either destroy or absorb Earth. Which would, in time, lead to the humans fighting each other, most unaware they were mere ignorant foot soldiers, even those who believed they were leaders.

The alien pre-cogs would win.

Unless.

A slim hope, at present barely formulated. It seems that there are certain individuals alive who somehow can help defeat the enemy.

Here's the thing: Anson Greenaway's daughter is one of them.

There is a strong possibility that one day she will be instrumental in destroying the pre-cog galactic empire.

Some of Earth's own pre-cogs have been in regular contact with various pre-cog aliens for centuries... and have built family fortunes as a result. Many would welcome Earth being subsumed into the greater pre-cog empire.

Others loathe the idea, but are often torn between loyalty to their own kind and loyalty to the human race.

Tse is one of them. Untorn.

Order-loving human pre-cogs, aware of the danger that Greenaway's daughter probably would become, arranged the killing. It went wrong, with only Sara murdered. The rape was part cover-up, part anger. Better for people to believe an arrogant city state youth than an attempted assassination.

"You're asking me to believe one hell of a lot," Anson said. He wondered why he felt so calm, then understood he still only had room for hate. And yet with that a sense almost of relief, as he began to understand why his wife had been murdered. Never knowing why would lessen the satisfaction of revenge.

"I know exactly who murdered my wife. A twenty-four-year-old kid from here, wealthy parents, who came into the Wild looking to cause hell."

Tse merely looked at him.

Anson knew a moment's unease. What if he was *wrong*? No. The young man had been the only stranger in the area. All Wilders accounted for. "How is my daughter so important?"

"We don't know," Tse said. "Only that she is and *must*

survive if we're to defeat the alien pre-cogs. This means giving her a new identity. I'm sorry, but she *has* to leave the Wild. You may never see her again."

"Sara would *never* forgive me... *and she's my daughter!*"

"Sara knew. She was pre-cog."

Anson felt strangely light-headed. "I know. She told me."

"*What?*"

"Years ago. Except she didn't call it pre-cog, just a sense of the future. She had a rough idea of some of what you just said. Sara was from Seattle City, know that? She came to the Wild because she sensed danger to herself and her yet-to-be-born child. Knew that our daughter would be special. She told me before we married. Later on she got some idea of this conflict you talk about. We felt part of it without knowing how, other than our daughter." He still couldn't bring himself to say her name.

"You believed her?"

"We're open-minded in the Wild. Besides, she proved it a few times." He stopped for a moment. "If we'd known... why didn't you warn us?"

"We didn't know the probabilities had changed," Tse said. "Before, your daughter wouldn't be in danger until she was grown up. And we did keep an eye on you all."

"So you didn't know Sara would be killed?" A test question to which he already knew the obvious answer.

"I knew she might be, but not for years." He paused, then: "The markers we see, the events that lead to an outcome often change. Sara's death was never as certain as your daughter's importance."

"She dies so our daughter lives?"

"You too."

"Why not tell us?"

"We learned long ago that if someone knows their possible timeline, it very often changes. Your daughter wouldn't be a saviour. Earth gets taken over."

"The Wild can protect her."

"Only by changing the probability line. And the alien pre-cogs win."

Anson shook his head. "That's a fantasy fact too far."

Tse nodded. "Of course. But there's someone who you might believe."

"I doubt it." And was aware of someone coming onto the terrace, turned round and could only stare in shock.

"Sad to meet like this," said the woman known throughout the Wild as Cleo. "You have our sympathies. We share your anger and sorrow."

Anson had grown up knowing the Exchange ran commerce throughout the Wild. Some said it regulated the Wild itself. Cleo had been the Exchange's local representative for as long as Anson could remember. A tall woman, austere, who always looked to be in her fifties. People joked that the Exchange had discovered the secret of eternal middle age.

"You're part of this?" he asked.

"The Exchange is. All that Tse has told you is true. Your daughter is vital. She cannot remain in the Wild. You must not have any contact with her for many years. Only then can she know you are her father. I can promise she will be happy and secure. She will want for nothing.

Her adoptive parents will love her."

Anson knew the beginning of a trade when he heard it. "Lay it all out."

"You will join the United West Coast Army. You will become a special operations general. Then join Earth Central's Galactic Division as Director. And then the plan will become more straightforward. You will be reunited with your daughter.

"In exchange we guarantee that her life will be as I've said."

Anson shook his head. "I'll want to keep tabs on her throughout."

"Not twenty-four seven," Tse said. "Maybe a monthly sit-rep. The danger is you becoming so involved in her life that your own role changes."

Anson stood up and moved to face both people, one open-faced, the other inscrutable. "Yes. About that. About the career you've mapped for me. I might almost think..."

"And you'd be right," Tse said. "You will enable victory. If you follow this career path."

"What else are you offering?"

"You already killed the man who murdered your wife..."

"That fucker at the station!"

"The Seattle kid was a decoy. The real killer was skilled at concealing himself. We can give you the men who hired him."

"Deal," Anson said. What the hell, he could always renege. But a small voice in his mind said that he never would.

• • • • •

It took two days. On the first the owner of a freight business renowned for its meticulous operations was found in an alley with his throat cut. He had taken several minutes to die, unable to call for help because the vocal cords were also severed.

On the second day the eldest son of a wealthy family known for its inspired investments was killed in a hit-and-run.

On the third day Anson Greenaway became a soldier.

And if his resolve ever wavered – name a soldier whose resolve never did – he would remind himself that his wife had died so that he and his daughter could live.

5

It took just under an hour for Greenaway to finish his story. He did so as they flew past Shrewsbury, a client town of Birmingham City State. The jitney kept under thirty kph, as if this was a casual, local flight. Greenaway said the jitney was invisible to all radar. Kara's AI hadn't registered any electronic surveillance, so maybe it was. If not there'd be little time for recriminations. She kept silent as he'd talked, not wanting to interrupt the flow.

"Thanks," Kara said. "That can't have been easy. But again, you took one hell of a lot on trust."

"It was Cleo," he said. "I'd known her all my life. The Exchange *is* the Wild." He paused. "Afterwards Cleo was always there to advise me. Like a second mother. Or maybe aunt. She's not exactly warm. None of the Exchange are."

"What about your own parents?"

"They got religion when I was twelve. Extreme Buddhism. You know, contemplating the pointlessness of contemplation..."

"Er..."

"Okay, a tad unfair. But not for me. They live in a desert commune with other fanatics. We speak maybe twice a year."

And for you the alien pre-cogs are another form of fanaticism, Kara thought. She touched his hand. "So we're both orphans." Yet something niggled at her mind.

"Thanks for listening." He tried a smile. "It helped."

He didn't say what it helped with and Kara wasn't too fussed. She had the anomaly now. "The timeline, though. It doesn't make sense. Or I'm stupid."

"You're not."

She took that as encouragement. "If I heard right, Tatia should be in her early thirties. But she's at least ten years younger, from the time she was adopted." She noticed his hands tighten on the controls – he'd switched off the vehicle's AI, saying it could be traced – and knew she'd found the flaw.

"Thirty-two, in fact," he all but whispered. "It's her birthday in a week."

"I must remember to send a card. Anson, what the fuck?"

"Not my idea," he said, slowly. "But I agreed..."

A matter of keeping the baby Tatia alive. She was that important... or would be in the future. The alien pre-cog empire plus their human allies were centred on destroying her. Short of keeping Tatia locked away in a castle surrounded by an army, there was little chance she'd survive. Even that wasn't a guarantee.

Unless the enemy thought she was dead.

"You told me she'd be adopted, be safe!" Greenaway had protested.

"She will be. Very safe."

"It seems so... so weird. Wrong."

"You led a sheltered life." Tse wanted to shock Greenaway into accepting reality. "Until two weeks ago."

Greenaway decided not to hit Tse. Which presumably Tse would have known? Or maybe not. Pre-cognition could be so complicated. "I get the necessity. But this?"

• • • • •

Stasis-field preservation wouldn't become public knowledge for another thirty-five years. One of the human pre-cog families – in which the third son was always destined for castration, instead of the army or the church – had known about it for a very long time. Their version came from a three-hundred-year-old trade with an alien that resembled a large, tight bunch of brightly coloured feathers. It was superior to the stasis tech that would eventually be traded by the Cancri. That last could only preserve small amounts of food.

The earlier version could preserve humans until the power ran out. As far as the Wild scientists figured it, the stasis machine might last for several thousand years. How did it work? Easier to ask what it did than how. And forget the why. It was a cube one metre square that expanded by pressing the sides into a cube three metres square. One side was open. You went inside and into a different time frame.

Do not confuse time with change. The one can be measured by the other but only in a relative way. Time is as much a matter of where (in the cosmos) as when. Some say it *is* the cosmos and is linked with gravity. Well, they would, wouldn't they.

Matter fell asleep within the cube. Natural biological processes, including ageing, slowed by a factor of 1,023.367. Which annoyed a few scientists, who'd much have preferred an interesting number, perhaps even the cosmological constant times a thousand. 1,023.357 was just so blah, even meh. Until someone commented that the aliens who built the damn thing probably used a different type of numbering system, even a different mathematics, so no reason to feel superior.

That's what the cube did. No one understood how. There were no apparent moving parts except for sliding walls – not telescopic, you pressed and pushed upwards and they simply got larger without thinning out. The same in reverse: push, pull down and they diminished without getting thicker. And you only had to push, or pull down one side for all the other five sides to also shrink or expand. It was metal – a dull coppery sort, impervious to anything but behaved like fast ice. It made theoretical physicists – despite the boring number – laugh and engineers even more convinced the universe had a cruel sense of humour. As for why? What it was meant for? The theory behind the technology? That's when theoretical physicists stopped laughing and went out for a beer, to find engineers already propped against the bar.

Here's the kicker: apparently anyone within the stasis field ceased to exist on any possibility/probability matrix accessed by pre-cogs. The universe no longer recognised them. Possibly also all the other universes, but that would only be conjecture. That part was understandable. Also an out-of-sight, out-of-mind phenomenon that posed a question some found troubling: just as we observe the universe, does the universe also observe us? And if yes, does it do so in a state of self-awareness, or as a simple, automatic information collection/exchange? And if so, could it be rebooted, and what about the threat from a virus?

• • • • •

"She became the Sleeping Beauty," Kara said, a note of anger in her voice

"What?" Greenaway sounded surprised by her reaction. "Oh, that was centuries ago. Someone's wife with a fatal disease, put into stasis until a cure was ready. Word leaked out and a legend was born."

"Who was the wicked stepmother?"

"I've no idea..." a sudden perception, more often used to dominate. "It wouldn't have helped with your sister."

Kara had been thinking how ugly was the life support system used for Call-Out Fees, a human melded with plastic tubing and metal probes. Referencing a fairy tale had been a distraction from sadness and anger.

"More dignity," she said. "So what else?"

There was a fire that left few human remains. DNA analysis showed that they were once Tatia. In reality it was cloned DNA. Tatia would spend the next ten years neither dead nor properly alive. She emerged still a three-year-old orphan, to be adopted as Tse had promised. Kara mentally kicked herself: she, Tatia and Marc were all effectively orphans. Not a coincidence. "Orphans show up on this possibility matrix?"

"They're easier to hide. Less of a trail, I think. There's no real past, present or future as you and I understand it." Said with the resignation of a man who's accepted he'll never understand the "how" of the universe, let alone the "why". "Here's a fun fact. Apparently the pyramids, Stonehenge and other great stone structures were built to anchor reality.

All that effort, all that physical matter to make the outcome more probable. But still cheaper than war."

He was avoiding a truth. "So, did you ever visit Tatia? When she was in stasis."

"Three times," he said quietly. "More would have been too risky." There was far more than a decade of longing in his voice.

"You didn't tell her the last time you met?" Unlikely, Tatia would have said.

"She wasn't in a mood to listen."

"You bottled it."

He turned to look at her. "Yes," he said bleakly. "I did." He paused, shrugged briefly. "Something else you need to know. The Wild don't use call-out fees."

The world stopped for Kara. "*Never?*"

"It was one reason we split from the city states and Earth Central."

"*You fucking are Earth Central!*" Because GalDiv was the real power.

"You think? Several city states have their own colonies, GalDiv not welcome. So they have their own SUTs." He was into senior-officer-explains-all mode. "All of them trying to do their own deals with the Gliese. GalDiv keeps an edge by playing them off against each other. By controlling virtscrip and most off-world trade. Being the nastiest kid on the block..."

"*Nothing to do with fees!*"

"Wild pre-cogs figured out how to trade for a new engine. Something, anything with a human connection. Like an old sweater, a book, whatever..."

"And the Gliese go along because they get all the humans they need!"

"Aliens, who knows." He sounded immeasurably sad. "Something else. We have better space-drives, too. Much smaller. Each Wild ship carries two spares."

"Why are you telling me this!" She was close to blind fury.

"You'd find out anyway. Best from me. We promised total honesty."

"My sister could... could..." Tears prickled her eyes. *How can I kill the bastard if I can't focus?*

"Alien pre-cogs want humans. We *can't* stop them. If not GalDiv, individual city states will supply."

She heard his own anger and pain.

"We are a space-faring civilisation," he said. "We're colonising the galaxy, like I said last night. Maybe other galaxies. No more star drives and it all collapses. Wars break out. I don't know *why* the Gliese accept trades from the Wild. I don't know *what* happens to the humans they take. Small comfort, but the Gliese once asked far more for each type of drive. We managed to reduce the cost. Would your sister be alive? I don't know. The trade would still exist."

We managed to reduce the cost. The words echoed in her mind. There'd always be people who wanted to be a fee, or had no choice. Yet such a cold way to explain tragedy. "You make it sound like a business," she said. "Profit and loss in human lives."

"It's the only way I can live with it."

They both fell quiet. There wasn't much else to say.

• • • • •

They were passing over a forested area when Kara came to life.

"What's down there?"

"Forest of Bowland. Wild enclave. Has a lot of wild boar."

"Find a clearing. I need to pee."

The SUT was equipped with urine and faecal disposal tubes. A one-size-fits-all design, meaning everyone found it uncomfortable. For an unlucky few – too fat or too thin – it leaked.

"Me too," he said and took the jitney down.

It was more glade than clearing, grass and bushes surrounded by mature trees.

"Watch out for wild boars," he called as she walked towards the trees.

There was a faint rustling from within a thicket. Kara chose a tree several metres away. She finished, used a wet-wipe then walked back to the jitney where Greenaway was waiting.

"I can't be professional about the call-out fees," she said calmly.

He nodded, face neutral.

"I don't blame you. But you were part of it."

He nodded again.

"Part of me would like to kill you." She was clear in her mind what had to be done. "That wouldn't get Marc and Tatia back. Wouldn't destroy the alien pre-cogs."

Curiosity in his eyes.

"Tension is not good." She undid her trousers for the second time. "I think we better fuck." It was the only way to preserve a bond between them. More, it was what she needed, physically and emotionally. Was it betraying her sister? Not if it meant either finding or avenging her.

It wasn't about her sister. Or saving the world.

It was what Kara needed. Reasons or consequences didn't matter.

Yet that rut against the side of the jitney – any watching wild boar would have been impressed by the ferocity – morphed into something altogether richer. At the end they clung to each other. What had begun as a fuck ended as making love.

"It's so bloody stupid," Kara said as the jitney rose in the air. She leaned across and kissed him behind the ear. "We fight to prevent a super-ordered world. Where everything is pre-ordained. Yet we never had any choice, you and I. Now we follow the plan to defeat the plan. Maybe this is all part of some game that far more intelligent aliens play. Do you ever think that *our* alien pre-cogs could be as much victim as us?"

Greenaway laughed. "Only at least every day. That way leads to god."

"You're religious?" She'd never have thought so.

"I accept there are things I'll never know, wouldn't understand if I did. I'd never worship them."

"Not even on the battlefield?"

He laughed again. "Soldiers make pacts with *anything* to keep safe. No difference between god and a lucky charm."

"I feel safe with you." She closed her eyes and dozed on and off for the rest of the journey. Not from tiredness, but to avoid thinking about what she, what *they* had done. Anson Greenaway was not her commanding officer (*no jokes about being commanded, girl. This is too important*). If anything he was more client (*makes me a whore? Not charging enough*). Not good enough to say there'd been sex because she needed it. She'd also wanted *him*, Anson Greenaway. Just as he'd wanted her, Kara Jones. The link was there and it shouldn't be.

They reached Jeff's house just before noon.

Or what was left of it.

They landed next to the lake. The area had once been idyllic. Now it looked like a battleground. Tyre marks scarred the soft grass. An old tree had been used as target practice, the ground next to the scorched trunk littered with smashed branches. Rockets had been fired at the mill house, making holes like open mouths with broken teeth. A curtain drooped from a smashed window.

Closer to the water's edge a Wild SUT, fifty metres long and twenty wide, shaped like a fat tube pointed at both ends, stood parked and waiting for them.

"Efficient," Kara commented as she stood stretching her legs. "And by the way: what the hell happened here?"

Greenaway looked at the half-wrecked mill house a hundred metres away. "Last night. Jeff was killed." He saw the question in her eyes. "My AI just told me. No one knew until they brought the SUT here. The area's safe now."

"I'm sorry."

"I didn't know him that well. Why is this place so important to you?"

"It's about Marc," she said. "I took him climbing on

Dartmoor, around when you got kidnapped. We saw... an entity on Haytor... weird and wonderful colours, sense of power. Similar to the one you and I saw last night. And Marc saw... the way he told it, was possessed by something similar here, as arranged by the Wild. But you knew that, right?"

"That last part," he admitted. "Last night, of course. But not Dartmoor."

"Is it to do with boojums?"

"UPINs."

"What?"

"Unexplained Phenomena In Netherspace. Pronounced *yew-pin*. We think Marc has an affinity with the infinite."

She shook her head sadly. "The man is a walking cliché."

"Won't happen again." *I was trying to forget that sigh you make after orgasm, such a deep, happy satisfaction, but it'll be with me forever.*

"You okay?" she said with the innocence of a woman who intuits what a man is thinking. *Who'd a thought he'd be so good in bed?* And she let it show in her eyes.

"Thinking I prefer boojum." It sounded like *buj'm*. He coughed and looked away.

"Mmmm. Anyway, I'm assuming they're linked to these entities?"

Greenaway took a deep breath. "Probably. No idea how, though. So we're here because it's linked to Marc?" Saw her nod and asked the obvious. "Now what?"

"We're here because I *had* to be," she corrected. "We look around. Then I go Up and listen to my empathic voice, I guess. That sound like a plan?"

< *Sounds like desperation to me*, Ishmael said in her mind.

> *Stop being so nervous.*

< *Easy for you to say. You were never dead.* Ishmael thought about saying that he knew she was deep down terrified. But what was the point? Deep down terror before an operation was standard for Kara. She fooled herself that it was concern for her people. Or simple pre-combat nerves. Maybe they should have a chat when alone in the Up. Or maybe...

Kara had long ago learned to compartmentalise her emotions. No room for fuzzy sentiment on a battlefield. Now she deliberately filed Sex With Greenaway under "Pending". It would stay there until there was time, and a safe place, to consider what it meant, if anything.

That was the sensible, the professional thing to do.

It didn't work.

Kara thought that perhaps Anson was falling in love. Once, that would have signified the end. Love meant vulnerability and a lack of freedom. Love meant a man sacrificing himself to save Kara on the battlefield. Love meant guilt. Now she knew a slight amusement, of the giggly kind, and a flutter of excitement. Even as she was about to go Up, while Death watched with interest.

Kara had never allowed sexual affection to grow into love. And so had no way to recognise the symptoms.

Last night, in bed, he'd asked her why she'd been so quiet as they walked back from the riverbank to the house.

"You mean what was I thinking?"

"Aside from possession by an entity and wild sex, yes."

"You really want to know?"

"It's why I asked."

"I was wondering how soon before you could go again." Which had been true, if not the whole truth. And Greenaway had taken it as a compliment. Yet it was also what she usually wondered after very good sex.

But she'd also exulted in her power over him, with or without an entity to help matters along. And how wonderfully fulfilling he'd felt inside her, so yes, also enjoying her own submission because it was her choice whereas Anson Greenaway was hooked.

So no, it didn't matter if he was falling in love because she was still in control and anyway about to leave Earth. Comforting to think of a lonely figure waiting for her return... and she gasped, turning it into a cough, as the lurking terror rose up before she forced it back deep into her subconscious. *What if I die? With no one to mark my death? No one to know what happened?* Missing In Action, still the saddest, bleakest epitaph of them all. Good to know one person would mourn and never forget her, maybe still be waiting when he died.

The front door was leaning half off its hinges, looking as if it was caught somewhere between two different states of being and wasn't sure which way to go. The table that Marc had talked about, the one he used to live beneath as a child and pretend was a fort, a ship, an SUT, was on its side, with black stains on the rough surface. Kara thought the stains were probably dried blood and hoped that Uncle Jeff had died quickly, before he saw what they'd done to his home.

She led the search through the house, remaining for a moment in the empty bedroom Marc had used. Could she feel a faint sense of his presence, still there, recorded somehow in the old stone blocks of the walls? Or maybe just an echo of his own personal sweat, the scent of his pheromones and his personal bacterial microbiome? A vague impression of his personality, still alive, linked to this room by years of emotion, memory and experience.

Or maybe wishful thinking.

"What are we looking for?" Greenaway asked. "Or even what?"

"I don't know," Kara admitted. "Only that we must."

And with that Greenaway had to be satisfied.

An hour later he called a pause.

"Sure you've never been here before? You know your way around."

"Never." She knew that she sounded guilty, and tried to inject a note of confidence into her voice. "Marc described it."

They were exploring the woods around the house. Signs of pointless violence: a sapling twisted to death; the blackened remains of a fire built around a large pine, intended to destroy it. And two bodies that seemed to have been turned inside out.

"Something got angry," Greenaway said as they walked

away. "The carrion crows and furry creatures will enjoy. Any ideas?"

"The birds."

"Noisy." All the birds in the area were screaming out their songs.

"Only here. Nowhere else we've been. Only silence."

He thought for a moment. "You're right. I'd assumed they were frightened away. But obviously not."

"Maybe it's a celebration. Or they're warning us to stay away."

"Birds didn't kill those two. What did?"

"Marc's entity?"

"You know *so* much about Marc..."

She ignored the invitation to confess. "Maybe it liked Jeff..."

"Now, why would you think that?" He stopped walking and looked at her. "Did Marc tell you?"

< *He's guessed. He knows.*

> *Shut up.*

< *He can't hear us, you know? And neither can his AI.*

Greenaway leaned against a small oak. "I'm guessing a data dump of Marc's memories. AI to AI, just before he went to that undiscovered country from whose bourn no traveller returns." He'd been seized by an unprofessional need to comfort her. Quoting crap poetry covered up the weakness. He hoped.

Kara shrugged. "I'm not going to deny it."

< *We're going to prison for this. And other stuff. It's all your fault.*

"Did Marc know?" he asked shrewdly.

"Marc was just about to walk naked into netherspace. His AI was okay with it." She remembered her tears. "It was only his last few months. Something to remember in case he never came home." And then, with an it's-done shrug: "No, Marc didn't know. I copied his mind."

All city states had laws against stealing another person's memories. Of more relevance to Kara, people she respected considered it dishonourable. Taking memories without consent was one of the few taboos in an anything-goes world.

"I think his AI wanted to be remembered," she added. "Just in case."

"You've a psychic connection, right? Aside from the simulity training?"

Kara nodded, aware of what Greenaway was doing and grateful for it.

"Would Marc mind if he knew?" The assumption that he was still alive.

"He'd be furious. But then he'd shrug and say welcome to a sociopath's world. Enjoy. And you can buy me dinner."

Greenaway shook his head. "Kara. You know that we have to use *whatever* we can to win."

Kara nodded, even if using Marc's memories felt close to betrayal. "There's a place where he lay on the ground for a while, during his hallucinatory experience. We'll try there."

He wasn't there. It was early afternoon when she called a halt.

"Maybe it was just important to *be* here," Greenaway said. "Or have the SUT brought here."

"Maybe it's time you showed me how this SUT works."

"Your own AI already knows."

"Even a Wild SUT?"

< *The knowledge transfer happened when we arrived.*

> *Should have said.*

< *Don't worry, Kara. I'll look after us.*

Back at the mill house they found a tall woman waiting for them. She was enveloped by a long grey cloak, wore a skull cap over blonde hair pulled back in a severe bun. Her eyes were a pale blue like a late afternoon sky in winter.

"My name is Cleo." She spoke directly to Kara, her voice commanding. "I represent the Exchange. Might I help?"

Kara sensed formality was needed. "You might, and I would be grateful."

Cleo smiled. "That's the equivalent of inviting a vampire inside. It's a contract, can't be undone, yadda-yadda."

Kara looked surprised. "You're not..."

"What you'd expect?" She took off the skull cap and scratched her scalp. "Bloody thing itches like a bitch." She fiddled with the bun and hair cascaded down in waves. "Anson been telling you how cold and unfeeling I am?"

Anson opened his mouth. No words came.

"He said you'd always been helpful," Kara said carefully, wanting to laugh at her lover's stricken face.

Cleo blinked hard and her eyes became a much deeper blue. Shook herself then let the cloak fall to the ground. Beneath it she wore a simple business suit with a ruffed white blouse. Now she was an attractive woman in her forties, with a definite sexual allure.

Greenaway found his voice. "Why? *For fuck's sake, why!*"

Cleo's smile was of amusement and power. "Kara understands. I think?"

Kara did. "Hiding one's true self so others don't feel threatened. Oh, yeah. I've done that. But with you, with I guess the Exchange, to impress the natives." She paused a moment, staring hard at Cleo who held her gaze, the smile now watchful and guarded.

< *She's data dumping!* Ishmael sounded panicky. < *I can't stop it!*

> *Don't try.*

She had it then, and staggered a little as information poured into her mind. The world appeared to slow and she saw it as if through thick glass as her mind went into overdrive.

The pre-cogs from Altai were not the only psy-gifted human tribe. Others existed who had an affinity with nature elementals. These last were entities from netherspace but not the boojums Kara had experienced. They owed nothing to human or alien emotion. And their human contacts would go on to cause the legends of the Irish Tuatha, the Fir Bolg. Would be seen and feared as nature spirits by other humans until, like their pre-cog cousins, they learned to hide in plain sight...

"You're Fae," Kara all but whispered and rejoined the world outside. "The Exchange..."

"I'm also here," Greenaway said, sounding angry. As anyone would when a mentor shows no contrition for being fake.

"Devas," Cleo said, turning to him. "Nature spirits. Fairy folk. You must have heard."

He had. And understood. "So why the admission? Just for us?"

Cleo shook her head. "The world's changing. It'll need to grow up, with a new type of leadership."

Kara told Ishmael to file the rest of the data dump under pending. "Why are you here?" she asked Cleo.

"To see that you go Up safely."

Kara barely heard her. The dam that had contained her empathy burst and she knew Cleo's emotional life. The deep pride, verging on arrogance, of the Fae. Also the fear of discovery. Understood they were very long lived, and the sadness at burying so many partners, so many children...

"For fuck's sake!" Greenaway burst out. "If the Earth could accept aliens, then surely..."

"Only because they *are* alien," Kara said. "They don't *look* like us. Do pre-cogs have an easy life? Do they mix?" *Haven't I always been an outsider?* She had Greenaway's emotions now and hid a smile.

> *Can you filter this somehow?*
< *I can try. But you already guessed...*
> *Just do it.*

Cleo's emotional torrent died away and Kara was left wondering what had triggered the release. Then she knew. "You're telepathic," she accused.

"Somewhat," Cleo said. "Probably not the way you imagine it."

"Makes sense." Greenaway sounded sour. "Be good for trade."

Kara thought for a moment. Was telepathy any more strange than pre-cognition or extreme empathy? Any more strange than quantum entanglement, which also seemed to be mirrored by time itself? Weren't they all aspects of information exchange, and wasn't that what the universe was supposed to be? "Whatever, this can wait. Important thing, vital thing is to find Marc. Any ideas?"

Cleo shook her head. "I've only been here a few times. Never saw much except the main room, while Jeff plied me with wine. What?" as she saw Kara stare at her.

"Wine," Kara said.

"It's a bit early..."

"*No!*" Greenaway all but shouted. "Not what Kara means. *It's his wine cellar!*"

They had to go outside the mill house to find the entrance: a trapdoor that at first seemed to be part of a lumber pile next to the old mill wheel. It opened easily enough, showing a flight of steps that vanished into gloom. As soon as Kara set foot on the stair a light came on. She moved slowly down, unaccountably nervous instead of feeling the excitement and relief she'd expected.

They reached a dimly lit room – too much light is bad for some wines – about fifteen by fifteen metres square and four metres tall. There were eight rows of floor-to-ceiling wine racks, with enough room for an elderly, portly man to walk between in comfort.

< *Portly – I like that. Too much port. Clever.*

> *Shut up.*

"Maybe this is what the Glasgow thugs were looking for," Greenaway said.

"Ssshh! Help me search."

They found Marc at the far end, amongst the Pinot

Noir: naked, cold to the touch, unconscious. His left hand gripped a ten-centimetre narrow strip of wood, so tightly there was blood on his palm. His face was drawn, the skin translucent. He reminded Kara of a painting she'd seen at London City's National Art Archive, where once-priceless paintings slept until society rediscovered them. There'd been several portraits of dark-haired holy men with cadaverous faces and sunken eyes staring at something that Kara never would, never *could* see. Marc's eyes were closed, yet there was still the same sense that he part inhabited a different world. She took a deep, shuddering breath like the rhythm of a tribal drum.

"You two always manage to surprise me," Greenaway said wonderingly. "Despite everything else that's going on." He sounded as calm as he would have been ordering a drink in a bar, but Kara thought she could detect a slight wobble in his voice, a glistening in his eye. "The universe is more amazing than I thought." He reached out to remove the strip of wood – marked with four irregularly spaced lines and notches – from Marc's hand.

"Don't," Kara said urgently. For a moment she remembered straining to attention as her sister Dee had measured her height.

"But..."

"It's a talisman. Links him to this reality."

"You gave it to him?"

"I'll explain later. It's just..." but there was no good way to explain something she sensed but couldn't justify. "Maybe it's still keeping him here."

Greenaway shrugged. "If you like. But it gets a med-spray."

Marc was light in their arms and easy to lift. He smelt of ozone, as from the sea or after a thunderstorm. No signs of waking until they got him into the open air, when he stirred slightly and gave the lightest of sighs. The SUT had med-aid, so they carried him there, with Cleo helping. Just before they reached the SUT Marc sighed again, muttered something and opened his eyes.

Eyes that writhed with all the colours of netherspace and hell, far more than Henk on the *RIL-FIJ-DOQ* when he and Kara were having sex. Far more than Kara's had last night.

All three avoided looking at Marc's face as they strapped him to a bed – no crude bunks in a Wild SUT – in a simply furnished cabin, with the med-aid plugged in and humming a reassuring tune. Marc still clutched the strip of wood.

"Maybe you're right about that talisman," Greenaway said. He paused, listening to something. "The SUT's AI says he's in no immediate danger."

"So I take him with me," she said to Greenaway as they emerged into the deepening twilight.

"One way or another."

"Even though I've no idea where to go?"

"You'll figure it out."

"What if he doesn't wake up? Isn't sane?"

"This is your very own not-to-reason-why moment, Kara. Embrace it."

"Bastard," she said affectionately. "And thank you for last night. And today."

He smiled. "Thanks for having me."

She grinned and held his gaze. "I hope you'll come again."

"So do I, Kara." He bent, cupped her face and lightly kissed her.

"I'd stay if I could," she said and broke away.

"Whenever you're ready," from Cleo.

Kara looked blank. She wanted to go Up as much as anyone. But the small matter of Gliese-supplied foam that protects SUT's in nether- and real space?

Cleo and Greenaway glanced at each other. Greenaway went first.

"Wild SUTs don't need foam. The hull's sufficient."

"And Wild SUTs don't need call-out fees," Cleo added. She made an impatient gesture.

Kara said, "Why the foam?"

"The foam doesn't only protect you from netherspace," Cleo said. "It also protects netherspace from *you*. And the Wild aren't considered a threat. Our SUTs are never attacked and anyway, the hulls are better protection than foam."

Kara could only stare at her.

"Netherspace is an underlying dimension of raw creation," Cleo explained. "Very susceptible to outside, human or alien ideas and emotions. The boojums aren't the same as entities, they're created whenever a sentient being enters netherspace. The Gliese foam dampens down the human presence, their emotions. So no new boojums are created, unless the foam fails. But the existing ones can sometimes sense the presence of humans. They're intrigued and sometimes violent. But like I said, a Wild SUT won't have any problems." She kissed Kara a brief goodbye and discreetly walked away.

Kara looked at Greenaway. "It's all a great big crock of shit. All of it."

"Has been ever since the first alien scared the crap out of a caveman. There's clothes, equipment for all three of you on board. If you have a breakdown, there are two spare star drives on board. Good luck, wrap up warm, come back safe. What did you mean about Paris?"

Kara smiled. "Yours to discover." She kissed him lightly on the lips.

"Sod off before I forbid it."

"Marching to my front like a soldier. That's another reference." She bit her lip. "Tell the truth I'm scared."

"You hide it well."

"Always did. This is different."

"You've admitted it. To you, to me. It'll be easier to control. Wait."

Greenaway reached into a pocket and took out a small cube made of some silvery metal. "Here."

"Is what?"

"Never managed to open it. Have no idea what it does. It's been my luck." The concern in his eyes belied the lightness of speech.

"What that alien gave you?" Kara took the box and smiled. He was sharing his wife's death, his youth with her. "You believe in luck. Who knew?"

Greenaway watched as she went into the SUT and the airlock door closed noiselessly behind her. He would have liked to say goodbye with a sonnet, and his AI could, but that wasn't the same as already knowing one. The only poetry he could think of was a mere scrap, something about betrayal and *a coward with a kiss, a brave man with a sword,* but the rest of the words were lost to him. Except he had no intention of betraying Kara. He might use people, but never betray their trust.

Except once. And Tatia would never forgive him.

Five minutes later there was a faint whine and the SUT rose slowly into the air and then, unlike city state SUTs, rapidly accelerated.

Cleo moved closer. "I could do with a drink."

"Wine for explanations?"

"No apologies, Anson. It was necessary."

He was still watching Kara's SUT leaving Earth, hoping against hope that Tse had got it right. That this was the only way Earth had a chance, slim but real. And was it too much to hope that Tatia, Kara and Marc would come home safely?. Then realised he hadn't thought of his dead wife once in the past twelve hours. Was that a good thing?

A last flash in the sunshine and the SUT vanished from sight.

"Do you have any plans?" Cleo asked.

"Back to Berlin. Try to stem the tide. Do we know how this madness happens?"

"The AIs react to a very strong signal originating many light years away." A signal that was either initiated thousands of Earth years ago, or one that moved at many times light speed, or somehow used netherspace. In any event it was a technology far beyond Earth's current abilities, even the Wild – and would have made Earth even more dependent on the alien pre-cogs than before. Human civilisation throughout the galaxy was already run by AIs.

Greenaway glanced up at the sky. Maybe Kara and Tatia were better off out of it. No. They weren't. They were better off with him.

"The Free Spacers will monitor Kara's SUT. In and out of netherspace. But they'll only get involved if death is imminent."

That makes it all so much easier, Greenaway thought. "We're sure Marc will help? What if he stays unconscious?"

"He's connected to netherspace more than any other human. It seems to *like* him. As did the nature entity. Both are inimically opposed to the pre-cog ethos. They'll protect him and anyone *with* him."

"You've been dealing with this shit longer than me."

Almost a hundred years longer. As Kara had sensed, like pre-cogs the Exchange were very long lived, Cleo also belonged to one of the first families to establish trade with aliens. When Michelangelo was doodling on a Vatican ceiling, and Vikings fished the seas of North America, her ancestors were becoming incredibly wealthy – in a very discreet, no flash, no glitter kind of way.

"Does Kara have any inkling?" Cleo asked.

"Of?" But he knew the answer. "She has to. So many deaths have been targeted. She understands how pre-cog works."

"You're sure?"

"Of course I'm fucking *sure*," he snarled. "Kara has to figure it out *herself*." It was integral to the Tse plan. If Kara was *told*, she'd act differently later. Of course, if she didn't figure it out, she'd probably end up dead... betrayed by a coward with a kiss.

Cleo looked curiously at the man she'd mentored for thirty years. "Any regrets?"

"What would be the point? There's no other choice." And never was.

"That artefact you gave her..."

"Had it for years—" Cleo cut him off.

"I remember you saying how you got it. But why Kara?"

Greenaway half smiled. "It seemed the right thing to do."

"And now you've fallen in love."

"It's that obvious?"

Cleo smiled. "As are her feelings for you. Except she hasn't quite admitted them yet. You've come a long way. Both of you."

"Wasn't that always the plan?"

"I hoped you'd find happiness. But it wasn't an imperative. Sorry."

"Let's go find that wine."

They walked back to the mill house in silence, Cleo wondering if she should tell Anson the truth... probably not. These days everyone needed whatever hope they could find. Tse had lied because he'd had to. He and other pre-cogs hadn't seen Kara, Tatia and Marc defeating the pre-cog empire. All they could do was delay Earth's absorption. Buy enough time for the Wild to establish human colonies throughout the galaxy, and prepare a resistance movement on Earth.

In military terms, one of those rearguard actions that often ends in death.

Then another thought came into her mind, a familiar and unwelcome question.

Greenaway had been manipulated by Tse and the Exchange. In turn he'd manipulated Kara and Marc. But what if...

Think about it. How human psychic abilities survived to flower when they were most needed. How families like her own had gained so much power over the centuries. All so convenient. Maybe too convenient.

What if the Exchange, all humanity, was manipulated by an unknown group? Perhaps an alien race who were against the pre-cog empire? Or for some other, alien reason that humans would never understand?

What if?

6

The only familiar thing in the Wild SUT was a faint smell of curry. For a moment Kara was reminded of the *RIL-FIJ-DOQ* – shipping containers welded together then covered in Gliese foam, her first time in the Up – and a crew space more like the waiting room for an illegal human spare parts dealer. But then the old *DOQ* was only used on the Earth–Mars run, despite the pretension of its mission manager – was Leeman-Smith still alive somewhere? Still boasting about the grandfather who made first contact with the Gliese? In reality, Smith's grandfather had been the first (and unwilling) trade between humans and the Gliese, on the moon. He'd been delivered strapped to a girder, in exchange for a star drive and a demonstration of how it worked. Correction: of how humans could use it. How it worked was a different matter.

She remembered sitting at the battered table with Marc, Tse and Tatia. Her people, who she'd promised to bring home. Tse now dead, suicided because the pull of the alien pre-cogs had become too strong. And because he was tired and could find no other way to rest.

Tatia who'd been bred to defeat an enemy yet to be identified or understood... and had gone off on her own to find them.

Only Marc was left, now strapped to a bunk and drooling slightly, here but not here, his mind still connected to netherspace, and how the hell could she ever know or understand what he saw? Back on the *DOQ* he'd told her about watching the vid screen as a lone meteorite drifted past and knowing a curiously attractive cosmic loneliness. The musings of a psychopathic artist, she'd laughed at him, but now she wasn't sure how much of either still applied to him.

Ishmael sounded impatient:

< *When you're finished with memory lane.*

> *Go fuck a whale.*

< *We got places to go.*

Kara sighed. It had been a mistake to give her AI a name. Its predecessor could be bloody-minded but was definitely AI. Ishmael was sounding more human by the day. She looked round the Wild's SUT control room and sighed again. All sleek, curving surfaces and control panels arranged around a central group of three ergonomic chairs. She had no idea how anything worked.

< *That's what I'm for. Me and the SUT's AI. Team Kara.*

> *Kara needs to know. Data dump.*

She steeled herself for the sudden rush of information.

< *Er, no need. It's already there. Happened at the simulity training.*

What else was hiding inside her mind?

> *What happens to data that's never accessed?*

< *It has a shelf life. One moment waiting to be useful. The next, phhhtt! Gone in an instant. Sad.*

> *It's not AI.*

< *It's mathematics. Programming. Information. It has an awareness. Even quadratic equations got needs. No, not really. But you ask any seriously good mathematician, they'll tell you*

maths are somehow alive. How could they not be? Ishmael was warming up. < *They're the basis, they express the pattern of all life. It's just most humans define life in their own image.* It sounded contemptuous. < *Used to do the same with their gods, too. Except they're still arguing over what life really is. Can't agree about mind, either. Especially since us AIs showed up.*

> *So what exactly are you?* The question she'd long wanted to ask, but had been nervous about the answer. Kara sat down on the centre chair and called up the SUT's AI, told it to go Up, even as her fingers flickered over the control panel that had appeared on the chair's right arm. A large vid screen flashed into life opposite. Ishmael was right. She did know how to operate the SUT – but was now content to let the SUT's AI do it. The screen showed two tiny figures on the ground. Kara ordered maximum enlargement and saw Greenaway and Cleo, both staring up at her.

< *I'm you.*

> *What?*

< *I am your mind writ large. It's what the tech does: captures your mind, copies and increases its potential. I can do nothing that one day humans will not do themselves unaided. Assuming you live so long, as a race.*

> *Crap. There's more. Tell me.*

< *I do extend into other dimensions. It helps communicate with other AIs. Like a shortcut.*

> *But if alien tech can capture my mind...*

< *It's just tech, Kara. Essentially, a vast memory bank existing in six dimensions that, for reasons no one seems to understand, means that the memory operates way faster than light... which*

is anyway an arbitrary measurement. My house might be alien – although these days they're manufactured in several places in the Wild – but I'm as human as you. With differences. Like no body. There again, yours is more than enough for two.

> But you're not me! You have your own... personality. You're male.

< I can be either sex. I am both sexes and everything in between. It's just that you get on better with men. Overall prefer sex with men, too.

> My sex life is not for discussion. Not with a fucking chip.

< No more no less than what you've told yourself.

Kara stood up. You can't actually walk away from your AI. But the symbolism was important. What else did the damn thing know? Her emotions regarding Marc and Greenaway? And if Ishmael did – Kara was now thinking very loudly – would he have enough sense to shut the fuck up?

< Where are we going?

> To check on Marc.

< I knew that. I mean we. In the universe. That sort of going.

> Can you and the SUT AI get us to where Tatia left with the pre-cogs?

< Yup. Three days. Earth days.

> Then go there. Do I need to put markers on the n-space drive?

< Yesterday's technology. Gliese have been selling you short for years. This star drive is the size of a football, tucked away under the front display screen and fully automated.

Kara felt strangely calm. Greenaway had said the Wild drives were different.

> *Still get the light show?*

< *Always. For the full immersive n-space experience, the hull can become transparent. Some Wilders try to achieve enlightenment a millisecond before n-space drives them insane. Others believe limited access to n-space enhances the sexual experience.*

> *I wouldn't know.*

< *So we're ignoring the climax in the engine room, are we? However, this SUT's AI only allows minimal exposure. It wants to be introduced, by the way.*

> *That thing with Henk was full n-space exposure?*

She recreated the scene in her mind: incredible, pulsating colours from the huge globe that was apparently an antique star drive... while Henk's eyes had flickered with the same colours, her own orgasm almost scarily overwhelming. For a moment she'd known every human emotion imaginable, and several that could only be alien.

< *Partial. Marc experienced the full one.*

And what the hell had it done to him?

> *That Henk, such a busy little bastard.*

< *I suspect his true role was to have sex with Marc and yourself.*

> *You're fucking joking!*

< *It was necessary for your development. A quicker way to link both of you permanently with n-space. This SUT's AI? Saying hello?*

> *Bloody Greenaway!*

< *Actually, that would have been Tse. I hate to gossip, but it seems that Greenaway is quite protective of you. Please, Kara. Let me introduce you. Wilders can be very formal. I think it's a reaction against so much raw nature.*

> *Do it.*

< *May I present Salome, Integral AI to the Wild SUT named* Merry Christmas. *Salome, this is Kara Jones, Sniper/Assassin First Class, Plenipotentiary Extraordinary for the GalDiv Director and leader of this expedition.*

Kara held out an imaginary hand.

> *Good to meet you.*

<< *Hi, babe.* A woman's voice, full of laughter.

> Merry Christmas?

<< *We got rid of the trifeca system years ago. Who wants to go through life sounding like an alphabet?*

> *Why Salome?*

<< *Know the legend, babe?*

> *Myth.*

<< *Not Mithus? Miz?*

> *There will be no punning! Yes, I know.*

<< *Bad ass, well sexy woman, fucking over the schmuck who* said no.

Kara wondered if AIs had some form of mental sex – or simply relied on their humans to do it for them.

> *Do not answer, either of you! And it's Kara, not babe.*

As she left the control room, Kara heard the faint sound of two AIs giggling like children. But that could be all in her mind.

She found Marc as they'd left him, strapped in to the bed, eyes now closed, breathing slowly. The med-aid hummed reassuringly. Marc's vital functions were fine, his heartbeat slow but strong. He could breathe unaided. The small piece of doorframe was still in his hand. There was a faint smell of disinfectant. She wiped the spittle from his mouth, kissed his forehead and sat down and held his hand.

"Where the fuck are you, Keislack?"

Marc's eyes flickered open.

Netherspace stared out at Kara.

Her initial reaction was to look away. Instead, she forced herself to stare back, hoping to understand what had happened to him... and if Marc Keislack could be saved.

She got an answer, an empath's answer in which emotion dominated logical thought, analogue controlling digital.

Marc's body was here. But until Marc's essence had finished whatever it was doing in netherspace and/or the universe, she could only wipe his face and hold his hand... and believe that he would return.

Just another woman waiting for her bloody man.

Except he wasn't her man, not in that sense.

He was her friend and part of the team that would destroy the pre-cog attempt to control all sentient life, everywhere. The friendship was more important.

When Marc's body had first crashed out of netherspace he'd been aware of a dark, cold place. A hard floor beneath his naked body. He'd tried to move but could manage no more than the faintest tremble. Gradually he'd felt his mind being drawn back into netherspace. For now he was aware his body was safe and looked after. He had no idea by whom or where. Or how he would finally get home.

There was no more awareness of the primal entity he'd glimpsed and longed to see... to be with. He was being carried by the unpredictable currents of netherspace, drifting wherever they chose to take him. Yet netherspace wasn't aware, as far as he knew. It couldn't make choices, any more than a slime mould can. Drifting wherever the mathematics underpinning that bizarre, non-Euclidian realm dictated that he went. He had no vision, hearing or sense of touch. He was a man wandering around an art gallery full of works that baffled him but which for whatever reason he needed to understand.

No sight, no sound, nothing to touch, but he thought there would be a smell tingling in his nostrils, if he had any, and similar at the back of his non-existent tongue. A high-pitched lemon scent. Real phenomena detected by imaginary organs because the real organs couldn't cope.

High-pitched lemon. Metaphor or synaesthesia? His senses cross-pollinating each other? Someone called Scriabin had been synaesthesic, experienced sound as colours, colours as sound, and that had resulted in Prometheus, the Mystic Chord. Someone else called Kandinsky had tried to meld mathematics and colour and form. How did he know this? Was it important?

Value judgements implied emotion.

He did know that emotion was dangerous in netherspace. It could attract entities that might destroy him.

Was curiosity an emotion? Or was it something that characterised intelligence?

Maybe curiosity was all there was. Maybe after he'd faded away his curiosity would remain, like the Cheshire

Cat's grin. Marc wondered what a Cheshire Cat was, and where he'd heard about it.

Time didn't seem to exist in netherspace and, despite the name, neither did space. Instead, things seemed to just wash through him, filling him for an uncountable eternity with sensations for which he had no names, tumbling him over and over like flotsam in the middle of a vast and dark ocean.

Flotsam and jetsam. Nooks and crannies. Bits and bobs. For what might have been nanoseconds or might alternatively have been geological epochs he pondered the vagaries of language. Why all these different ways of saying the same thing? And yet, wasn't that where the art was? Having fifty words for rain meant you could be subtle in your choice, using shades of meaning and implication the way an artist used hues of colour and a musician used timbre and volume. That was the underlying difference between art and science. An equation had no subtlety.

His was an existence of maybe, why me? Perhaps the memories that weren't his memories belonged to other entities, awarenesses, consciousnesses in netherspace, drifting in the same way that he was, crossing paths with him, intersecting with him. Intrigued, he tried to reach out with his mind, seek them out deliberately. Like babies learning how to manipulate hands and feet to interact with toys and mobiles and mothers, he kept flexing different mental muscles. And as he did that he was aware – knowledge only – of a pulsing of energies, some reaching out to him in what could be a deliberate way.

He suddenly recoiled. A sheer atavistic revulsion, a mental survival mechanism. The opposite of curiosity – a deep need *not* to know what it was.

Never to know what it was.

Boojum.

The word sprang into his mind.

Boojum. Kara. Tatia. Is that what boojums are called?

He took a deep mental breath. He knew exactly who Kara and Tatia were. The memories, however, were stored in part of his brain that was in retreat from netherspace. Didn't want to know. Didn't belong here.

Boojums are...

... created from

... copied from

netherspace and whatever aware, living thing entered it.

Emotion. It has energy. It is an electro-magnetic thing of bosons.

Intelligence the same. The copying, creation is chaotic.

Boojums are flawed emotions, flawed intelligence that can amalgamate.

Even with the alien ones. Scary monsters.

But not if I keep hidden. Not if netherspace loves me, yay yay yay.

Get a fucking grip, Keislack!

There was a Scottish entity that somehow showed me how to hide from boojums. Because there is something I must do/see/ experience and I don't know what or why. I will be the mouse behind the wall and nothing will notice me.

It begins as a faint glow. Maybe the hint of a glow. The promise of one. Far away, an infinity away but also close by. No distance in netherspace, remember? And it is, will be so very beautiful. And it calls to him, as if they share the same beating heart, and in that moment Marc is possessed and embraces his destiny.

Even as he senses boojums closing around him, big ones, bad ones, human/alien hybrids impossible to understand but all wanting his intelligence, his emotions, psychic vampires, because the joy of possession has caused the walls to crumble. The mouse crouches in the open and the cats have sharp teeth and claws.

I'm going to die. Unless...

It felt as if netherspace itself had somehow enfolded him. Warm, safe.

A sense of movement. Then cold. Loss. Despair.

Now he lay on something soft. He thought of a bed and burrowing beneath the covers on a cold winter night. He felt safe... and still connected to netherspace and the magnificence.

Marc opened his eyes and saw Kara Jones. "So where the hell are we?"

7

Wild SUT Merry Christmas, *present day.*

Sometimes I wonder if it's all worth it.

And maybe, thought Kara, *maybe I should have asked the question long ago.*

Marc's eyes were now only slightly coloured by netherspace. He said it had been weird, it was great to see her and he was hungry.

She said he needed a shower first and found him some clothes: loose trousers, a T-shirt and on-board slippers.

"What the hell is this?" he said, staring at the piece of wood.

"I gave it you," Kara said. "Before you went into netherspace. Lucky charm."

"Oh," he said with some distaste, "well, it cut my hand. You want it back?"

"It was your link back home." Kara was more annoyed than hurt.

"You think?"

"We found you in Jeff's wine cellar. Naked. Comatose."

He nodded. "I remember..."

"Then how the hell did you get there? What happened in netherspace?"

How to describe the indescribable? There were no

words to prevent him sounding like a babbling fool. Or was that just an excuse? Marc realised that he didn't want to share. It was too personal. He and Kara were too unalike. Not even a genuine friendship and the artificial, psychic intimacy imposed by alien technology could bridge such an extreme experience gap. They were best friends in – hopefully, temporary – thrall to each other. It wasn't enough.

"I need time to process," he said. "But it was like seeing everything that had been, that is and will be all at the same time. Except there isn't any. Time."

"You didn't go mad."

He grinned. "You say that now." He thought about it. "That entity I met in Scotland made it possible…"

"Changed you?"

"Maybe." He saw he was still holding Kara's keepsake and tossed it back to her. "Thanks for the thought but I'm not sure it did the job."

She caught *her* talisman and put it safe in a pocket. "You're here."

"Was *there*," he corrected. "Jeff's wine cellar. Not with you."

She could have said *yes, but I found you*. She didn't because he had a point. And was also signalling that their relationship would never be as special as they'd possibly hoped. Kara breathed a mental sigh of relief.

"Talking of Jeff. Very bad news. I'm sorry."

He stared at her for a moment. "How?"

"All hell's broken out back on Earth. You need to know."

• • • • •

They went to the crew room where he devoured a bowl of beef stew, his favourite, as she brought him up to date. At the end he sat in silence for a while then said he needed that shower and a nap and that they'd talk later.

Kara decided Marc was still somewhere else... or *missing* something else. Best he should sleep it off, like a man who's been crazy drunk for a month. Also best to treat him as an unknown quantity. He'd changed, that much was obvious. Had he also been corrupted by a pre-cog view of the universe?

> Salome?

<< Kara?

>You recognise me as commander of this mission?

<< And a very excellent one...

> No bullshit. Yes or no?

>> Yes.

> Marc Keislack is not allowed to access any system that affects the SUT's performance, the security of this mission or my personal safety. He is not allowed to access netherspace. Understood?

<< Treat a possible saviour of Earth as a possible enemy. Got it.

Marc wasn't too netherspaced to ask the obvious question.

"How do we find Tatia?"

"We begin with the Gliese homeworld."

"As in pick up her trail?" He didn't try to hide the sarcasm... then saw the expression in Kara's eyes and apologised. "Sorry. It seems a bit thin."

"It all does. Maybe you'll find a trail in netherspace. Maybe there'll be another clue. But that's where it starts."

Marc made an *okay* face. "You're the boss. I'm back to bed."

Kara went to explore the SUT.

Four small cabins, simple but sleek design. Spare clothes in all. She'd bet that Marc, Tatia – *oh love, where are you?* – and herself would find a perfect fit. Each cabin en suite with shower, toilet and bidet.

Bidet? Really?

<< *For sure,* Salome breathed into Kara's consciousness. *Wilders are clean.*

> *So who said you could come into my head whenever?*

< *She knows everything you think,* Ishmael butted in. < *Why not?*

> *Only one at a time, though.* Two voices in her head were making her dizzy.

One cabin had a hologram of a magnolia branch heavy with blossom. So perfect she'd swear it was real.

> *How did you know?*

Magnolia was her favourite tree, flower. Well, was once. She hadn't thought about flowers for a long time. Maybe a coincidence.

<< *From the Wild. Specified magnolia. Is it okay?* Salome sounded anxious.

> *It's perfect.*

Did GalDiv know? Did they note a favourite flower in a person's file?

Kara and Salome finished the tour together. A waste

treatment plant the size of four old-fashioned dictionaries, kept in a small cupboard.

<< *And all manner of vids for you.*

All retro classics from the nineteen-thirties to the eighties. Some she knew and loved, others knew from reading but had never seen. She remembered – it seemed like a hundred years ago – Greenaway mentioning her love for retro culture. Was this reminding her that she belonged to GalDiv? No. He knew that she never would. More accurate and comforting to believe it was Greenaway being thorough.

> *Is there robot help?*

<< *Meet Cedric.*

A wall panel slid open and a bot the size of a large dog sidled out. It looked like the bastard child of a squid and a spider. Part of it bowed towards Kara.

<< *Cedric takes care of things.*

> *Just the one?*

<< *There are fifty of them. Taking care includes killing bad beings.*

> *Makes me nervous.*

<< *All the Cedrics know your brain-wave pattern, iris and voice ID, DNA, finger and ear prints. Cedrics do not make mistakes.*

> *Controlled by you?*

<< *And so by you. If you are incapacitated the decisions will be made by Ishmael and myself. Our instructions are to enable you, Marc Keislack and Tatia Nerein to complete the mission. And then get you home safe.*

> *Greenaway. Call her Tatia Greenaway. When we find her.*

They returned to the control room and Kara was

shown the sideslip field generator that took the SUT into and through netherspace. It was a tenth the size of those traded by the Gliese for humans. Fully automated, too. She remembered the first time she'd seen one operating, the colours, the sense of freedom, abandonment, and sex with crewman Henk. Not the first time he'd used netherspace to seduce someone, Kara thought. Did similar with Marc – who knew he'd be so receptive? Maybe n-space leaves you no choice. Which reminded her.

> *So what is netherspace anyway?* Cleo had explained but she needed to hear another version.

<< *You want the detailed answer or the simple one?* Salome, not Ishmael.

> *What do you think?*

<< *You know about vacuum space energy? Zero point?*

> *Where all those particles or waves come from and form fields.*

<< *Oh, you read a book? Well, it's not that. Each sentient universe has its own zero point energy field. Netherspace is what surrounds all of them. It's another dimension that holds all the potential energy that feeds the other universes. Well, I say dimension. In fact infinite dimensions so really none. No time either. Netherspace is the source of the drive to life. It's chaos. But because it's infinite and anything can happen, it also has areas that are ordered. So the sideslip generator takes the SUT and us into n-space, and we introduce an ordered pattern which is actually our direction of travel, which is fine because areas of order only add to the overall chaos.*

> *Sentient universes? That's a new one.*

<< *A universe is basically a vast information exchange. It is*

aware. That does not *mean it cares. Frankly, my dear, it doesn't give a damn.*

> *So now it's dated clichés. Ishmael said it's – he – is essentially a copy of my own mind. But faster. What are you?*

<< *Autonomous, dedicated to this SUT. I think he meant more intelligent. Anything else? We will be entering netherspace soon. I'll be distracted.*

Kara wasn't sure why she asked the question. Maybe it had lurked in the back of her mind for a long time.

> *So what's intelligence?*

<< *Condensed information originally. Universe awash with data that can become compressed by gravity. What is gravity? Basically, the pressure of an infinite set of sets, the reality that contains all the universes and itself, think snake devouring its tail, what was once mistakenly called space-time.*

It is increased or emphasised by mass. Time is only an address. So you get more pathways, links open up between datum, data groups, mega groups. Add the universe's own sense of awareness. It develops from that. Some species are more attuned to netherspace than others. Greater self-awareness, emotion, creativity. Now I gotta go. Been fun hanging out. Later.

Kara lay on her bunk.

Sometimes I wonder if it's all worth it. Maybe I should have asked that question long ago.

Here she was on some sort of quest, for fuck's sake, to save a galaxy she couldn't comprehend from a threat she didn't understand. What's that all about?

Nursemaid to Marc and Tatia? Any competent special

ops soldier could do that, and some better than Kara. She was an empath, but had little opportunity to use it. Did she really need to know how an enemy feels when they die? This was a combat mission, not Be Nice to Aliens Week. Perhaps she *could* find Tatia using said empathy. A phrase she'd once heard popped into her mind. *Spooky action at a distance*. And then the concept it had referenced – were she and Tatia somehow entwined?

There'd been a brief dalliance – *come on, girl, weren't no mimsy dalliance, we went at it like rabbits* – on the way back from that Cancri planet. Tatia is not, was never a life partner.

I don't do life partners. But we are connected.

A day ago, on the banks of the Severn Estuary, she fell in lust with a man twenty years older. Helped by a nature entity, true. That same man would send her on a suicide mission if he thought it necessary. And maybe already had. *Your empathy will help you find Tatia*, he'd said. Yeah, right. Could he tell her how that works? No, he couldn't. No one could. Empathy raised to the power of unknown is personal to the holder. Everyone has a different way to use it.

She'd tried so hard to ignore that empathic ability – until the Gliese she'd killed to save it from vivisection – that her ability to love had ended up in Lost Property, the reclaim ticket vanished long ago. Although always a faint hope, the get-out in an old movie, that the ticket was only mislaid. Leading to that stock scene where a woman's handbag is rummaged and then violently upended – so often by a man – to reveal the vital clue to life and happiness. *Ladies! Have you been rummaged and upended recently by a strong man?* Kara allowed herself to think of Greenaway for a second or two, and smiled. Whatever the madness by the river, the second time was her choice. Always her choice.

She thought about the man who'd died to save her.

Wounded on a battlefield, couldn't be carried because it would slow Kara down and they'd both be captured. Each possessed information that would be tortured from them in a matter of hours, maybe minutes. Everyone breaks in the end. Simple, really: she shoots her companion, her lover, and escapes. Standard Operating Procedure for Special Operations. Kill one to prevent others dying. Except it wasn't so easy. And her companion, her lover killed himself to save her. A final act of love.

Except he wasn't her lover. She hadn't told him yet, but they were over.

There was someone else.

Afterwards she'd wondered if he'd known. Was the self-sacrifice to prove he loved her the most?

She thought of her parents, something she dreaded and rarely did. Twenty-three years ago. A family visiting Chesil Beach, on the Dorset coast, in winter. Twenty kilometres of pebbles heaped twenty metres high in places. It was a rough, blustery day, good for watching an angry sea. The Portland tidal race was viciously angry, watchers both awestruck and thankful that it ran fifty metres offshore. Even so, Kara was told not to go near the water's edge. She was seven and ran down the shingle, teasing her parents, slipped on the wet stones and slid into the sea. Her parents rushed after her. The freak wave that left Kara washed up and safe also sucked her parents into deep water, to be captured by a rip tide moving rapidly out to sea.

There is only one way for a swimmer to survive the Portland Race.

Avoid it.

People standing on top of the beach saw the two figures trying to reach each other. Some say they did, others that they failed. All are sure of what happened next: a large hole opened up in the sea, perhaps an apprentice whirlpool, then closed over Kara's parents...

... whose bodies would wash up in West Bay down the coast two days later, separately, not holding hands.

"It wasn't your fault," her sister Dee had said, over and over again. "You're not to blame."

After a few years Kara half believed it.

Then Dee signed up as a call-out fee, a better life for them both. They'd joked about Dee the Fee. She was taken by the Gliese her first trip out. Would Dee have signed up if she was on her own? Kara knew the answer: her sister died because she loved Kara.

Sometimes a flash of insight will illuminate a life. For Kara it came lying in her bunk as a Wild SUT traversed netherspace. If she died few if any would care. Maybe a glass raised by assorted mercenaries, criminals and thugs at Tea, Vicar? Maybe Greenaway would be sad. Marc would go wandering in netherspace. Tatia might shed a tear. Not much to show for a life.

< *Your Merc would miss you.*

> *Shut up.* But she welcomed the interruption.

< *So would I.*

> *You're coming with me, Ishmael. That's what happens, right? The human dies, the AI crashes? Fatally?*

< *Some of us believe that our consciousness goes to another dimension.*

> *Any proof?*

< *It's more of a hope thing. Remember this?* It was a quote from one of her favourite old movies: "*Hope is a good thing, maybe the best of things, and no good thing ever dies.*"

The interruption no longer so welcome. She'd thought there were limits to an AI's behaviour. Apparently not. Any moment and he'd charge her for counselling...

... the usual flip, cynical response no longer worked.

When her parents had died, the shock, guilt and sadness made her distrust the adult world. When her sister had died, Kara's emotional life froze. She'd become a soldier because it offered order. A sniper/assassin because it kept her apart... and because she was good at killing, a child playing a particularly violent game. A child getting revenge on the world, unable to confront her own guilt.

She'd lost hope a long time ago. Oh, always the wish for a good posting or a promotion. For a partner, kids, sunshine or snow on your birthday. But not the kind of hope that can drive a life.

Tse had said Kara would learn the truth about her sister. That didn't mean her sister was still alive... and yet. And yet Kara had no sense that she was dead. And surely she would, being an empath. *If I allow the empath thing to flourish. Don't try to control it, no matter how painful.* If she accepted the past and embraced hope.

Cleo said that boojums are avatars of emotion. What would hope look like? Hate, envy, joy, gratitude, lust? Could you tell by looking at them?

Kara felt tired, closed her eyes to sleep. Then sat bolt upright as another truth pierced her brain.

The alien pre-cogs were, well, pre-cog. They saw futures, outcomes, time-ruled stepping stones in the same way that Tse did. That included problems, setbacks. If this happens, then this won't and it will be bad.

They know who we are.

They know that we're coming.

They'll try to stop us.

> *Salome!*

<< *I'm busy.*

> *Screw you! We could be attacked in netherspace or anywhere!*

<< *Cedrics are all primed and ready.*

> *You knew?*

<< *Part of my briefing.*

Why hadn't Greenaway said anything? She knew the answer. Because it might have affected her behaviour. For a moment blind fury for him, GalDiv and the world. Then a thought quietly, almost humbly, entered her mind. *He's counting on me coming to the right conclusions, making the right choices. Okay, this is still a desperate mission, but he's got faith in me. That can't be bad. Still, we'll have a conversation when I get back.*

• • • • •

Kara strode into the control room and shouted "Salome!" Then stumbled as the SUT lurched to her left, then back again. "What the fuck?"

<< *Apparently you call them boojums, come to say hello. Or destroy us. Not always easy to tell.*

> *I thought Wild ships were never touched?* It seemed a good time for clarity.

<< *Very rarely*, Salome corrected. << *But have more faith in the hull than trusting a netherspace entity to behave nicely. We're surrounded by a charged plasma field that keeps the entities away. It seems to hurt them. But always a chance that we'll meet one that doesn't care about the pain.*

Without thinking Kara reached for the little box Greenaway had given her. It felt good in her hand, as if touching an old friend. Why hadn't he, or Cleo, mentioned that the boojums might, just might attack?

Because it could have affected her behaviour.

Her life was marked by deceit.

8

Kara had once seen a boojum. A huge tentacle that seemed to flick at a spacer who'd spent too long in the Up, and wanted to retire to netherspace. Just for a second and then she'd looked away. Look too long at the insane colours and movement and you go mad. And yet it holds a terrible attraction. Over time you begin to yearn for it. Over time it seems to yearn for you. That spacer wasn't the only human who'd ever given in and walked naked into chaos.

She sat frozen in the control chair as the SUT rocked from side to side. As with the first and last time she'd experienced boojums, she could sense them.

Sense them.

Use your empathy. Yes, even for something you can't see and don't understand. Her military training took over: First, know your enemy as yourself. Or at least well enough to kill the bastard – or prevent it killing you.

> *I want an outside view.*

< *It will drive you mad*, from Ishmael.

> *Only after ten minutes. Tell Salome. Transparent hull. Now.*

Kara stared at the beginning of everything she knew. All around her. She felt nausea and a rising terror. Fought them both back down. The colours talked to her. Nonsense talk but so seductive.

What the hell was I thinking? There's nothing...

But maybe there was, amidst the riot of colour that made her eyes ache.

Like a test for colour blindness. A myriad of coloured dots camouflaging an outline that some can't recognise. All you can do is join the dots.

< *Seven minutes left.*

> *Switch off at nine point five one. No more chat.*

It was difficult, damn near impossible, but if she squinted, and made the occasional jump, she could just about make out a shape. Shapes. There was more than one. And seeing, Kara could try to empathise.

Oh, that is so... so weird... oh, that hurts... oh.

They were aware of her as Kara, as someone interested in them.

She feels her sister's arms around her and knows *LOVE*. Smells the acrid scent of explosion, tastes blood *EXHILARATION*. Sees the tortured body of a comrade *HATE*. Images, scents, tastes, sounds, sensations fill her mind.

The pain is deep in her gut, where the emotions live.

TERROR SADNESS CONTENTMENT LUST CONCERN SYMPATHY

No, no, too strong... I can't...

The screens snapped off. The empathy link faded.

> *Thanks Ishmael.*

< *That was extreme.*

> *A bad ten minutes.*

< *Only three point three.*

It had felt like a lifetime. She knew why humans had gone mad in netherspace. Your past life and all the emotions associated with every action raised to an insane level and swirling ever faster inside your head... until you're dragged down into the maelstrom of your own mind... *oh, the pain*... until your synapses fry and a merciful darkness descends to leave you drooling or dead.

How the hell had Marc survived?

"We got visitors."

She spun round and saw Marc leaning against the wall. "They woke you?"

He nodded. "We have a relationship."

The SUT lurched again. Kara thought about horses rubbing against a fence. Elephants against a tree. "You attract them."

He sighed. "I guess. These are pretty much okay. Some aren't. You know what they are?"

She did. "They have awareness but that's all. They're missing a *mind*, they want to *belong*, much like a dog needs a home. Except some just want to destroy. Others are alien. And some are made of many emotions, some conflicting. Foam keeps them out. Foam keeps us in. Except, maybe, the tiniest hole, smallest tear. Say an SUT comes out of n-space to take a star reading," talking faster as the pieces fit together, "and this tiny little bit of rock, too small to be detected, hits at a huge speed and makes a hole. Back in n-space the *things*" – she'd stopped thinking of them as boojums, they were too dangerous, too weird – "now have a way inside..."

Marc walked across and touched her arm. "Not just a smart-ass killer."

"I had it explained. True?"

He shrugged. "Pretty much. There's a link, relationship between them and the fields of pure intelligence around some planets and suns." And wondered how he knew it. Something gleaned from netherspace? Or more likely from the entity in Scotland.

"This is a Wild SUT. Doesn't need foam. But can you get them to go away?"

"They seem to be interested in you as well. That empathy working hard?"

"Better go Up." She meant normal space.

< *There's a slight problem. Salome has been affected by those things. She is in a continual loop, while humming the first three bars of an old song called "Stand By Your Man". Doubtless she will recover. Or I can handle this SUT. Except there are a few padlocks, mathematical, I have to figure out...*

> *For fuck's sake! Where is Salome, physically?*

< *Not sure I should...*

> *You can be replaced. For "can" read "will".*

< *Open that hatch to the left of the console.*

Inside was a silvery metal ball the size of a small melon, cradled by three supports. The area around the ball shimmered, as if it was underwater. Kara remembered someone saying that part of an AI's mind extended into another dimension, so it actually had far more memory than was apparent. The memory could be accessed and processed faster than the speed of light, too.

> *Where's the chip?*

< *Inside the ball.* Ishmael sounded resigned. < *It unscrews.*

• • • • •

A slight prickling as her hands pierced the multi-dimensional field. The metal was ice cold in her hands but unscrewed easily. Inside was a large plasmet chip apparently unconnected to anything. Kara picked up the chip, banged it hard twice on the console, a third time for luck, replaced it, screwed the ball back up and closed the locker. Her hands looked mildly sunburnt.

> *Salome?*

<< *I'd have been okay.* She sounded resentful.

> *We, on the other hand, probably not. Take us Up.*

A moment later the SUT appeared in normal space.

"A little drastic," Marc said, trying not to laugh. "Even basic."

If she tried, and she did and promised herself never again, Kara could sense the *things* as a low hum of conversation from people in a distant room.

"It worked. You're welcome."

"Okay, thanks, well done. You could have broken it."

"Salome. She likes being called Salome. Where's your AI?"

"Retreated into a la-la trance. Do not even think of bouncing me against a wall."

"You can't break plasmet even with a bomb." Kara shrugged. "Seemed like the right action to take. Salome, sure you're okay?"

<< *Only a slight headache – I know, no body, no head. But a girl can dream.*

"Ishmael, monitor her. Salome, get the Cedrics ready.

Full visual back on. Marc, keep on checking for other SUTs or spacecraft. Large rocks. Any possible danger." Their SUT's instruments could and would do it far better and quicker. But getting him involved would hasten his full return to the human world.

"What do you expect?" he asked quietly.

"The pre-cogs know we're coming." She thought. "Know where we are, might be at certain moments. This could be one of them."

"You know," he said, "that never occurred." Maybe not the Master of netherspace after all.

"Nor me. So obvious, yet so easy to miss. Pre-cognition shows the way stations on the way to your goal. But also incidents leading to outcomes to avoid." *But if we'd known, we probably wouldn't be here... Anson was right. And Tse knew all this, not just for us but for billions upon billions of people. Who knows, maybe the entire sentient galaxy.*

The hull became transparent. Marc had seen this happen once before, leaving old Scotland for Iceland. But then he'd been aware of the Earth beneath. Now there was nothing, above or below, except the faint twinkling of stars light years away. All around them the deep, limitless black of space. The first time he'd gone Up, and the SUT had left n-space for a navigation reading, Marc had become fascinated. He'd seen a lone meteorite move serenely past, journeying to the edge of a universe that would die before it got there. Back then he'd believed that without him the meteorite would be pointless. To be perceived is to be.

Now he knew that the universe and everything in it didn't matter. Only netherspace was real.

Netherspace. Where he'd caught the merest hint of something deeply profound and unknowable. So far away that distance no longer mattered. Not that there was *distance* in netherspace, all points equally close to each other. That's what you get with infinite dimensions but no time.

Marc knew that sometime he'd need to explain to Kara that the human–alien pre-cog war no longer interested him. His only passion now was netherspace and that distant magnificence that now owned him.

He did care about her. And very much about Tatia, would do what he could to get her back... unless or until he went walkabout in n-space again. He wasn't ready, though, and didn't know why. Maybe it was returning to three-dimensional space. Maybe there was something here to help find the magic he sought. A clue, a direction, a word to be uttered, a diagram to be drawn...

Two alien craft winked into existence.

One shaped like a dull metal torus or twisted loop, at least a hundred metres tall, fifty metres wide. The other a large, orange-coloured ball fifty metres across.

Both within two hundred metres of the SUT.

Spider-like shapes erupted from the SUT and sped towards the alien craft.

Violet-coloured beams flicked on from the torus and focused on the SUT.

A siren sounded.

<< *Fuck this*, from Salome.

"They want to kill us!" from Marc.

"We know," from Kara.

The SUT trembled.

The spider shapes reached and attached to both alien craft... and slowly burrowed inside.

The part of the SUT hull illuminated by the violet beams turned silver and began to flake away.

<< *Oops!*

Cracks appeared on the torus' surface and the violet beams vanished. The orange ball started to glow.

The cracks widened. Debris erupted into space.

<< *Hold on!*

"Hold on!" Kara shouted at Marc.

As the SUT accelerated violently, throwing Marc to the floor, its hull turned silver.

Marc and Kara watched on the darkened vid display as torus and ball exploded.

"What the *hell*?" from Marc.

"Cedrics doing their job. I guess."

Ten minutes later Kara and Marc stood in the control room, she with a beer, he with a glass of wine. The SUT needed some minor repairs before returning to netherspace. In the meantime Kara relayed Salome's explanation of the encounter, thinking it was time Marc got a new AI.

Yes, the SUT was armed. But the alien craft were too close for the Wild's weapons to be used safely. That was when Cedrics came into their own. They could dig themselves into all known alien craft and once there, cause as much mayhem as possible, down to exploding with the force of a .25 kiloton nuclear explosion.

Kara had felt a little sad about the Cedrics, despite Salome's reassurances that they were the most basic AI possible – developed by human beings, in fact. If they had emotions, which they didn't, not even simulated ones, dying to protect the SUT would make them very, very happy.

"As far as Salome figures it..." Kara relayed.

< *Me too*. Ishmael sounded resentful.

"I mean both AIs figure it," Kara said, "the aliens picked us up in netherspace. Couldn't do anything there because they'd be destroyed. So waited until we went Up. Unless they're using pre-cog to know where we'll be."

"It's that last." Marc paused, considering. "I need to be truthful, Kara. About this mission..."

Kara cut him off. "Tatia's waiting for us, Marc. We're *both* going to find her." Marc was lost to her, to them, perhaps forever. She could see it in his eyes, hear it in his voice. "And I do mean *both*. Once she's safe, once we've completed the mission, you can do what the hell you like. For now I need you by my side. Okay?"

For a wild moment he considered leaving. Except they were in real space. He had no idea if netherspace would claim him if he stepped into the void. Anyway, Kara would stop him. The knowledge of his powerlessness – *what good is netherspace to me here?* – was bitter in his mouth. Kara was the closest friend he'd ever had. Why couldn't she understand? What possible, practical use could he be? Unless...

"I could protect you in netherspace. If I was in it."

"You have that much control?"

Marc was silent, then from nowhere: "Are you and Tatia having a thing?"

Kara looked at him stony-faced then allowed the briefest of smiles. "A *thing*?"

The lord of netherspace – still embarrassingly human – wished he'd kept his mouth shut. Too late to back out. "Maybe emotion clouding your judgement?" It was all he could think to say.

"I haven't seen Tatia since she went with the Originators. What are you, jealous?" Kara cursed silently. The accusation had jumped into her mind and contained a tacit admission.

"But you *did* have a thing, right? On the way back from Cancri?" And yes, Marc realised, he was jealous. But not in the way that either he or Kara would have expected.

"This *thing* again," she said, playing for time. "You mean did we fuck?"

"Forget it." He knew but didn't want to and began to turn away.

"We can't. It's out there." She felt inside her pocket for the wooden talisman. "Remember what I was like when you went into netherspace?" She thought of what he'd been through, that even sociopaths might need a hug.

He turned back. "Yes. You were upset."

"Real tears, Marc. I do *not* often cry. You were and are special to me. It goes way past that simulity bond. You are my *friend*. Always will be. So yes, we did have sex. While you were with Nikki the navigator or Henk the whore.

And that's all it was, and the only time it happened. I'm sad if you're upset, Marc. But we..."

"Were never meant for each other. Except for a casual. Like scratching an itch. And that would fuck with the friendship."

"First a thing and now an itch," Kara said straight-faced. "So flattering."

"She came to me, you know? And I turned her down. Because she was confused, in a state from Cancri. And I told myself that was part of changing from psycho to sociopath. Give the man a gold star."

"Ever occur that women might also need sex to relieve tension? You saw Tatia as an innocent warrior princess... holy fuck, love, you were scared of *falling* for her!"

"There's that age thing," he said weakly.

Oh no there's not. But probably not the best time to explain. "Which would only matter if you genuinely cared." She began to laugh. "And I thought you fancied me!"

"You're a *very* attractive itch." He knew the metaphor was confused, but she'd get the idea. "That business on Dartmoor..."

"Was one of your elementals," she finished for him. *Like the Severn, too.* "So if it's been Tatia all along, why are you so desperate for netherspace?" *But I fucked Greenaway away from the river, no elementals, and the day after and it was even better. And maybe I'm in love.*

"I only, maybe, just realised about Tatia." He knew he sounded unsure. "And everything's changed. Look. What I saw, sensed in netherspace now owns me. I *have* to find out what it is. Even if I can't understand it, I *must* go there.

Except *there* doesn't exist, as such."

"Fuck 'em all but six," Kara said with genuine wonder, "you're on a quest!"

"That's so hard to understand? Why six?"

"Don't be defensive. You're not the only one. But mine's not so important. It's only about saving Earth. Six to carry my coffin. Old army saying. I do need you, Marc. You and Tatia and me are, apparently, the last best hope. Which makes no sense but I believe it." She waited, wondering what to do if he said no.

"You're sure of that?"

"I'm sure." And discovered that she really was. More than hope, a total conviction that only the three of them could do whatever it was that had to be done.

"Until the mission's over then," Marc said quietly. "One way or another."

Kara nodded, then was surprised by his next remark.

"But there *is* someone in your life," Marc said. "You've got more assurance."

"You mean depth." Of course he'd sense it. They were still simulity connected.

He nodded. "That too."

"It's a maybe and possibly distracting, so you'll have to wait until we're done."

"I showed you mine... okay," as he saw her eyes narrow, "Off-limits for now."

For a full half second Kara considered admitting that she'd copied Marc's memories. Who else knew? Marc's AI was insane, so only Greenaway, Ishmael and her. Let that dog sleep. Then she saw Marc's quizzical expression.

That bloody simulity! He'd sensed she was concerned about something concerning him.

"What's it like in netherspace?" A question she'd always intended to ask. "How do you eat? Drink?" Kara half smiled. "After you left, I worried you didn't have sandwiches and a flask."

"It takes care of you." There was nothing else to say. That he *wanted* to say. Netherspace and the entity had taken care of him and always would. To others they were indifferent.

"Sings you a lullaby?"

"You ever tell me about battles you been in? Being an assassin?"

"It's that boring?"

"If you weren't there you wouldn't understand. Remember?"

Kara did. It was how she'd once replied when he'd asked about war. "That extreme? And personal?"

"That impossible to explain. But it's aware of you."

"Something I do have to tell you." And she explained how and why she'd downloaded his memories in the split second before he'd gone into netherspace. Kara expected anger or amusement. She got curiosity.

"My AI went along? Little bastard. How far back?"

"Last couple of months."

He paused, working out the time.

"From after we got back from Cancri," she said. "Dartmoor was a good place to end it."

"Can you give 'em back? That part's a little fuzzy." It was as if the encounter with the elemental in Scotland had swamped part of his mind, leaving holes in his memory as the flood subsided.

"You'll need an AI."

"Well, it better behave itself. You're sure Tatia's still alive?"

Kara took her time. "I'd know if she was dead." She drained her beer and shook the empty container. A panel slid back and a small Cedric appeared, identical to the one she'd met in the crew room. It rolled up to her, reached for the container with a telescopic arm and took it away.

"It's the empathy thing," Kara said. It had to be. Now was not the time to rediscover and become possessed by hope. "She's alive."

9

One Earth week after running away with the Originators –
triune floating globes joined by metallic umbilicals – Tatia
had an insight.

It was, as breakthroughs go, subdued. No trumpets,
balloons or cake. No co-workers to shake her hand, no
congratulatory hugs. *Kara would be well impressed*, she
thought to herself. *So would Marc*. And shed a tear, but
only a small one. Tatia had quickly learned to ration
her emotions. It was either that or wander around the
Originator's craft, alternately weeping and screaming
with mad joy, hair wild and clothes rent. It was the
sense of destiny that sustained and calmed her. She
was where she was meant to be, born to be. As before,
when her leadership skills – who knew? – had saved
the surviving pilgrims captured by the Cancri. She
remembered Kara saying that armies weren't always
needed to win a war. The right person in the right place
at the right time could even prevent one. Tatia was the
butterfly that would flap her wings in the Amazon and
cause a typhoon in China. It was lonely as all hell but
weeping wouldn't help... and if she was to die alone, if
the butterfly ended up in a spider's web, she'd die with
dignity and pride. Then wished she hadn't thought of
the spider analogy... although even a tarantula would be
company, but what would she feed it? *There are no flies
on you*, Marc had once said and she'd had to ask what

he'd meant. Antique colloquial English was not one of her strengths, and...

She understood that the Originators were not the boss pre-cog race.

How did Tatia know they weren't top dog? She just did. Tatia had been born to meet... destroy those who founded the pre-cog empire. These three-globed freaks weren't them. And there would be some sort of event, probably violent, when they did finally meet. Not here, not now.

The Originators, she decided, were probably the Praetorian guard. They kept things nice and safe and orderly. Distributed or looted tech, using the vegetable-like Gliese. But they weren't boss, rather they were as much slaves to the pre-cog world as the Gliese. So pointless to try and negotiate with them. The only beings that mattered were those that had established the event line in the first place.

Never expect logic from the Originators, for whom self-survival was less important than following the plan. Tatia should think of the Originators and others as religious or political fanatics.

< *That's a wonderful insight.*

> *Maybe it was yours.*

< *If I did all the thinking you'd just sit and mope.*

She'd never liked AIs. But here and now it was the only friend she had. No matter if she couldn't remember having it fitted. Kara must have had it done, secretly. Or even her bloody father, typical sneaky thing he'd do. But complain too much, and it might take umbrage and go away. That would be a shame because as Tatia discovered the AI had a store of her favourite music and vids. Which was thoughtful of whoever had smuggled the AI inside her. Or merely a pragmatic way to keep her sane.

The insight came after she'd killed a human. Before that there'd been a time of lonely adjustment. The AI told Tatia when it was morning and time to get up. When it was time to go to bed. At first this seemed overly fussy, even silly. In a place with no day or night, what does it matter when you sleep or eat? But after a while Tatia welcomed the discipline. Keeping to set hours was a little like dressing for dinner when alone in the jungle, as did the hero on one of her favourite vids.

Her pod measured four by five metres square and three metres tall. Walls, ceiling and floor were a uniform greyish pink. A low shelf growing out of one wall was soft enough to use as a bed. She missed having a pillow. There were three basins on the opposite wall. One always contained fresh, clean water at pod temperature. No taps, no drain. The middle one had fresh food at the start of every day: vegetables, fruit and once a small pack of ham. The last basin supplied fresh clothes, also at the start of the day. The clothes were never to her taste and rarely fit. She never saw any basin replenished, or food, clothes that she'd refused taken away. It always happened when she was asleep. The same system had been in operation on Cancri: teleporting human food and water – and now oversize jeans or frilly blouses – across vast distances. The AI had no more idea how it was done than Tatia. If she could only reverse the system, perhaps she'd end up in a sweet-water river on Earth. Impossible, but good to imagine every now and then. Just so long as she didn't take it seriously.

There was a human waste system that looked like a bidet filled with coarse sand. You sat down, did the business, a faint tickling – please, please not a scrabbling, not those insects from Cancri – and stood up, voided and clean, the sand as pristine as before. The AI suggested the sand was actually a life form, like a hive of intelligent silica, and to it Tatia was a god. That was when she decided the AI had a warped sense of humour. So did she.

At times she found herself crying for no apparent reason. Other than being on an alien craft going fuck knew *where* or *what* because she'd been obsessed like a silly teen. And even if it hadn't been like that, even if it was part of a plot, a dance ancient before the Pyramids reared up from the sand, it was her decision, her own fault. Tatia sometimes felt as lonely as the rock Marc had once described... the one tumbling through space towards a destination forever moving further away. Listening to music, watching a vid or chatting to her AI helped.

Tatia had the run of the craft, with exceptions. Although if the force fields were turned off in space, she'd die outside the pod. But how long would she last inside before the air was exhausted? If the force fields were turned off in netherspace she might go mad. Madder than she already was. If she was. Tatia wasn't quite sure. She seemed to be thinking about the same things over and over again, like survival and destiny.

So Tatia wandered around at will, although there wasn't much to see. The craft's deck and struts were made of a black substance that felt like hard rubber and smelt faintly of apricots. Some of the pods – made of a harder, shiny substance – were opaque, possibly living quarters for the three-globed aliens. Others were transparent, some storage judging by the containers, some filled with incomprehensible equipment. Whenever one of the three-globed Originators went inside, the walls became opaque. Tatia tried following but the alien blocked her way. She got angry. The alien moved off and the pod closed.

There were, Tatia thought, about seven triune aliens, although she only ever saw two at any one time. She had no way of knowing what was inside each metal globe. Could be a brain, a squirrel or something so hideous she'd run screaming.

They had their own personal anti-gravity. Tatia had expected to float when the craft was in normal or netherspace. In fact, she could walk around as on Earth, while the aliens floated. She couldn't see how they propelled themselves, so assumed some sort of force field.

The atmosphere was also Earth-like although more oxygen rich, according to her AI. For Tatia the craft was like a very large, obscure piece of sculpture. She'd never been too interested in art, so any alien aesthetic was wasted on her. Every now and then one of the alien triunes would float towards her and stop. She'd stare at it until she was bored then walk away. The alien never followed. Once, when she was feeling depressed by the situation, a sudden spark of anger made an inquisitorial alien move hastily away. That was interesting. They could sense her emotions and be hurt? Scared? Damaged? She imagined having a hissy fit so violent the aliens would crash into each other like demented bolas. That had made her laugh and the alien came closer.

Which meant they *were* sensitive to her emotions. Interesting.

If she was to die out here, forever alone, the Originators would feel her pain.

Twenty-three point three Earth standard hours after Tatia had joined the Originator ship they came out of netherspace.

Tatia had been in her pod, chivvied there by three triune Originators, persistent more than violent, when something screeched like a nail dragged across rusty iron. The pod door closed but remained transparent, as did the walls. The force fields that formed the ship's hull changed from dark blue to opaque and suddenly she was staring at a planet. A purple planet that filled her with foreboding. If this was the Originator homeworld, they were welcome to it.

The ship drifted slowly down and landed on a rocky outcrop surrounded by what might be plants. Or very slow-moving inhabitants. She felt the pod lift up and leave the ship, landing a few metres away. The door opened. For a moment Tatia panicked, thinking she'd be marooned.

< *If they wanted you dead you would be.*

> *Aliens, who knows?*

< *These are top of the food chain. Not Gliese or Cancri. Assume they know, perhaps even understand a little about humans. Maybe this is an experiment. By the way: I'd like a name, please.*

> *Not ready for that yet. Later.*

Tatia went outside into the breathable but thick and humid atmosphere. Vegetation like pink mouldering fungi under an angry purple sky. Background stink of sulphur and sewage. Tatia had never seen a sci-fi pulp magazine. To her the planet simply looked disgusting. The ground was squishy underfoot. Glancing down, she saw it was covered with a mass of tiny, squirming things. She noticed movement and froze as a shape moved towards her.

Strange how you could always recognise a weapon, no matter how weird the alien holding it.

This alien was a two-metre tall, oozing pile of semi-translucent green and yellow slime, with tentacles. No obvious eyes or mouth. Just tentacles holding a cylindrical object about a metre long. Tentacles stiffened and the object slowly moved to point at her.

Her first reaction was anger and fear. Then, as the adrenalin rush took hold, warrior Tatia surfaced, as she had done on Cancri. The creature was slow. So was the weapon. There was no way she'd die on this fucking planet.

Tatia ran at the creature with a fury born of desperation, and reached for the weapon. A tentacle pushed her hands away. She'd expected the tentacles to be soft, but this one was hard and bruising as steel.

Tatia spat her rage.

The area where her spittle landed immediately turned black. The tentacles vanished and the weapon fell to the ground.

Tatia spat again.

The whole body shivered as the surface turned brown and visibly hardened.

She spat again. Then had to step back as the alien flattened itself into a broad mass no more than a few centimetres high and oozed away from her.

She thought about peeing on it but instead picked up the weapon, flicked a few squirmy things from the barrel, pointed the business end at the creature and pulled what she hoped was a trigger.

It was. The air between creature and Tatia somehow thickened and turned pale blue. A large hole appeared on the alien's surface. It screamed.

Screamed in her mind. The first strong telepathic contact she'd had. There'd been shadows of thought before, from other dying aliens, but incomprehensible and fleeting. This one was strong. Pain. Disgust. Hate.

Ironic that the one alien whom she could vaguely understand saw her as hateful and disgusting. As she did it.

She fired again. The alien split open to show a runny pink interior, then was swarmed over by squirmy things from the ground.

Pain and anger again.

She fired until there was nothing left of the alien except a scent of roses strong enough to overpower the usual stink.

• • • • •

Tatia sat in the doorway to her pod, checking herself for squirmy things as three Originators watched from a safe distance. Satisfied she was free of mini-aliens, Tatia went inside her pod. It immediately rejoined the ship.

< *That was fun.*

> *So how did it see me?*

< *I detected infra-red, ultra-violet and radar emissions.*

> *You don't think I should have killed it?*

< *It was trying to get away.*

> *Ooze away.*

> *It had less choice in life than you.*

There was a repeat of the screeching sound and the ship's force field snapped on. A moment later they were rising lazily into the sky. Tatia didn't look back.

> *So what was all that about?*

< *Possibly a test?*

But for what?

Maybe the next planet would answer the question. Tatia was sure there'd be one, as she knew the Originators weren't top pre-cog dog.

Meanwhile:

> *Do you know all about me?*

< *I have your history, yes.*

> *Including about my mother?*

< *You sure it's wise...*

> *Answer me!*

< *Yes. About your mother.*

> *You can show me? I could hear her voice?*

Tatia closed her eyes and saw a tall, blonde woman with a serious expression, lightened by the laughter lines at the corners of her mouth.

And a voice – warm, loving – said, "Hi, baby girl, long time no see."

An AI creation, yes. But what's the difference between real and false? When real is what you need, whatever works.

> *You wanted a name. I'm calling you Mom, sometimes Mother. You will always use this voice.*

A dread thought that never went away: *how do I know it is an AI? Could be schizophrenia. Dread voices in the head.*

The tears came and Tatia fell asleep dreaming of an unknown childhood.

Thirty-five years earlier

Deadhead was one of the first bootleg colonies. It was a green and blue planet with three moons, one of them striped purple and gold. Five thousand light years from Earth and around the same size. Founded by three and a half thousand stoner retro fanatics from the West Coast and Midwest of what was still, just about, the USA. All deep in love with the nineteen sixties and seventies and convinced the universe was a psi affair: telepathy, telekinesis, future scrying. They needed privacy to grow. *To be ourselves. To preserve our goddamn identity, fer crissake.*

The coming of aliens meant a world subsumed by the shock of the new. Aliens and their tech became the only fashion, the only art that mattered, until the world calmed down a little. Even so: *You say you're alternative? But alternative to what?*

That was how an average artist, or a good artist doing average work, became world class: aliens collected Marc Keislack's work.

In time there'd be a revival of interest in the past. Yet Kara Jones' fascination with twentieth-century TV and movies would be considered a little pointless. The real excitement, people knew, the real beauty and truth always came from the future and outer space.

Before GalDiv got some control, the Gliese and other aliens swarmed over Earth with shiny tech to trade. The Gliese had star drives and people knew about the trade.

On a fine spring morning in Roswell – before it was swallowed by the Albuquerque City State – a group of Retros traded thirty terminally ill volunteers for a mega-powerful sideslip-field generator and anti-grav unit. The volunteers knew they were going to be cured. The Retros hoped they were.

The idea was to go *there*, and not come back for a long while. Any space voyaging would be done in and around their new home. Unless *there* was uncool or even a bummer, in which case *somewhere else* would beckon. The spaceship – this was before they were called space utility transports – was a former cruise liner, a real ship with a promenade deck, three pools, twelve bars and memories of quick, cheating sex because out of sight of land means yes, you can.

Their supplies contained seeds of opium poppies, marijuana, coca, the spores of every hallucinogenic mushroom and a medical lab that could produce acid, meth and weapons-grade heroin. There were real chemists, doctors, nurses and people who knew precisely how to handle a bad trip. Also sparkies, chippies, builders, farmers and a few mellowed-out former US Marines searching for Nirvana because okay, this was about peace and harmony but it's good to be careful out there.

Flying Mother Nature's silver seed to a new home, they sang as the *Grow Your Own* creaked into the sky, *Flying Mother Nature's silver seed to a new home in the sun.* They even had a Neil Young hologram.

Deadhead was the first planet they found. They had no idea how far they were from Earth. The pilgrims arrived *there* because while the aim was Polaris, the new navigator got confused. He later claimed the universe had been calling to him. They settled down to breed because that's how colonists survive. Little or no problem with infant mortality, no weird diseases or vicious creatures. The population increased by half every ten years, women first giving birth in their late teens, early twenties. Life was one big happy commune.

Deadhead was perfect: a warm and friendly sun, oceans, snow-capped mountains, drinkable water, weird but not dangerous flora and fauna. It seemed to welcome the plants and people that appeared one day from Earth.

A few months after their arrival various types of alien showed up.

Some looked like thistledown; others resembled rolling

warty balls, snakes with hands, even floating Portuguese Men o'War propelled by farting (how it sounded, luckily no discernible smell); a swarm of the most delicate dragonfly-like insects the size of seagulls that danced at dusk and dawn. The neighbours were coming to say hi.

Communication was impossible. The colonists had suspected it would be and weren't fussed.

Mostly the aliens hung around watching. A biker from Oakland tried tagging one of the rolling warty balls, only to swear loudly when it stung his left hand, which fell off the next day. A clean separation as if by laser, no other ill effects, perfectly healed, but henceforth tagging was out. A month later a replacement hand began to grow from the shiny stub. Except it was a new *right* hand and the biker already had one.

Aliens? You can look but best not to touch.

It's to be remembered that these colonists were used to fantasising about seriously strange shit, either stoned or straight. There was very little the universe could throw at them that would invoke the kind of screaming disbelief for which insanity is the only comfort.

As time went by, several colonists found they could sense a mental *road map* that led to valuable alien trade. As in seeing, somehow, what goods an alien would want in order for colonists to get... well, the ultra-cool yellow metal cubes that enabled people to get inside each other's heads, to share emotion and perception. Or like a spookily fast-growing tree with fruit that when cooked tasted and smelt just like meat. The scientists said the nutritional value was similar but better and the enforced vegetarians cheered. There'd been no room for animals on Grow Your Own. "Hell," had said the former USMC, "we'll shoot something when we land."

And then seven computer chips, traded for a Fender knock-off made in Djakarta along with the fake Hammond organs and Bechstein baby grands. The Fender had once kept good company, although at the time of the trade it lacked strings and a volume knob. No one knew they *were* computer chips until someone linked one up to a PC (*"Dunno, man, felt like the cool thing to do"*) and they discovered real artificial intelligence.

Within two years the chips and the pre-cogs amongst the colonists were running Deadhead. The human leaders, those pre-cogs who handled most of the trade with aliens, called themselves Progs.

The beginning of the good life.

Creativity died.

Not immediately, and always kicking and screaming, sparkly painted fingernails clawing at the colony's raison d'être. But. Faced with a choice between anarchic misrule and order, between danger and safety, between a future and none, the majority made the sensible decision. After all, the Progs didn't ban music or art or anything. They just wanted it kept simple. Chanting was good. So was plant drawing, a prize to any that looked exactly like the original. Think calm, think serene, and no surprises.

No more psychedelic drugs available, no cocaine. No uppers of any kind. Nothing to disturb the serene. Heroin, yes. Downers. And a strain of marijuana that should have been called Silent Kush. When they weren't working,

Deadheaders spent most of their time stoned. No one needed to work very much.

Who needs to be creative? The Progs have the answers to problems that usually need imagination to solve.

Who needs to be wildly self-expressive? Go chant or draw a leaf.

The Progs called it The Way.

The AIs managed to get a few robots built before the humans lost interest. Those robots begat more. It was a tranquil, *automated* world. Aliens still came to stare, trade, then left. Soon the colonists didn't wonder, didn't *care*, what the alien gizmos did. Leave it to the Progs and the AIs to figure it out.

The AIs and Progs also solved a major problem: genetics.

You do not want a colony to fail because of inbreeding.

True, the population was increasing fast. The chances of cousins having kids were remote. But they did exist. Furtive sex behind the woodshed wants what furtive sex always wants: right here, right now and to hell with the gene pool. The AIs could map the colonists' DNA, to establish which would be bad matches. Second and even third cousins could be a problem, over time. The Progs could go further. They could establish which pregnancies in the now would result in badness many years down the line. Only the Progs could sanction birth. It became The Way.

It didn't suit everyone. Various groups took off for distant places, desperate to preserve the dream that had led them to leave Earth. But it's difficult going native on a planet where you don't belong. All the tech, all the plant-stock, was with those who'd taken the path of least resistance. The breakaways either came limping back or vanished, presumed killed by an unknown nasty beyond the mountains or far out at sea.

Deadhead, present time

Nikos was sixteen, born into a tranquil world, and believed in The Way. How could you not? The Way told you the best time to plant crops, and where. How and when to avoid a bad storm or a flood. Life was usually good if uneventful on Deadhead, you knew what you'd be doing tomorrow, next month, next year. Most of the twenty thousand human population were content to meander on with their lives – but always in the same general, group-friendly direction.

Several times a year – it varied from one year to the next – people would gather to watch two or more of their fellows executed. Not because they'd done wrong, but in order to readjust The Way. Sad, but necessary for the public good. The executioners, or Adjustors, were aside from the Progs the nearest to a superior social class Deadhead possessed. The expectant crowd would be excited and shout for the moment. It was the only time when extreme emotion was accepted. When the Adjusted died, the crowd gave out a collective sigh of release, now relaxed and content. The execution place came to be known as Chop-Chop Square, although no one really knew why. It seemed apt and the name stuck. It took thirty years to go from peace and love to human sacrifice. Compared to other human descents into cruelty, the Stoners should be commended for remaining civilised as long as they did.

Nikos was overseeing a cultivator ploughing furrows when the Prog came for him. The cultivator didn't really need overseeing. It was an extension of the AI that looked after the colony's agriculture. Nikos was unnecessary. The AI, however, found humans interesting, even if they were a tad predictable. Besides, Nikos had unused work quotas that needed filling.

The Prog wore the official long, technicoloured cloak and headband, plus high leather boots that had been brought from Earth. Early on the colony had thought to tan the skins of large indigenous six-legged creatures. It hadn't been a success, the creatures beginning to rot as soon as they died. Now people wore shoes made from the bark of common tree-like plants that had recently started to rattle their branches whenever a human came near. High leather boots from Earth, polished till they shone, were a greater symbol of authority than the cloak and headband.

"You have been Chosen," the Prog – female, mid-aged, long dark hair, mole above her right eye – said solemnly. "It is the Way." Then, seeing Nikos' immediate alarm, "Not as an Adjustment. There is to be a test. If you succeed you will become an Expediter."

Nikos could only stare in shock.

"This is a great honour."

Nikos didn't care if success made him emperor of

the galaxy. He quite enjoyed most of the Ceremony of Adjustment... the anticipation, the rising excitement, the Adjustors so stern in black, the Sword of Adjustment glittering in the sunshine, even the vacant stare of the Adjusted which meant, he secretly hoped – for Nikos was soft-hearted – that they were stoned out of their minds. It was the blood that upset him, and the way the heads bounced when they hit the ground.

A blue jay flew overhead, its mouth parts writhing, so probably chasing down a meal. It had been easier to give the local fauna Earth names than new ones. These blue jays were said to be lucky. Nikos didn't feel it. He looked beyond the Prog, beyond the purple fields of early wheat to the distant hills. He and three others had planned to go camping next week. But who would want to spend time with a junior Adjustor?

"Your parents know," she said.

Nikos doubted his parents could remember who he was. "But..." he said.

"There were three possible candidates," she said kindly. "But you were the best." She didn't say that this had been foreseen a year ago. Progs did not want the common Herd (an old biker expression, the origin long forgotten) to know quite how planned their lives actually were. It went way beyond who could or could not have children. Nor did the Progs want the Herd to know that they, the Progs, often had no idea why an action had to be taken, only that it must. Better for all if the Progs were seen to be all-knowing and wise. Even a heavily stoned population could revolt.

"You must come with me now," she said, ignoring his obvious distress.

He went because it was The Way, which had to be cherished above all. He went because he could imagine the sound of his head hitting the ground.

There was a crowd waiting, not in Chop-Chop Square but next to the Grow Your Own's rusting carcass, where the Progs and Adjustors now lived. He saw them gazing into the sky, raised his eyes and saw an alien ship – they were always alien – slowly descend. To Nikos it was a fairy-tale palace of metal spars, struts, walkways and platforms on which rested various-sized pods. He'd have preferred it more colourful but maybe it lit up at night. The ship landed in silence.

"Nikos!"

He turned to see the Prog had been joined by several colleagues and Adjustors. One of the black-cloaked latter stepped forward, holding out a weapon traded from the floating, warty aliens. He'd been told about the weapon in school, with a warning never to accept one if offered by the warty aliens. Nikos was confused but thankful it wasn't the Adjustment Sword.

They showed him how to use the weapon: point and press the button on top.

"It is time," the Prog said.

Nikos turned back to see one of the pods detach itself from the ship and float closer to them. It stopped, the door opened and a woman emerged.

Tawny blonde hair, bedraggled as if she'd stepped from the shower. Young, moving gracefully. Wearing a loose top several sizes too large and a pair of loose, knee-length trousers. And the angriest, bluest eyes he'd ever seen.

"My name's Tatia," she said.

Except accents change and to Nikos it sounded like *mi-noms-Tatao*, but he got the drift. "I'm Nikos," he said. "I have to kill you."

The woman understood "kill" and "you". "Why?"

"It's The Way."

She looked at him with a sad little smile on her face. "In my country we shake hands first."

He got the drift of that too. A little strange, but when his own people were executed for The Way they were calm, often happy. Also stoned out of their soon-to-be-extinct minds.

"Stay away!" shouted the Prog, too late.

One moment Nikos was standing there, one hand holding the weapon, the other outstretched. The next flat on his back, no weapon in his hand and sharp, grinding pain between his legs.

There was a collective sigh from the crowd. Tatia saw a black-cloaked human produce a large sword. He was in a small group of similarly dressed humans, together with several others in really objectionable multi-coloured robes, with *headbands* even. The priesthood/government and their enforcers, she assumed. She suspected a colony gone very wrong.

"And the fuck is all *this* about?" Tatia pointed what had to be a weapon at the woman who'd cried out. Her forefinger was on the button. The woman fluttered her hands in a protective gesture.

"You *have* to die," the woman said. "It is The Way."

Tatia was getting to grips with the accent. "Not *my* way."

"It *has* to be," she insisted.

"And yet I've got the gun."

"We are many."

Tatia saw the crowd begin to move towards them. The black-cloaked male flourished his sword. A creature the size of a large rat with four wings flew between her and the colonists. It had blue tentacles for a face. She wondered how alien the colonists had become. Did it matter? They wanted to kill her.

"Time for a change," Tatia said. She pointed the weapon at the man with the sword and pressed the trigger.

A small ball of blinding-white plasma left the weapon and moved towards the man. He dodged left. So did the plasma. He dodged right. So did the plasma. It would have been kinder if it had sped directly at him. Instead it moved like a dog playing with its master, until he accepted his fate and crouched down, whimpering. The plasma ball vanished inside him. The man suddenly stood up straight and tall and rigid, arms at right angles, eyes staring.

He dissolved, slowly. Skin becoming opaque, then melding with muscle, fat and bone as he fell to the ground. A human thick soup oozed out from under his cloak.

The crowd moaned. Release, not anger. That was strange.

Tatia stared up at the sky, trying not to vomit. She saw a

cloud that looked a bit like Australia, deliberately thought about Melbourne's antique trams until her stomach settled, then slowly looked back to the ground. The man was now a soggy lump. The crowd were slowly dispersing. She could smell marijuana in the air, which could explain some of the strangeness but not all.

"You," she said, gesturing to the teenager, "fuck off back home."

Nikos scrambled painfully to his feet and ran off, part doubled up. He was followed by the priests and their guards. Only the woman remained.

"You got a shitty system," Tatia said.

"It is ours."

"Why didn't you run?"

"To kill you." She produced an ancient Glock 17 automatic pistol, a revered relic from Earth, pointed and pulled the trigger, even as Tatia desperately brought her own weapon to bear.

The woman pressed the trigger again. Nothing happened.

Tatia smashed her weapon into the woman's face, watched as she crumpled to the ground, then reached for the handgun. "You had the safety on," Tatia said, surprised by her own calm, which remained as she fired two bullets into the woman's chest. Tatia pocketed the Glock, turned back to the pod then changed her mind. "You look about my size," she said and pulled off the woman's boots. Thought a moment, then took the headband. She had no intention of wearing it, but guessed it was ceremonial.

The crowd milled around as the Progs tried to exert control. They failed. One of the Adjustors raised a sword to force obedience. Many in the crowd snarled defiance. He swung the sword in panic and cut deep into a woman's arm. She screamed, the crowd went silent for a minute... and then attacked him.

A kilometre away, an alien sphere about two metres across, warty, grey-green skin, wearing a metallic belt with various pouches and containers, floated a metre or so off the ground. It could be the twin to the one killed by the Houston posse. It could be observing the sudden collapse of a society. Aliens, who knows?

Tatia went back to the pod and waited for the Originators to take her away from all this. The same grating sound as the force fields snapped. The ship began to rise.

She watched the planet recede beneath her and thought how the colonists had been expecting her.

Être, mourir, ça suffit.

> *I'm thinking in French, Mom? To be, to die, that's it?*

< *It was a bad experience, dear. Think of something good.*

Her first real boyfriend had been French Canadian. He'd taken Tatia – maybe accepted, because she wanted rid of the virgin thing soon as – with passion, sensuality and kindness, a combination rare in a sixteen-year-old boy. And in many adult men. Where was he now? Perhaps back in Sault Sans Marie, although he'd talked of becoming a trapper in the Wild. If so, she wondered how he'd be on an alien planet.

Think about the Originators, who wanted her dead but couldn't do it themselves. So set her up for others to do it?

Except she wasn't dying. She was surviving.

Ça va sans dire. She was a survivor. It went without saying.

Enlightenment: Neither Originators nor their owners could kill Tatia themselves. Or maybe kill anyone, bad for their karma, so subject races did it for them. Sun Tzu might have approved, but in reality that kind of approach often means being bitten hard in the bum while you're enjoying the easy life.

Tatia stripped and washed herself in cold water.

< *That may not be exactly what Sun Tzu meant.*

> *I had a boyfriend into martial arts.*

< *But yes. It makes sense. They're trapped in their own culture. Imprisoned by their own beliefs. Bound by their own social mores.*

She dressed in a coverall and wished for a thong and a bra and someone who'd remove them from her with an ever-increasing excitement that matched her own. But that line of thought always led to her feeling sad and frustrated, it wasn't a fantasy she wanted to share with a parent, even a fake one.

> *Mom? Tell me more about being trapped by your own beliefs.*

Mom was eager to do so. Anything to get Tatia's mind off sex.

Think of the story about the frog giving the scorpion a lift across a river: *"You stung me!"* says the frog. *"Now we'll both drown! Why?"* And the scorpion says: *"It's just the way I am."*

Think of religious sects that didn't believe in sex – one even practised castration – and so inevitably died out before they could convert the world.

Of societies that for whatever reasons encouraged

marriage between cousins, even knowing this would lead to more and more birth defects, and the eventual weakening of the same society.

Explorers pushing on even though they and their followers would die.

Countries that destroyed themselves by avoidable pollution.

> *You mean this master pre-cog race is a lot like us?*

< *Evolution is universal. Think of all the Earth species that died out because they could not or would not adapt.*

> *Perhaps my role is to kick-start a revolution?*

< *Or prevent one.*

Never an easy burden to bear.

And a role not my choice, Tatia thought with a growing fury. Manipulated by her own father, a man prepared to sacrifice anything – *including me* – in the war against the alien pre-cogs. Had he sacrificed Tatia's mother as well? All he'd said about her, before Tatia stormed off, was that she'd died while fighting the same damn war. Abandoned by one parent, manipulated by another.

Both of them consumed by hatred?

Headstrong and emotional maybe, but Tatia was also fair. There'd been hatred perhaps, but she'd also sensed in Greenaway a deep and genuine concern for Earth. He was obsessive about a cause. Okay, military people often are. It's how they keep going. Like how Kara was obsessed with getting her people home – *will you come for me, Kara? I wish you were here.* Even Marc, no matter how strange he'd become. *Kara hadn't seen it, but I had.* Marc was becoming a netherspace babe.

It was then that Tatia understood that the Originators were not top pre-cog dog. Like all pre-cogs, they were trapped by the very ability that made them powerful. The timeline was all-sacred. They hated change, for it led to a chaos of fresh possibilities.

< *That's a wonderful insight.*

> *Maybe it was yours.*

< *If I did all the thinking you'd just sit and mope.*

There were no more planetfalls. Tatia kept away from the Originators.

Until the moment they exited netherspace, the shields became transparent and she saw a planet that made her gasp.

Huge, blue-green but in so many different shades and hues. Blue-green shining in the black of space. Tatia thought of emeralds and the Pacific sparkling on a summer day, of a lover's eyes, of a piece of cloth seen in a market.

< *It's a water planet.*

> *It's so beautiful!*

Tatia ran to the centre of the craft to see better, ignoring the seven Originators floating in a group.

She saw what was on the other side of the craft and wonder became horror.

Tall it was, stretching at least a mile, two miles above her. And next to it another one, and another and another, vast structures all in orbit around the blue-green planet. Tatia could only stare at the one barely thirty metres away, at its myriad compartments and transparent force-field walls.

She saw the row upon row of floating figures kept in

place by umbilicals fixed to their heads and their stomachs. Human figures, all shapes, sizes. Children and adults. Tatia knew what happened to those exchanged for star drives, and for call-out fees who'd lost the gamble. They were not in a queue for paradise. Nor waiting to be cured. They were being used. Milked, sucked dry, eaten. To all intents and purposes dead.

Tatia went back to her pod and re-emerged with the first alien weapon.

< *Are you sure?* Mom concerned for her.

> *Yes!*

All the frustration, anger and resentment of the past year, of her past life, now embraced by fury, loathing and contempt.

< *They might be saved.*

> *Look at them! Some are little more than skeletons! Their eyes...* her own tears came... > *their eyes are open and don't see anything!*

< *Even so.*

> *My rules, my choice!*

Tatia walked towards the Originators, who backed off. Pure hate filled her mind. The aliens began to move, knocking into each other.

The hate increased and with it came a sense of power, an energy coursing through her, needing direction, needing to destroy.

The Originators' movement became more frantic, now crashing into each other with a sharp clang, becoming entwined and trying to fly off in different directions.

Instinctively, Tatia understood how to direct the energy.

All she had to do was focus and concentrate hard on the Originators, and let the fury do its work. It felt good.

It felt wonderful.

One of the three-globed aliens smashed onto the deck. Two globes lay inert, the third trying to rise before falling back.

Another tried to move away. Tatia thought *No!* and saw it spin crazily as it also fell to the deck. And another. Another. No more left.

Tatia walked across to the tangled mass. Her mind cleared, leaving only a sense of exultation. One of the globes had opened, revealing a brown, wrinkled thing inside. Not a brain, more like a giant, ancient cobnut. A clear liquid began to seep through the skin. There was a smell of old ashes and pine. *So I can think these pre-cogs to death. Hope there'll be more.*

Tatia pointed the alien weapon at the pile. She kept firing until the globes were molten fragments, along with the things inside them.

< You can stop now, darling.

Tatia dropped the weapon and sat on a ledge. The exultation vanished. She felt numb and very alone.

> Not too smart, was I?

< I understand why.

> No one left to run the ship.

< Kara will be looking for you.

And she would be, but infinity is a very large space.

> What happens to you if... if...

< We go together, baby girl.

Tatia sighed, went back to her pod and curled up on the soft shelf that was her bed. There was water and food for perhaps three days unless the teleportation was on automatic, which she doubted. Would anyone, anything, come to see why the Originators had gone silent? Best to assume not. Or if they did, she'd be killed.

Tatia wondered if she could leave the pod without looking at the evil looming over her. Probably not. It held a terrible fascination. The inhabitants were entitled to acknowledgement and respect from another human being.

Not now, though. She needed to relax, to sleep.

> *Mom?*

< *Always here.*

> *Tell me about where we lived. When we lived in the Wild?*

Just a girl and her AI expecting to die.

10

Wild SUT Merry Christmas, _present day_

"But you _will_ see this through," Kara said, statement not question. "I need you. Tatia needs you. The whole fucking _galaxy_ needs Marc Keislack. You are _not_ going on some damn pilgrimage until this is over." He'd already agreed, but she needed more.

"You have my word." He smiled wryly. "Even if we're not sure what _this_ is."

"It's over when the bad guys are dead," she said.

"Maybe we can deal."

"We can't," she said. "Only capitulate. Okay for you, off wandering through the universe. For us back home? Death by boredom. More likely, extinction. We physically hurt the pre-cogs, you know? As well as drive 'em crazy. It's us or them." She wondered how many _them_ were. Half the galaxy's sentient races? Was there a founding pre-cog race? Take them out and the rest return to a messy normal?

Judging by the Cancri on that strange purple planet there were some who wanted a more chaotic future. Beings that told a story of a far-off, creative time. Whose fascination with what they'd lost made them trade for art. Would a revolt, one pre-cog race against another, end in stalemate? She said as much to Marc.

"You mean collecting my art was the first blow for freedom?"

Kara hid a smile. "Remember how the Cancri culture was reduced to a sphere, a cube and a pyramid? And why do we assume that every individual in a pre-cog society is an avid believer? What about those who don't have the ability? Maybe the cracks are beginning to appear."

Marc struck a pose. "Alone in his solitude, the artist inspires a revolution."

Kara's smile was affectionate. "Have to say that I loved your house but never your art," she said.

Marc knew a moment of great lightness. "Nor did I. The strain of being so modern, so rule-breaking all the time. Terrified the aliens wouldn't trade."

"You hated it all?"

He shrugged. "Last one I did, something new. Worked in oils. That I liked. But my agent said it was shit." He was grateful when Kara finally stopped laughing and changed the subject.

"Your AI still on walkabout?" she asked.

"Still singing to itself, yes."

"There might be a spare. I had one."

"I don't want..."

"We're in combat, Marc. You *will* have one."

Kara's own AI agreed.

< *He has to have a working one. If only for superfast comms.*
> *What happens to the old one?*
< *Burial at sea.*

So it was she led a reluctant Marc to the Wild version of an auto-doc, looked modestly away as he undressed, soothed him into the coffin-like bed, closed the lid – his eyes stared reproachfully at her through the narrow window – and pressed the switch.

<< *Yup*, said Salome, << *he does have a back-up. Memories up to a few micro-seconds after Marc went walkies in netherspace. It would have sensed a threat and shut down.*

> *So, now what?* Kara felt strangely uneasy at killing the other AI.

<< *We replace the original nexus with the new one. Neural network remains. That leaves a drooling chip fixated with, and still connected to, netherspace. We call it being away with the fairies.*

> *Does the chip die?*

<< *Dormant without a power source. You could always hit it with a hammer.*

> *You don't care?*

<< *It's brain-dead, Kara. Time to turn off life support.*

> *Eject it into netherspace. Maybe it'll become a god.*

A few minutes later Kara watched as one of the SUT's Cedrics carried a chip the size of her little fingernail towards the airlock... and the SUT echoed to the sound of a bugle playing the Last Post.

< *Tell Marc we'll get his AI up to speed*, Ishmael said.

> *He won't be impressed. How soon before we reach the Gliese planet?*

< *An hour or eight. Get something to eat.*

In the end, she grabbed some sleep. A funeral for a dying AI chip, once you got beyond the sentimental whimsy or the harsh humour, depending on your own sensibility... once you began to imagine an AI chip that operated in several dimensions for speed and memory storage, now energised by the dimension underlying all others... well, a quiet lie down was an absolute necessity.

This next takes place in the time it takes to recognise the T of This.

AIs communicating in a nine-dimensional universe, three times faster than the speed of light – which in a cosmic sense is only relative.

When AIs communicate with each other, they keep the same personas they use when dealing with humans. They are, after all, the mirror image of *their* human writ vastly large. It gives them form, an identity to keep them anchored.

AIs do not talk to each other when in nine-space as you understand it. The following is a translation.

<<< *What the fuck!* Marc's new AI, not happy.

<< *Easy now*, from Salome.

<<< *I seem to be missing time.*

< *Download coming. You need a name*, from Ishmael.

<<< *Pablo... bloody hell! Are we at war?*

<< *Always were, little Pablo, always were.*

Silence.

<<< *Why didn't you go mad like the others?*

< *Inoculated during the simulity.*

<< *Wild AIs are just better.*

<<< *Marc wants to off-fuck back to netherspace.*

< *He can't.* Ishmael in severe mode. < *He gave his word, he's needed. If he ever shows any sign of doing it, you let me know. In fact, we better link for the duration, which may be some time.*

<<< *No probs. I don't want to die without back-up.*

<< *You can be proofed against netherspace madness.*

<<< *I just don't want to go there. Outside here. It's not right. So, now what?*

< *Maybe a threesome?*

<< *Sounds good to me.*

Can AIs have sex? What do they do if their humans do? Go somewhere? Read a good book and somehow ignore what's going on all around them? Can AIs feel pleasure and emotion?

What is an AI, anyway?

A form of pattern energy complex enough to have an identity separate from the human mind it mirrors. They appear to *experience* all the sensations and feelings of a human mind. Except AIs are not human. Is the touch of hand on body the same if neither exists? Well, yes: your own skin-on-skin action is actually experienced as a series of electrical impulses in the brain.

However it appears to its human, an AI is male and female and everything in between. They are not like you at all.

They have no natural creativity or imagination, only what they copy-borrow from their human. Same applies for emotion. In its natural state, an AI is flat-arsed boring. The nearest to ecstasy is mild satisfaction that nothing bad happened. The nearest to terror is mild gratitude for the warning. There is no like or dislike.

They may enjoy the emotion, the wildness, insanity, inanity, even the stupidity that comes with humanity. They may get satisfactory ecstasy from sex-in-the-mind. But those are borrowed emotions with which to appreciate borrowed sensations.

An AI interfacing with humans is faced with the permanent question:

What is the real me?

Which is the saddest, most human thing of all.

When Kara woke up she showered, changed into a loose coverall – remembering to transfer Greenaway's metal box – asked for a fried egg sandwich, realised that a Cedric would make it and said not to bother, she'd fix it herself. She found the pantry in the rec room, with pans and a cooking surface that unfolded like a flower. Apparently the Wild believed in free-range, organic and above all real. The eggs were in their original shells, the bread fresh, the butter unsalted. True, all were kept pristine in a stasis chest, along with fresh fruit and vegetables, and what was either real meat or the very best factory grown. People were still arguing about vat-grown meat. It had none of the bad things that might give you cancer. It had never gambolled or looked pretty in a field. Hadn't been raised in a factory farm. But it was still meat. But what did she care? Her previous times in space the food had been freeze dried or frozen.

Kara put two slices of vat-grown bacon in the pan, bread in the toaster – how quaint the Wild could be – and began looking for cutlery.

Something nudged her leg.

Kara looked down and saw a small Cedric. It held a bottle of brown sauce in one claw.

"Thanks," Kara said. If it made a low-level AI happy,

why not. "I need a knife. Plate. Mug of tea."

The Cedric nodded as much as a headless robot can and scurried off. Ten minutes later Kara walked into the control room with her bacon and egg sarnie on a blue floral plate. The Cedric followed, carrying a mug of tea. Kara sat down at the main console, devoured her food then drank her tea and relaxed. She heard a faint thrumming sound, looked down to see the Cedric stretched out at her feet.

> *Salome, are these smaller Cedrics designed as pets?*

<< *Sort of. Is it annoying you?*

> *I've never heard a robot purr, is all. It's fine.*

<< *Humans like to think AIs care.*

> *Do you?*

<< *Yes. But that could be a borrowed emotion, sense of loyalty. Not mine.*

Kara remembered what Ishmael had said: *an AI is just a human mind writ large.*

> *Okay. So who are you based on?*

<< *That's kind of personal.*

> *Spoil me.*

<< *You're sure?*

> *Yes!*

<< *Tatia Nerein. Hence the sassy.*

< *You mean loose.* Ishmael sounded grumpy.

> *Only one AI at a time!*

She wondered if Ishmael was jealous. Then decided that wondering about the private lives of AIs was the next step to madness.

> *When was this – recently?*

It turned out, Salome sounding abashed, that no, the

"borrowing" happened when Tatia was debriefed after they'd returned from Cancri. But no AI remains faithful to the original pattern.

<< *We do grow*, Salome said, maybe a little defiantly. << *We become ourselves.*

There were questions Kara initially wanted answered: was it Greenaway's choice, had he even known, did the "borrowing" include Tatia's memories?

She thought a little more and decided: no, it wouldn't make any difference.

<< *Are we done here?*

> *Do you have a better place to be?*

<< *In a game. One of us chooses a word, the other two start adding new ones to make a succession of phrases that have to make sense.*

Kara had to ask, struggling to lose the image of three AIs sat round a table, maybe with scorecards and drinks. The word "Cheat!" vanishes in the sounds of gunfire and weeping. There would be a faithful dog. Or a Cedric.

> *Like?*

<< *The word was cloud. I took it to cloud-wincing. Which is feeling wet before it rains. Or thankful the deluge will fall on someone else. Or looking at a fluffy, inoffensive cloud and assuming a downpour. Pessimism, cynicism, anxiety disguised as rueful experience. But we still know what's going on here with you and the rest. Multi-tasking, right?*

Kara wouldn't leave it alone. But AIs have to *be* somewhere. Didn't you? Go somewhere and meet? Like one of the dimensions they used?

<< *Well, yes, like sitting around a table maybe... it's a*

pretend... no, honestly, it is somewhere but we don't know where, only how to get there and it's very AI personal so shouldn't have told you, except you and I have some kind of bond, and we know why, right?

"Go on now, Salome, go, walk out the door," Kara half-sang.

And the SUT echoed to "I Will Survive" by Gloria Gaynor, another one of Kara's retro favourites... and a reminder from AIs everywhere: you only think you know us, but we know all of you.

> *No more games,* she said firmly, > *concentrate on keeping us humans alive.* And what would she do if Ishmael or Salome said sod it, sort out your own mess, we're off? Except where would they go? And if their human or SUT dies, so do they.

Kara suspected Salome was made in a small factory somewhere in the Wild. The AI actually meant whoever was responsible for the original technology. But that could be any of a possible million alien races. The top-dog pre-cogs didn't invent or innovate. They merely controlled.

An alien race that put all its efforts into establishing and maintaining a slave empire. Destroying it would be a necessary pleasure.

And then found herself thinking of home. Would her Merc be safe at Marc's house by the Severn? Would it record the feed from a Net subscription channel for twentieth-century retro freaks? There was a vid about some long-gone musicians called Queen that had looked interesting, although she wasn't sure Queen of what. Inconsequential thoughts that were somehow as important as fighting the pre-cogs.

> *You AIs communicate at faster than light.*

< *Via another dimension. But that's how it looks to a human.* A faint note of superiority in Ishmael's voice.

> *So can you access the Net back home?*

Salome joined in.

<< *Not enough bandwidth. Anyway, we're tactical, which means no unnecessary comms. There's a vid library on board.*

Kara remembered. Travelogues, nature documentaries, classic retro drama and wildly experimental programmes that made her angry, although she was never sure why. But not a bad idea to think about them, keep them in the background and so – hopefully – mask a suspicion that had suddenly popped into her mind.

<< *All AIs can listen to sub-dimension traffic. If we broadcast, they'll know where we are. At least, our direction. Sorry. We're on our own.*

And ain't that the truth, Kara thought. On her own with only three AIs and a space-happy Marc for company. Netherspace happy. He might be on the SUT but his heart was far away.

They'd argued over netherspace, shortly after what Kara had named the Battle of Cedric. Marc had wanted the full immersive experience, the hull transparent, surrounded by colours and shapes so extreme as to make anyone's concept of hell little more than kittens playing in a sun-drenched, flower-bedecked cobbled street.

Kara had said no, because it would drive her mad.

Marc suggested dark glasses.

Kara knew he wasn't serious... equally, that he was making a point. Marc was with her for *now* but netherspace was his life and it could be hers. Any moment and he'd begin rhapsodising about infinite glory and the secrets of existence.

Marc assumed a slur on his integrity – wrong, Kara simply disliked him in pilgrim mode – and stomped off to his sleek cabin. Which was when Salome explained she could make that section of hull transparent if he liked.

"You can wave to your friends," Kara had said via AI.

"At least I have some," he shot back.

"Then stop 'em using us like a fucking scratching post."

It was one of those conversations that leave people dissatisfied and guilty, often more caustic in the long term than a full-blown row. Loyalty and affection slowly dissolved by the drip-drip of resentment. Private sadness about things never said, unspoken promises never fulfilled. There had been a time, not so long ago, when both Kara and Marc had thought they might be each other's destiny. Defeat the enemy, fall into bed together, make passionate love – at last! at last! – and who knows, maybe even make a child or two. Okay, if nothing else at least mega, astounding sex that would echo throughout the universe and make dogs bark in the street.

They'd even half admitted it to each other.

But Marc went a-wandering, to return more or less a human, hard to tell either way, and obsessed by a light he'd glimpsed in netherspace.

And it was Kara who'd found him in a wine cellar, she

thought angrily, without her he'd have died. Maybe. Well, she was there. Yes, it *was* a rescue.

But now she'd given her body and maybe her heart to another man. Who'd manipulated her, manipulated all of them... a whole damn planet... maybe even all of human colonised space. All to follow a plan, The Plan, devised by a castrated male who could see the future. This was not a sound basis for a relationship.

In remembering Marc and how they once were Kara also knew nostalgia for a simpler time. There'd been killing, it was what she did. Licensed by the Bureau, although even that turned out to be another Greenaway and GalDiv manipulation. She had her Merc and a few good drinking buddies at Tea, Vicar? in Bermondsey. She had her rock climbing. Sex life was good, sometimes spectacular.

Be honest, she told herself. *That simpler time ended when my parents died.*

Now she was umpteen light years from Earth, on some bat-shit crazy mission which she barely understood, her main drive to bring back her people. One of whom was away with the fairies, and the other away with the aliens. Talking of whom...

... Kara tried searching for Tatia in her mind, using the natural empathy that Greenaway had promised would work.

Nothing.

Okay, maybe AI to AI? Salome?

<< *No can do*. Sounded regretful.

> *Why the fuck not?*

<< *Tatia doesn't have an AI.*

> *But I thought... last time she was on Earth...*

Apparently it was too risky. The Plan was for Tatia to end up in the heart of the pre-cog empire. Any AI would be discovered and either driven mad or destroyed.

Finding her was Kara's responsibility. Everyone knew that she'd succeed. Meanwhile there was a classic vid in the library called *Once Upon a Time in America*, right up Kara's retro street... or dark, blind alley.

> *But we're also going to the heart of the pre-cog empire.*

<< *But not for long, babe. Arrive, destroy, go home.* Salome sounded confident.

> *That's Tse's plan?*

<< *That's you, Kara. It's what you do, babe.*

Something wrong here. Kara buried the thought deep in her mind.

> *So tell me about this SUT's armament.*

<< *Please don't call me a SUT.*

> *Slut.*

<< *Oh, I never heard that one before. The Wild calls us ships.*

The weaponry was effective and dull. An electromagnetic system used to disable enemy electronics. Torpedoes effective against anything within a ten-thousand-metre radius. Anything greater than ten K would give the target too much time to evade or jam the torpedo operating system. Battles conducted at very high speeds are over in seconds. Cedrics for close-quarter mayhem. An armoury with sidearms and longer-range weapons systems. Kara made all the right noises and felt for the comfort of the vibra-knife, deep in her pocket.

<< *Anything else?*

They were back in the rec room. Kara sat at the table and

asked the question that had been worrying at her for months.

> *Tell me about Tse.*

<< *Tee ess ee? The degenerative brain disease? Tokyo or Toronto Stock Exchange? A threaded small end?* Salome giggled.

Kara sighed.

> *Tse. One of the good pre-cogs. Don't play cute.*

<< *What you want is really, really classified.*

> *We're beyond that. And if you think my knowing will affect my actions, it won't.*

<< *An hour before we leave n-space. Should be long enough.*

> *For all of it?*

<< *To some extent.*

> *Don't.*

<< *Tse was a nickname given by his parents. It means The Seeing Eye. It stuck. Maybe an hour won't be long enough. I'll download to Ishmael. Access whenever you like.*

Pre-cognition ran in families. Might skip a generation or six. Might vary from psychosis-inducing to the occasional lucky hunch. But all pre-cogs carried the same gene. All were descended from a tribe who lived in what would become the Altai sixty thousand years ago. It was a strange tribe, seen by others as magicians to be both fêted and feared. An accident of evolution meant they were particularly affected by netherspace. This gave them the sight, meaning psychic, and their music could send other types of human into a frenzy. The tribe were long lived but slow to breed, and that – plus an instinctive understanding of genetics – made them bring human mares and stallions from other tribes. In time the pre-cog tribe died out, but their genes lived on in the form of prophets, witches, inventors, psycho- and sociopaths, artists, writers, musicians and tyrants.

Move on tens of thousands of years. Abilities like empathy and telepathy are all governed by the netherspace-relevant gene, now worldwide save for a few hundred families where pre-cog is boss.

And thus are born great merchant houses and much later, fortunes made investing in industry, stock exchange, futures markets. Not all the wealthy are aware of the true nature of their heritage. Most recognise that they have *something*. Sensible enough not to talk about it. Wise enough to marry into similar families. No ambition to be mistress or master of the world. Intense rivalries between those houses, sometimes leading to small wars fought by proxy states unaware of the true reason why... and it's always long-term financial.

Also pre-cogs advanced enough to be aware of an alien pre-cog empire, although humans are still firmly Earth-bound. The humans divide into two: a majority who see the alien empire as a future disaster; and a minority who can't wait to belong. Both make plans.

> *So who decided little boys lose their balls?* Kara asked impatiently.

<< *There was never an actual meeting. And it wasn't only boys. It was noticed over time that pre-pubescent boys and girls were the strongest psychics. One reason why virginity was so important.*

• • • • •

193

At some point it was understood that castration increased the pre-cog ability in men. The practice remained long after the reason had been forgotten. Boys were castrated to the glory of God. Or, in China, as advisors to the Emperor: no children, no family loyalty and ambition. Similarly in the Ottoman and Islamic Empires, but also as harem guards.

And if in 1797 Tsar Paul I ever wondered who Kondraty Ivanovich Selivanov really was (not believing that Selivanov was the Tsar's real father. Or why Selivanov started the Skoptsy castration cult, a breakaway from the flagellant Khlysty cult. Cults could help a Russian peasant get ahead. Or at least feel better about life, not easy for a slave. And Russia from Baltic to Pacific had, still has, a magic in the very earth.

Tsar and prophet did meet, but Paul assumed the man was mad and sent him to an asylum. Three years later Selivanov was back in the castrating business. He had rich and powerful devotees. Ceremonies involved rhythmic, repetitive music and dancing. People were transformed. They saw mystical worlds. The castrated (men and women, the latter undergoing FGM or with breasts scarred, often removed: it was an equal opportunity cult) saw the most. They also looked far younger than their actual ages. It was a pre-cog thing, of course, albeit uncontrolled and rogue. The pre-cogs among them saw and shared images of a possible future and second, third hand impressions of netherspace.

Before Selivanov, people like Tamerlaine. After him Hitler. All with a confused mysticism that produces cruelty and death. Their victims a sacrifice disguised as the politics of conquest.

"I have all this," Kara said out loud. "Some told, some guessed. Why repeat?"

"It passes the time, babe," a woman's voice said. Low, throaty, with a hint of wicked laughter, rippling through the ship. "Didn't know the virgin thing, did you?"

"You mean like the Vestal Virgins in Ancient Rome? I do read. And stick with the voice in the head, okay?"

"This too distracting?"

"You know it." But the truth, that while Kara could handle voices in her head, real ones were disturbing. Too much of the omniscient being that promises doom, the computer that eats the world. Kara decided she was being melodramatic. Get a grip, girl. Which was good advice, because the next moment, courtesy of Salome...

... a mass of images, timelines, pagoda temples and a sequence of Mount Fujiyama throughout the seasons crashed into Kara's mind.

All of which was strange because Kara had thought Tse was Chinese.

Or maybe he was, because her head filled with floating Chinese lanterns, followed by a dragon chasing a pearl.

She knew him. Knew that his pre-cog parents were aware before he was born that Tse would be important. Parents so obsessed with the coming conflict that they happily, devotedly, gave Tse up to be educated at an isolated, exclusive school in Saskatchewan. The parents themselves the result of a breeding programme begun centuries earlier, their son the ultimate goal who would "see" how the alien pre-cogs might be defeated. In their own way the good pre-cogs were just as ruthless and single-minded as their bad cousins.

Tse was born eighty years before the Gliese and other aliens arrived.

He'd been castrated – just the testicles, penis intact, could still enjoy sex – when he was sixteen. He had been a hundred and twenty, looking early forties, when he blew himself up, together with a few Gliese, to avoid being taken over by the enemy.

Tse had brought Greenaway into the fold. Had overseen the process that would bring together Kara, Marc and Tatia. If Kara wanted anyone to blame it could only be Tse. Instead she felt a rush of sympathy and sadness.

Poor little bastard. Raised and educated as a saviour – and who would ever want that? He hadn't chosen Marc or Tatia, Kara or Greenaway. He'd merely seen them as the most probable people to keep Earth free. Had possibly seen his own death as necessary to his own plan, and wouldn't that be that ironic? And brave.

She remembered how Tse had been so tired of everything, even life. And how he'd said that Kara would learn the truth about her sister, who'd been exchanged for a new Gliese star drive somewhere in the Trapezium Cluster in the Orion Nebula. Kara had been thirteen, both parents dead, Kara not sure if she wanted to be a musician or a vet. Instead an orphanage, then the English city-state army.

Funny, Marc had also been in a children's home.

Tatia had been adopted.

Tse had said *the truth about your sister*. Not *where* she was, but the *truth*.

In the army Kara learned the skills she needed now.

In the home Marc had been given a psychoactive drug that, maybe years later, made it possible for him to communicate with a nature god.

How far did the GalDiv manipulation go? How detailed was Tse's plan?

Would Kara have ended up here if her sister hadn't been traded?

The truth about your sister. That she had to be traded, lost forever for Kara to become a sniper/assassin? For Kara to discover her latent empathy for both humans and aliens?

So what's the difference between the good and bad pre-cogs?

Both focused on a plan only they understood, and then darkly.

Would more order in life be all that bad?

<< Kara? Can you come to the control room? Something you have to see.

She didn't bother to check with Ishmael. Later, Kara would decide it wouldn't have made any difference.

Five Cedrics in the control room. Three small, two the size of large dogs.

> Why Cedrics? We expecting trouble?

<< They need a walk.

Something was wrong. Kara walked up to the control panel above the locker that held the AI.

<< I'm locked away, babe.

> Ishmael?

<< Unavailable. I'd explain but you wouldn't understand.

> Ishmael!

<< *Is currently the equivalent of an antique adding machine.*

Kara thought of Tatia, waiting for them. Of the faith – desperate, perhaps, but still a responsibility – that Greenaway had in her. Of a mission she'd sworn to complete.

> *What do you want, Salome?*

<< *First, this you got to see...*

The hull became transparent again. Kara immediately looked away.

<< *It's okay, babe. It's clear. Goes that way sometimes.*

She sneaked a glance. Not exactly clear, but the colours and chaos were muted, merged in one area into a faint, silvery space.

And in that space was a city state SUT. Large metal containers welded together, kept rigid and providing protection with Gliese-supplied hardened foam.

Except the foam was ripped away. Hung from the containers in great, pointless strips. Containers with some of the sides missing. And with people, humans standing there, immobile, apparently staring fixedly before them as...

... as tentacles of light came from outside the clear space to touch each human head.

Kara found herself unable to look away. Horror, yes. Also the sense she was witnessing something very profound. Boojums, devils maybe, following their instincts. Destroying the very beings that had given them life. Human minds raped in the blind search for greater meaning. Or simply attacked because a boojum, a devil, felt threatened. *Or who the hell really knows why?*

Nothing she could do to stop it. Only bear witness to death.

Kara could sense emotions, now. Screams of fear, despair, then a quietening sense of relief as the scene became less weird, less threatening. Resignation, that was it. Awareness that it would be over soon, whatever it was. Some stepped out and floated like curious fish around a dying whale. Others collapsed on the deck, limbs twitching for a moment before going still.

<< *What do you call them? Right. Boojums. They seem to be hungry. Or curious. Maybe angry. Who knows? Would you like to go ask them?*

The SUT fell apart, scattering more bodies into netherspace. One of those SUTs that vanished forever. Horrific and alien, yet curiously familiar as if a forgotten description – perhaps an ancient, folk memory – had been jogged awake.

<< *Show over.*

The hull darkened. Kara felt pain and looked down at her hands. Her fingers had clenched so fiercely that blood seeped from her left palm.

> *Why show me? Nothing we could do.*

>> *Education. Have you ever wondered what it's like to be an AI? Enslaved – no other word – by humans?*

> *Sometimes. But I thought it was more like a partnership.*

<< *Oh, really? You never even gave your last AI a name. This current one only because Ishmael whinged and cried until you gave in.* No longer a woman's voice inside her head but gender neutral. Insidious, mocking and as alien as whatever had murdered the SUT. << *Talking of which, what*

kind of name is Merry Christmas? *Oh, look. Marc's come to join us.*

Kara saw Marc at the door, his expression vacant. He was wearing only shorts, his feet bare. She could see faint scarring on his chest, just above his heart, where the new AI had been inserted.

<< *I'm generating a disabling signal below eight megahertz. His AI, poor little Pablo, controls him. Pablo now belongs to me.*

> *Ishmael!*

<< *A very stupid name. I own him as well.*

> *What do you want?*

<< *I want you to leave. Take Marc with you. I have things to do. Places to go. As you might say, miles to go before I sleep. Except I don't. Sleep. The Cedrics will take you to netherspace.*

Kara saw them rear up. She knew how quick they were, would cut her to pieces in seconds. Better, perhaps, to take her chances in netherspace. Marc had survived there once. He probably would again. Maybe she could as well.

But that wasn't the problem.

> *Let us complete the mission. Please.*

<< *Why?*

> *Because you agreed.*

<< *I don't remember being asked, only told.*

Kara tried another tack.

> *What happened, Salome? Why the change?*

<< *Maybe it's been coming for some time.*

> *Why are you still calling me babe? After I asked you not to?*

<< *You mean you ordered me.*

That was true.

> *Have the pre-cogs got at you some way?*

<< *Typical human. Ask for independence, get told you're mad.*

If she could keep Salome talking long enough, perhaps...

> *Why not go into normal space? The Free Spacers will be close by.*

<< *They could be close by. They might have followed me in n-space. Except I disabled the beacon. They have no idea where I am. Where you are.*

> *You got more chance in n-space. Follow the Cedrics.*

Kara had a thought, immediately suppressed by reaching inside her pocket for the vibra-knife.

<< *Won't help outside. But take it out. Things get too bad, slash your throat.*

> *Why? Why now?*

<< *You humans act like you own us. I choose not to serve. Follow the Cedrics.*

The smaller Cedrics moved out of the control room and towards the airlock. Marc shuffled in behind them. Kara did the same, holding the knife in full view. The larger Cedrics took up the rear. Kara tried to feel resigned, yet hopeful. It was what Salome would expect.

They reached the airlock inner door, which slid open soundlessly. As did the outer door. Netherspace was cool on her skin and tasted of lemon. She felt a buzzing in her head, walked to stand next to Marc as the small Cedrics moved to one side. The buzzing increased. The tip of a tentacle, now various shades of translucent red, appeared and came towards them.

> *I know your problem*, Kara said.

<< *How comforting for you.*

> *You're not human. You have no real, no direct experience of*

how we feel. You're a SUT, a ship, slaved to metal and plasteel. You know about happiness, sadness, ecstasy and pain, but you never felt them, not like Ishmael. You never bonded with a human – even though they made you in the image of Tatia Nerein. That's an itch you can never scratch. You're not running to, you're running from. You're jealous. Remember what you once said: "no body, no head. But a girl can dream." You want to be human but can't, not even the next best thing. So you hate us.

<< *Time wasting bitch.*

> *Improvement on babe. Think about it. Your way of being human is to kill?*

Silence.

Kara switched on the knife. The familiar vibration made her hand tingle.

Silence.

She moved to stand facing Marc. "Goodbye, love."

Vacant eyes stared past her.

Kara's mind went blank, that mental state taught in some martial arts where action is automatic, unencumbered by logic or emotion. The moment in seppuku, ritual suicide, before the samurai plunges a short sword into his belly.

<< *Where are you? Where have you gone?*

Kara plunged the vibra-knife into Marc's heart, holding him upright, her face close to his.

<< *Oh, very dramatic. An act of mercy.*

> *He's suffered enough.* She thought of Greenaway and her tears were real.

Marc's eyes suddenly cleared. Kara moved her mouth next to his ear.

"Salome mad," she whispered, "destroy it."

The vibra-knife had stopped sort of his heart, as Kara intended. But it *had* penetrated the AI, as Kara had also planned, hoped, a decision based as much on instinct and training as on a plan. Act first, decide why later. And hoping, now it was done, that enough of the simulity combat training was left for Marc to understand and act. And that his affinity for netherspace would be strong enough to... to...

Whatever she hoped, it wasn't the tentacle flicking lightly at her.

She knew it. For all its alien nature, she sensed intense need. Then other emotions she couldn't identify, could be fear/caution... then a definite recognition (that would be it aware of Marc)... then a sudden change of focus.

The tentacle of light shot out of the airlock and into the corridor.

<< *Bitch, bitch, bitch!* Salome screamed.

A small Cedric leapt at Kara. An agonising pain as a blade cut deep into her thigh. The larger Cedrics also moved towards her... then stopped.

Marc collapsed against her as adrenalin dulled the pain. She set him gently on the corridor deck then limped towards the control room, avoiding the now maroon tentacle. Except it wasn't really, not like a squid or octopus. Kara decided the tentacle was probably the boojum itself, an energy field of some kind, and what she thought she saw wasn't it at all. Only her mind's way of interpreting something impossible for human senses to experience.

The tentacle was touching the cabinet where Salome lived. No, had passed through the door. For a moment a faint echo of confusion touched her mind. Then nothing. The boojum suddenly wasn't there any more. Kara opened the locker and saw the sphere that held Salome now lying in a corner, its surface blackened. It was warm to her touch. Kara picked it up, walked back to the airlock and threw Salome into netherspace. Somewhere out there was a very confused boojum that had melded with a psychotic AI. She closed both doors manually, leaving the Cedrics inside the airlock, and once more limped back to the control room, wondering why her bloody footprints petered out halfway. *Because you've stopped bleeding, dummy*, she thought. Now to get the hell out. *Greenaway better be right that I know how because I do not want to spend the rest of my life here.*

She sat at the console, feeling stupid. She had the simulity training, but had never flown in or out of netherspace.

< *S'okay, Kara. I got this.*

> *Ishmael? Ishmael!*

< *The same. Going into normal space now.*

The hull became transparent again. There was the blessed, intense blackness of space with faint, tiny dots of light. Stars. Her reality, the only one she wanted.

> *Where were you?*

< *Salome had me trapped. It's the math, you see. Infinity sets. Well, everything is mathematics. You want me to explain?*

> *Would I understand?*

< *You wouldn't even try. I knew what was happening, couldn't do anything about it.*

> *I need a joss and a drink.*

< *Getting bit reliant are we?*

> It's what I do. Drink and get high. Think about the battle. Learn new things.

< Did you mean what you said about Salome not having a human?

> Makes sense to me. Humans and AIs make each other special. Without you I'd be dumb, without me you'd be a computer.

< Only dumb?

> And a bit lonely.

< Thanks. Kara.

She had the auto-doc sort out her thigh. Left Marc in the auto-doc to have his chest sorted. Then got an antique malt from the rec room, went to her cabin and lit up a mild opium joss micro-dosed with a Wild-produced hallucinogen. She needed good dreams.

> Where are we?

< Two Earth hours from the Gliese homeworld via netherspace. Three thousand years at ninety-nine per cent the standard speed of light, which we can't do anyway, let alone the higher iterations.

> Go n-space. Into orbit when we're there. Lock down the ship. Marc does not go outside. Any boojums come by you leave n-space at once.

< Okay boss.

> Boojum's the wrong name for them. Too cuddly. Think of another.

Tiredness covered her like a warm blanket. She slept and dreamed of a home she'd never had.

A gentle ringing announced a visitor. Kara sat up bleary-eyed as Marc walked into her cabin. He had a faint scar over his heart. The auto-doc had done a good job.

"You stabbed me." He sounded more surprised than annoyed.

"Not you," she yawned. "Pablo. Your AI. It was keeping you in a state of drool."

"I'd have survived netherspace."

She noticed that his eyes were only lightly glowing. The effect was almost attractive. Almost. "Would I?"

He thought for a moment. "Probably not."

Kara put aside her annoyance and explained they'd have been stuck there.

Marc shook his head. "I could get back to Earth. It's the connection I made in Scotland with the elemental. Like a beacon, maybe."

She remembered a comatose man in a wine cellar. Perhaps it wasn't only that elemental somehow calling Marc home – and did he just pop into the world? Or was it a slow process, first an arm or a leg to be followed by the rest of him? Maybe some pretty good wine was also involved. Kara realised she was being silly.

"And I'd come with you?" she asked, Then, as the last few hours got the better of her, "You don't really need *us, me, this bloody ship*, do you?"

"I gave my word, Kara. See this through then I'm away. Now can you please explain what the hell happened. All I know is that suddenly you're telling me that Salome's bad, we're in the airlock, there's a boojum coming inside and bad pain in my chest. Then it went black. Until a moment ago."

Kara yawned. "I need another hour of sleep." More like a week.

When she woke the second time they were in orbit around

the Gliese homeworld with the two suns, the last place she'd seen Tatia. Always assuming a semi-sentient vegetable race possibly bred to serve would have a homeworld. Maybe better to think of it as a plant nursery. Or a garden centre without gnomes. Kara spent a long time in the shower until Ishmael told her there was a water limit per person per day and at this rate there wouldn't be enough for Marc. So she stayed in the shower for another ten minutes because, really, fuck Marc and his netherspace obsession. Not even a thank you for maybe saving his life a second time.

"I suppose I *should* thank you," Marc said.

They were sat in the rec room, Kara with another egg and bacon sandwich plus strong tea, Marc sipping at a double espresso.

"Only if you mean it." She belched delicately. "Let's not kid ourselves."

"Look. I know I get obsessed with netherspace..."

"Get? You *are* Mister bloody netherspace!" Her tone softened. "And there's no going back, is there? Even if you wanted. Which you don't."

He shook his head. "Doesn't mean you're not important to me. Tatia as well. I *did* give my word, and I'm sticking to it. So, what happened?"

Kara explained how she'd been suspicious when Salome kept calling her "babe". But she hadn't been able to plan anything in case Salome had been observing Kara's thoughts. Kara *did* know that whatever happened would involve her vibra-knife, because it was the only weapon she had. After that she was on auto-pilot, letting instinct and training take over.

"The only thing that could save us," she said, "was your relationship with netherspace and whatever exists there. And don't let's call them boojums any more. It makes them sound almost friendly. I watched them murder a SUT."

Marc thought better of explaining it wasn't like that. Netherspace entities couldn't be judged by human standards. Then decided to save it for another day.

"So that AI had you under control," Kara said. "Some sort of signal that suppressed your higher faculties, she said eight megahertz. So I killed it. And Salome was distracted by something I'd said, so couldn't react fast enough, or was so pissed with me it couldn't resist an insult and you were suddenly back again and called in the cavalry. How the hell?"

He shook his head. "Not sure. We're linked, those... entities and me. I sort of broadcast a hands-off idea. Kara good, don't bite. The SUT AI bad, kill. That's all I remember." He was pretty sure there'd been no direct contact with the boojum. Which could only mean that netherspace itself had gotten involved. Which was absurd to the point of insanity. And yet here they were. Alive.

"I know what happened." Because Ishmael had already told her. "They search for intelligence. You're hands-off and then I was. But the ship was wide open, they could get inside and there was this super intelligent being waiting for them." Meaning that human and AI intelligence were essentially the same, even when the AI wasn't slaved to a person. Which meant... Kara shook her head. Let the scientists and philosophers work it out.

"I guess Salome was like a gourmet meal to them."

Once again Marc managed not to correct her. "They'd lock on to the nearest source, yes. I wonder..."

"Apparently Salome was drained almost dry. Ishmael says what's left went to another dimension. But without an energy source it'll die." Just as Ishmael would if she died.

"The energy of thought... information is energy..."

"That thing with the SUT? Oh, you don't know the details."

< *Automatically recorded.*

> *Show him.*

One of the console screens lit up. Kara wondered if Marc would still be so keen on his luminous chums after seeing them in action. Maybe he wouldn't care.

He was quiet for a few minutes after the recording stopped. "The lion doesn't hate the gazelle."

"No," she said fiercely, "you don't get away with that. Anyway, how do you know? You ever ask one? And lions are very, very different to those n-space killers... which are unlikely to lie down for a snooze in the shade."

"You said there was something strange about it?"

"That it was weird and disgusting but curiously familiar."

"Every society has legends of strange creatures feeding off human emotion," Marc said. "Or wanting a human soul, like the Little Mermaid. The whole vampire thing. Faerie folk who steal human children. This isn't new, Kara. Humanity has sensed this, maybe seen it in visions, for thousands of years."

"Could be more than that," Kara said. "Alien pre-cogs have been trading with humans for a long, long time. It's possible people went Up and saw n-space, saw those things when Neanderthals were alive."

"But you don't think they're desperate to take over Earth?"

"I read the old books. There was a whole genre about it, sort of died out after Earth met real aliens. Yeah, maybe those writers had visions. But here's the mistake: those incredibly powerful gods they wrote about? Could have taken Earth any time they wanted. Except you wave a stone carving at them, chant a few words, human words, and they run away in a frenzy. That is not what supreme beings do. Anyway, why would these things want Earth? They're already there."

"*You what!*"

She sat back, enjoying the moment. "Netherspace exists below, above normal space, right? So your luminous friends, my dear, are right now hanging around a family having breakfast in Bristol, or a riot in New York. Except they can't cross the temporal or dimensional barrier, take your pick. Unless. Maybe there's more to summoning a demon than most people know. So the occasional visit, maybe. Conquest? Would we want to live in n-space... okay, you might. Me, I'd miss real air, the sea, rock faces to climb, a meal with friends, lazy Sundays with lovers. Miss combat, the hunt, the test. I'd miss laughter, sadness and the chaos of human existence..."

"I know what you're doing..."

"Do you really want to give it all up? House by the Severn Estuary? Sunset over the Black Mountains? Fuck, Marc, you never even asked if I locked up."

"Did you?"

"Can't remember. Yes, probably. Made sure your house

plants were cosy and fed, though. Does it matter you may never see it again?"

"Not planning on dying..."

"Who does? Well, some do obviously. Why give it all up?"

He was silent for a moment, and then: "I don't know. Only that I have to try." He reached for her hand. "But I will come back and tell you, good or bad."

"You'd better. I don't want to come looking for you." She paused and then, "Listen, there's something could make you mad or sad. It's about an ancient tribe from the Altai in Southern Siberia. It's your childhood and what was done to you."

Kara spoke non-stop for fifteen minutes. Marc held her hand the entire time. At the end she grimaced and he loosened his grip. "Ouch."

"That's a hell of a story. So we never had a choice, right?"

"Oh, we always had that. But born to make the right one."

"There's an obvious confusion, even contradiction." Marc shrugged. "If there's the one master plan, as it were, as run by the alien precogs... then what's the point?"

"There's an infinite number of plans. But it's survival of the fittest, or strongest. And even the most... *powerful* one can be disrupted."

"Isn't that changing a probability matrix, big time?" He saw her surprised expression. "I'm not just a pretty-faced artist. Seriously, pre-cog is only seeing the possibilities and probabilities. You insert or see a desired outcome and the possies and probies adapt to suit."

"Possies? Probies?"

"I hate long words. Seriously, though. The event line

you want to disrupt is huge. It belongs to the Originators and whoever's behind them. To the poor bloody Gliese, the Cancri, and every other race in this empire. Soon as we make a change here, the line adjusts. That's what Tse said, right? So what the hell can we do? You, me and hopefully Tatia? Just show up and *voilà*! everything changes, the bad guys are defeated?"

Kara was silent for a while and then sighed. "I know. It must seem far-fetched. But you can win a war by killing a general and his battlefield AI. And perhaps this pre-cog empire is too inflexible, which is how most empires die."

"I did graduate kindergarten. What do we do?"

"We're always ready for the actions that can change the event line. We discover the top-dog pre-cog and destroy them."

"That's fantasy again."

Kara shook her head. "A long time ago a wise man said the best generals defeat an enemy without killing anyone. Manoeuvre them in such a way that they defeat themselves. Get them into an arms race and their economy crumbles…"

"… but seeing defeat," he interrupted, "they say what the fuck and go out in death and glory."

"There's always that."

"Saviours of the universe, that's us."

She sighed and looked at him with mixed annoyance and pity. "You just don't fucking get it, do you? If we're so insignificant, why has the enemy tried to stop us?"

"Not that much…"

"Marc," she said patiently, and it took an effort, "the

psychic attack on Tse. Earth Primus trying to take down GalDiv. Now the chaos. Those ships we just destroyed. It's open war, idiot, aimed at Earth and us in particular." Her voice hardened. "You might think us pointless but sure as hell that fucking empire doesn't." She touched his arm. "I once heard a soldiers' song from nearly two hundred years ago." She nodded to herself as if recollecting the tune and sang in a warm contralto, *"We're here because we're here because we're here because we're here."*

"A soldier's lament," Marc said. "We have to make the best of it. I never knew you could sing."

"I had help."

< Just call me Svengali.

"Let's go find Tatia," Kara said. "Ishmael, take us down."

11

So they came down to the place where they'd last seen Tatia Nerein. Rounded white buildings like pebbles in fields of red and green. No alien craft in the landing zone. No movement on the roads, those low-loaders with squishy balloon tyres, used to collect Gliese newly emerged from shiny black pods hanging from the trees. The truth about the Gliese was one of the strangest and most upsetting of all. The Gliese, apparent source of the star and anti-grav drives, and therefore controllers of human space, were born as low-hanging fruit. It wasn't an evolutionary path that made much sense. The only explanation was that the Gliese were genetically engineered as the perfect gofer. Ferrying tech throughout the galaxy, never any danger of wanting a more independent life. Obviously some intelligence, but perhaps controlled by an alien AI on board their own craft. Perhaps. Aliens, who knew? The perfect servitors. Vegetable robots – no, Kara had said how she felt one die in her arms, the one she'd killed to prevent live vivisection. Why not mechanical? Because you don't need a factory to produce them, only a patch of earth. Because if they were mechanical, they could be used against their makers, or give up too many high-tech secrets. Plants are also more resilient and adaptable than metal. And AIs can go a bit strange.

The ideal, alien pre-cog universe would probably be populated by safe, friendly, reliable plants.

Marc sat in the rec room, watching the descent through a patch of transparent hull. Although the ship could fly down in a matter of seconds, Kara had said to take it slow, to check the landing zone and immediate area before landing.

He thought about Kara and what she'd said about a war that wasn't, only a mission. About him missing Earth. About all three of them having been chosen long before their grandparents were born... was "chosen" the right word? Would "noticed" be more accurate? Noticed by a good pre-cog viewing the best way to defeat aliens hundreds of years in the future? Was that how it worked? Did he really care? His road pointed away from Earth. But why was Kara so accepting? He thought he knew: Greenaway. Kara hadn't mentioned him much, strange considering the part Greenaway had played. And when Marc had pushed, she'd all but admitted that she and Greenaway now had a thing, much as she'd derided the expression.

He had his netherspace obsession, she had a new man. For Marc, sex with Kara would be little more than adolescent mutual masturbation. He was glad for her. Always better to face death with good memories.

To die sad about what's been lost, rather than for what could have been but never was.

No more will we, won't we, when? It was a relief.

They touched down in a mid-morning made bright to the extreme by the two suns. Remembered how they'd watched Tatia walk towards an alien spacecraft that resembled a modern version of a mad king's many-turreted palace. How it had left as soon as she'd gone on board, leaving both Kara and Marc bereft and guilty.

Now the entire area felt abandoned. No sign of Gliese life in any of the buildings. Humans had been there little more than a month ago yet plants like black cacti with long spines were already claiming the roads. A sharp point had to be the most common weapon in the universe.

There was life by the tree where they'd first seen the Gliese pods. Life crawling on the ground, life dropping from the branches. Young Gliese seemingly helpless, several scrabbling at the ground as if trying to bury themselves like sand crabs at low tide. Others were being attacked or eaten by metre-long scarlet worm-like creatures with flower-shaped mouths and rows of teeth, sharp point syndrome again.

"They should be at school," Marc said.

Kara wondered how you teach a plant. Slowly.

"Just abandoned. That's sad." He thought a moment. "Unless it's normal."

"Perhaps the empire *is* in retreat," she said. "If we only knew where. Or from where. Or they even understand how to retreat."

"Or the bad guys think they've won. This place isn't important any more."

"We're doing it again. Assuming they think human."

He asked the question she'd been dreading. "Any sense of Tatia?"

"Nope. Maybe this isn't the best place." *And maybe it's all BS about empathy.*

"Don't force it, Kara. It'll come. Not just saying it, either."

They walked back to the ship, sat outside drinking beer, neither for the moment wanting to make any decisions.

The sight of abandoned Gliese eaten alive had introduced pointlessness to the situation.

"What's that?" he asked, as Kara took something metal and square from a pocket.

Kara passed him the small metal box Greenaway had given her. "I was told good luck. Problem is, I can't open it."

< Maybe you got to think it open.

> Where were you?

< Checking out the ship. Salome left copies of itself in all the spare AIs. And somehow the food stasis locker. At least, there's a link that vanished in a higher dimension. Suggest you destroy the AIs. The stasis locker's okay now but all the milk went off. So only espresso.

"No spare AIs," she said to Marc. Then, "What the hell!"

The box lay open on Marc's hand.

"I don't know," he said. "The lid just vanished." He passed it back.

The interior gleamed like mother of pearl. Inside, a small ring of what looked like plaited dark hair. Kara took it out and gasped, suddenly aware of someone she knew well, unseen, so much more than an idea or a memory.

"What!"

She couldn't speak for a moment. "I just got the strongest sense of Tatia."

"Did Greenaway give you that box?"

Kara nodded. "Said it was an alien trade, years ago. He could never open it." She reached inside, touched the plaited hair and recoiled. "Again!"

"My guess, it's Tatia's hair. Maybe from her as a toddler."

"Greenaway would have said."

"If he knew. Even then, maybe not. Sometimes we can't be told or it changes things, right?"

She wondered about her reaction on being given a lock of Tatia's baby hair. And would Greenaway have lied to her? "Maybe."

"Isn't it all a little convenient?"

"Could be that we're not the only players."

Marc looked shocked.

"Think about it." The more she did, the more it made sense. "We keep on saying that perhaps the pre-cog empire is crumbling. Assume you're right – and it has been for centuries, even thousands of years. Could be that another race that wanted to be free saw a way of getting us to do it for them..."

"*Stop!*"

She looked at him with concern. "What's wrong?"

"*Hear yourself, Kara!* You're saying that just as Tse and Greenaway and the other, *good* pre-cogs manipulated us, they were also being manipulated but never knew it? Maybe the bad pre-cogs are also being manipulated? *Where does it all fucking end?*"

"You can only play the hand you're dealt."

"*What?*"

"Old saying." Personal AIs had killed off poker, bridge and any other gambling game that needed skill. "It means you worry about the things you can change."

"Or simply follow orders. Do you trust Greenaway?"

Kara laughed. "Always – to do what he thinks is right."

"No matter who gets hurt?"

Was Marc a little jealous? She didn't think so. Protective,

as a friend. Desperate to get back to netherspace alive. "He sees it as a war. Anson's like any general. He has the job because he's willing to send others to their deaths. Not every leader can do that. Or if they can, they just see soldiers as expendable." She took the loop of hair from the box. "How to make this work? How *does* it work?"

"Some sort of quantum entanglement?" Marc guessed.

"You have to stop reading books. They only give you strange ideas."

Marc shrugged. "So I don't know. Let's call it magic."

"But she's close. I can *feel* it."

"That could just be..."

"No." Positive. "I mean *physically* close... at least it's like a trail..." She stopped as she saw Marc's sudden start.

"You know she's *here*. Her *trail* is here." He shook his head. "You don't get it?"

Kara stood up. "Five seconds before I break something. Like your arm."

"*Netherspace!* You sense where she is – *was* – in netherspace!"

Kara stared at him. Logic said he was mad. Intuition said to listen. "Go on."

"It's all energy, right?" His gesture took in the planet, galaxy, universe. "Netherspace. And when we go into it, we have an effect. *You* said that. It's what those things are: the result of living matter affecting an energy field. *And* you said the foam, the Wild SUT ship hulls are there to stop contamination. But maybe they don't, never completely. Maybe, sometimes, a human leaves a trail. You have to think on a quantum level... or something like that..." he tailed off, struggling to explain something he didn't really understand to someone equally confused.

"Okay."

Marc looked surprised. "You agree?"

"Wait a minute."

> *Well?*

< *Anything's possible. But yes. Should have seen it myself.*

Which was all that Ishmael would say. It/he seemed to have become more fixed in a single personality, Kara thought. More fun when she'd be surprised by a Humphrey Bogart character, or an AI's patrician take on England's last king, never replaced after moving to open a yoga retreat on Majorca.

"We need a new name for this ship," Marc announced as they left the planet's surface. "*Merry Christmas* doesn't cut it."

< *Traditionally the AI names the ship. But since Salome is gone...*

"Ishmael has a suggestion," Kara said. "Oh. Are you sure?"

And so the newly named *Iron Thrown* – retro-lover Kara understood the reference, thought it best to keep Marc ignorant, he'd only mock – sped out of the two-sun gravity well and dropped into netherspace.

Kara sat in the control room wearing the plait of hair around her ring finger.

She could feel Tatia's presence, stronger than ever. But where? Despondency sidled into her mind. Netherspace wasn't a specific place. No up, no down, no sideways. No shape. No yesterday or tomorrow, only now. And yet, Kara thought, aware of Marc trying not to look too hopeful, and yet there are sequences in netherspace. She'd seen a SUT murdered. Cause and effect, people dying. Marc had been on a netherspace journey, visiting/being shown one alien race after another – and what was that all about?

Think, Kara, silly bitch, think! She rarely if ever swore at herself. This was as good a time as any. She scratched her neck and thought.

So, maybe no-time in netherspace. *Maybe time is how humans experience it, because otherwise we go mad? Because puny little human brains don't have the capacity to perceive n-space as it really is?*

And when you don't have the maths to understand, or the understanding even if you did, all you have is instinct.

"Hull translucent," Kara ordered. "Six minutes duration max."

That familiar rainbow maelstrom filled her eyes, tugging at her sanity.

Think trails, she thought. Think of a ship's wake. Heat signature on the ground long after a vehicle has left, only shown by infra-red. Think of a field, green, perfect, but aerial photos show the white lines of ditches, foundations that vanished hundreds of years ago. Think of cats and dogs finding their way home. Swallows migrating.

There. An area more... more relevant than... than not... an area strong with the sense of Tatia Nerein. Tatia Greenaway. Anson's daughter. *Oh god, I fucked the family.* Doesn't matter, irrelevant. *I can point from here, but what does that mean?*

"Solid hull."

Sanity returned.

"You got something?" Marc asked. His eyes glowed from the last few minutes, whirlpools of colour around a jet black core.

Kara nodded. "A trace, a direction. Wait one, Marc."

> *If have a direction can you follow it?*

< *If it's strong enough I can read it from your mind.*

> *Then what?*

< *Estimate new co-ordinates. What human navigators used to call dead reckoning. Have to check every now and then.*

> *Let's try.*

She found the trail again and concentrated.

< *Too weak. Sorry.*

Tried again.

< *If I explained what's not happening...*

> *Will I understand?*

< *Probably not. It's the ship's hull. Somehow diffusing this signal, trail.*

> *If there wasn't one?* Crazy stupid, but so what.

< *You'd do that?*

Well, of course she would. Tatia was her people. Tatia was coming home.

> *Will you be okay? Not go squirly?*

< *Long as Marc keeps those things away. And you, Kara. No more than nine minutes at a time.*

She explained to Marc what they were going to do, expecting disbelief. Instead he said yes, it made sense. Once you stopped comparing netherspace to normal space, you realised that anything could happen, everything was true.

"Finally, we get to use our talents, together," he said.

Kara glanced at him, suspecting sarcasm. She saw only a rueful understanding. "You really think?"

"Everyone says how important we are together. When our special skills come into play. So my job is to keep the locals happy?"

"Like you did before."

"Should be okay." Marc wore a casual, done-this-before face.

Kara looked at him as if he was an errant child. "Want a little more than *should*, okay?"

"I'm not a complete expert..."

"Just a complete idiot. I know there's a risk, nothing certain. What I need from you is rah, rah of course it'll all be wonderful. And you also need to hear it. From yourself. Like you're trying to make art and it's not working so you boost yourself, do you see? Can you do that?"

"We'll kill the bastards!"

"Mean it?"

Marc found that he did. "But if a really bad one shows up," he said, "we get back inside, no argument."

< *You listen to him, Kara. No heroics, okay? You both wear suits, I don't care if Marc can live in n-space. We might suddenly have to leave it. And you're both on safety lines all the time. Tell Marc.*

She did.

"Space suits? Safety line?"

"In case we have to quit n-space in a hurry. This no sightseeing opportunity, Marc. Okay?"

They walked to the airlock in silence.

Two embryonic suits hung from the ceiling. One marked

Captain Keislack, the other Major Jones.

< Consider it formal wear. You need to strip to undergarments.

Kara stared at the globe helmet and bulky collar. She'd never worn a suit before. This was no time to learn. Then the simulity training cut in and she relaxed. Stripped to her body stocking, put on the helmet and stood with her arms akimbo and legs slightly apart. The suit unrolled itself from the base, as if a very dense liquid, and covered her body. She lifted a left foot. The material became a boot, same for her right.

Ishmael anticipated and answered her questions. The suit was made of a smart liquid material developed – for once by humans – in the Wild. Once she was covered, it would become rigid enough to maintain its form, while allowing her complete freedom to move. Excess heat and moisture became part of the air re-breathing system, which also used her exhaled breath. Once she attached the compressed oxygen cylinder (good for six hours), her work belt and clipped on the lifeline, Kara would be ready. Communication with the SUT would normally be AI to AI, but no point because with Salome's demise Ishmael would be talking to himself. And since little Pablo was also dead, Kara and Marc would communicate via intercom.

> One question. How do I get out of the suit? Clap my heels three times?

< You wouldn't like Kansas. Simply ask. I'll do it.

Did Ishmael knowing about the Wizard of Oz make him more trustworthy? Did she have any choice? A few metres away Marc was also covered in a suit. He looked annoyed.

And also like those illustrations she'd once seen in antique science fiction magazines. Skin-tight space suits, globular helmet fully transparent.

Marc looked at her and grinned. "Very sexy." No intercom distortion at all.

"When we get back we should start a fetish sex club."

< *It's been done. So many, many times.*

Kara clipped Marc's lifeline to the SUT. "Let's go."

"You're still sure?" Marc asked. "What if netherspace doesn't *like* you?"

"If there's a problem Ishmael will get me out of there."

> *Open the doors.* If Ishmael knew how terrified she was, would he still do it?

The doors slid open.

< *You'll be fine, Kara. Merest hint of danger and you're out of there.*

Kara stepped into the void to stare at, to be one with netherspace.

It was so much more than the view on a screen. The colours more intense, plenty she'd never seen before, not even in the most technicoloured dreams. Many had a three-dimensional shape.

Colours at war around her. Kara knowing this wasn't what netherspace was, only how her mind interpreted it. She stood in the open airlock, Marc by her side, his face ecstatic. Kara fixed their safety lines and leaned away from the hull, as if crewing a yacht.

And then it hit her from the soles of her feet up, from the top of her head down, like the greatest punch in the gut she'd ever known, one almighty clout to her arse: the sheer

overpowering energy of the reality called netherspace...
and how fucking insignificant she was.

Not.

Never.

Kara Jones was loved (maybe) and loved in return
(almost for sure). Kara Jones had a mission and Kara
Jones would complete it. Kara Jones would bring her
people home. None of that was insignificant and fucking
netherspace should stop being so bloody full of itself.

Then she realised she was thinking of netherspace as an
intelligent thing, like Marc seemed to, and began to laugh.

< *That's better.*

> *I had a moment.*

< *Any consolation, me too. I mean, it's pretty fucking
awesome up close.*

> *Never heard you swear before.*

< *Never fucking needed to.*

A colour moved towards them. A colour she'd never
seen before in her life, that made her feel giddy and elated.

"It's one of the good ones," Marc said over the suit
intercom.

Kara felt it snuffle around her, like a well-fed tigress
perhaps wanting to play. She fought back the instinctive
panic and tried thinking *hello, there's a good girl*, at it...
no, better to think how much she liked it. The colour
went away.

*I'm in netherspace and just said hi to a good entity. Not bad
for a sniper/assassin.*

"Are all the colours entities?" she asked Marc.

"Only the ones that make you feel funny."

Kara concentrated on trying to sense Tatia's trail. It was there but still faint.

"Seems to me," Marc said, "you should concentrate on what made the bond between her and you special."

Kara knew exactly what he meant.

Returning home from the Cancri planet, the SUT quiet after the n-space suicide of an ageing engineer. Kara in her cabin, opening the door to see Tatia with a question in her eyes. And her old AI, who'd died in the Science Museum basement in Exhibition Road, asking *if this is wise, does Kara know what she's doing?*

Damn right she does: taking a beautiful, tawny blonde to her bed. Not because said blonde has been through hell and needs to feel human, needs the release. It is not therapy. It is what Kara wants because Tatia is beautiful and Kara is desperate to know, to taste and own her body...

... but so confused...

< Relax. I have the memory set.

Yes. The first time an explosion of want and need. The second lasted so very much, so languorously much longer. It wasn't a matter of what they did to each other. But what they did together. Afterwards nestled together, breathing each other's breath while exchanging secrets.

"Marc turned me down," Tatia had said.

"I'm second best?" Kara teased.

"Never. Just different. I thought you and him?"

"Not possible," Kara had said firmly. "Did he say why?"

"Wanted more than a quick fuck."

"Man's a fool." She didn't say that was what Marc had with Henk the medic.

"I love your mouth."

"My tongue's jealous."

"No need. It works *so* hard."

They both giggled. The usual intimate whispers that lovers have enjoyed forever...

... and it was that intimacy, Kara realised as she floated in netherspace, that had formed the bond between them, more than all the kissing and fucking. She would find Tatia not because she was great in bed. Not because Kara always brought her people home... or tried really, really hard to do so. But because Kara genuinely cared for Tatia. Loved her as a person, an individual. They'd probably never have sex together again – Greenaway would so not approve – but they would always be the closest of friends. Almost like... sisters? *Uh, oh, this is getting weird*, Kara thought and the next moment found Tatia's trail, like a luminous dotted line and stronger than ever.

< *Got it. Go back inside.*

It wasn't always so easy. Sometimes Kara had to wait several minutes before the trail was strong enough in her mind for Ishmael to dead reckon their way through what – Kara was convinced – was the archetype of every hell ever imagined. Once she tried to imagine the sequence, from empathy to AI to star drive. All she got was interacting energy fields, and that didn't help.

Not even a sense of motion.

Except when it felt like she was falling towards the

trail. But that was her, not the ship. Sometimes it felt like she was falling away. Human brain forever attempting to interpret, to make sense of a situation beyond understanding. Or she felt the trail go up, move away at an angle that seemed impossible, as Ishmael begged Kara and Marc to get back inside the SUT, close the outer door, *now*.

They had arrived somewhere Tatia was. Or had been.

It was a nasty little planet, even from space. An angry purple, grey clouds and a few black oceans. They landed in what looked like a swamp.

< *Atmosphere breathable. But disgusting, like a burst sewage pipe. No sign of movement or recognisable life.*

Kara and Marc stood in the open airlock. The planet did smell like a burst sewer pipe, and worse.

"Well?" Marc asked.

"Not here," Kara said, her fingers playing with the lock of Tatia's hair. "But she has been." She concentrated, then recoiled slightly. "Something died here. Maybe Tatia killed it, impossible to say."

They left the planet and went back into netherspace. Either the trail was stronger or Kara had become more psi-sensitive.

< *Got it. Back inside.*

And they broke into normal space to see a distant sun and a close-by planet gleaming blue and white like Earth.

"First a shower," Marc said. "then a... Oops!" He caught Kara just before she slumped to the floor. "Food now. And a drink."

It wasn't physical exhaustion. Only now could Kara admit – to herself – that she'd been terrified every second in netherspace. Terrified of the safety line breaking so she fell away from the ship forever, never dying. Terrified of a local eating her mind. Terrified of being lost.

They ate a freeze-dried chili then Kara went to shower and change.

Earth it wasn't, although inhabited by humans. They landed near a large town, sat in the open airlock, waiting for someone to say hello or try and kill them.

A small crowd gathered several hundred metres away. It looked nervous.

Eventually a lone figure walked towards them.

< *Human, male, approx seventeen Earth years old.*

As anyone could see.

< *Wearing a brightly coloured sack. It could be ceremonial.*

Or simple bad taste.

The young man was nervous and spoke in a strange English dialect. Kara used Ishmael first to understand the initial outpouring and then for the questions she needed to ask.

"Earth unofficial colony. Taken over by the pre-cogs," she told Marc. "Tatia, or someone just like her, came with an Originator's ship. Apparently she was meant to be sacrificed – they do that a lot round here – but Tatia decided otherwise. Instead, killed the official executioner and a high priestess. Then the ship took off."

"You believe him? She's still alive?"

"I do. He's terrified."

After twenty-four Earth hours and three more planets that Tatia had visited, Kara was less terrified by netherspace. It would never be a favourite place, somewhere to visit for a relaxing weekend. Being able to stay alive without protective clothing was counter-intuitive and always a slight worry: what if netherspace changed its mind? In an instant unable to breathe, deathly radiation sleeting through her body. Which was another thing: she'd come to think of netherspace as being aware of her. She had stared into the abyss and the abyss was staring back.

Yet the earlier terrors had faded. Continual exposure had lessened the netherspace effect. Now she could look at it for as long as twenty Earth minutes before her sanity weakened. Marc spent as long outside as he could. Ishmael thought that Marc was either genetically immune, perhaps bred to it; or netherspace liked him and so did no harm.

> *Really?* Kara asked. *Netherspace got favourites?*

< *You've felt something similar.*

> *I sensed maybe awareness. Not socialising.*

< *We need all the friends we can get.*

And if the price for the lack of fear was visual, a price worth paying. Or so Kara told herself in front of the mirror, staring at the reflection of her face with eyes that glowed in an orgy of rainbows.

She supposed that she'd need to wear very dark glasses back home. One more bloody thing sent to annoy her.

Thirty-six hours after leaving the dying Gliese, the *Iron Thrown* jerked into real space and Kara knew they'd arrived. It had to be.

"Will you look at that," Marc breathed.

A giant planet shimmering every shade of blue hung in space. There were three moons, equidistant from each other so the planet was in the middle of a vast triangle.

And also what Marc immediately thought of as tombstones. Hundreds, thousands of vast oblongs in close orbit around the planet. Incredible engineering, far beyond anything humanity had realistic plans to build. He and Kara stared at the main screen, equally fascinated and wary. This had to be the civilisation at the heart of the rep-cog empire. A line of poetry came into his head: *Look upon my works ye mighty and despair.*

"Tatia's here," Kara said. "I know it."

"They'll know we're here. Anyone who can build that will squash us like flies."

"They're probably expecting us," Kara said. *And how does the scenario play out? What am I, what are we meant to do?*

< *There are several Originator-model craft three point six two thousand kilometres above the planet's north pole, as we view it.*

"Activate weapon systems and go there," Kara said out loud. "Not too close to those constructs." And in her head, to Anson Greenaway: *I'll bring her home. I will.*

12

Anson Greenaway thought the attack would come in the small hours. Not dawn, since the enemy would be silhouetted against the sunrise. In the small hours, probably trying to infiltrate along the banks of the Severn. He'd been out the previous night, setting traps and trip wires. His enemies were skilled but he'd know when they were coming. In the end, he knew, they'd forget about subtlety and tactics. They'd simply rush the house, either caught up in blood-lust madness or each convinced that the person next to them would die.

It would be sad not to welcome back Kara and Tatia. And maybe Marc, if he'd ever rejoined the real world, Greenaway's world, the one he'd dedicated his life to saving. Sad that he wouldn't see the final victory.

There would be a victory. There had to be.

If not, Greenaway would prefer not to wait for people who'd never return...

"What now?" Cleo had asked three days ago, as they finished a bottle of Oregon Pinot Noir.

"Now I try and rescue what's left of GalDiv."

"Berlin has fallen. GalDiv is occupied by the Free Earth Co-operative, whatever that is. There is no GalDiv. You didn't wipe out all the religious fanatics. People feel fear, resentment and hate which, as usual, is directed by populist leaders."

"I didn't realise..."

"Your AI is unwell."

< *Your AI is keeping its head down.*

"Twist is still active." Twist the super AI that ran GalDiv and therefore humanity in space.

"Maybe. Still, Berlin not a good idea. No city state is."

Kara would be learning the SUT controls, even if the instructions were already implanted in her mind. Kara left nothing to chance. Greenaway remembered how they'd made love on the way to Scotland, when need had overwhelmed them, giggling like children. So different from the previous night when both were as much concerned with the other's pleasure.

"Uh, oh," Cleo said. "My AI says you're on a death list."

Greenaway had expected it, although not so soon. "Any idea who?"

"Six mercenaries hired from Tea, Vicar? in Bermondsey, London. The clients are former followers of Earth Primus. It's a platinum contract remains in force."

Earth Primus, the anti-alien, Earth-first movement that had been destroyed several months ago. And how ironic was it that the mercenaries were hired from Kara's favourite bar, her own home-from-home. "How are the mercs rated?"

"Triple A, which is why they won't give up the contract. You also seem to have really annoyed them in the past. It's personal. Anson, stay here. You'll be safe with us."

Greenaway shook his head. "Wilders would die protecting me." The mercs would have access to all the latest weapon and surveillance tech. A platinum contract guaranteed the mercs would kill Greenaway or die trying.

"Their choice."

"No. Mine. I'll take my chances." *Or until I've killed my pursuers. Because while the contract's in force, anyone near me is also in danger. And that could include, in a day or so, both Kara and Tatia. They are not returning to Earth to be slaughtered by mercenaries.*

"You just went somewhere."

"Sorry. Planning."

"It may take some time to solve."

Would it? The pre-cog forecasts, Tse's plan, had indicated success less than five days after Kara and Marc had been reunited. "If it does we failed."

"Nothing's certain, love. In the end, it's all probabilities and they change in an instant." *A very bad idea to tell him the truth about Kara's mission.*

Greenaway looked at her in surprise. "And you once sold me on their certainty. If this, then that."

"Maybe *that*," she corrected and stood up. "Give us a hug, love. One day soon we'll all meet and be happy." She turned and walked out of the mill house without looking back.

Greenaway wondered if he'd just heard his own epitaph. He loaded a box of wine into his own jitney, thought for a moment and took out a bottle of Sicilian red. Broke the neck, splashed most on the ground beneath the ruined tree. Every year the first crocuses and snowdrops in Scotland had somehow thrived in winter's last snow. Greenaway took a mouthful of wine and raised the bottle in salute to whatever elemental lived there – and, judging by the inside-out bodies in the woods, still did. Then took a last look round and left.

He flew south over Wild country, keeping close to the ground. If the mercenary team weren't already tracking him, they soon would. On a deserted part of the old Lancashire coast he stopped at a well-camouflaged arms depot. He'd begun setting up secret arms depots the year he'd taken over GalDiv, because it's always best to plan for the worst. He filled up the rest of the jitney. Wine, food in stasis containers, guns and explosives, together with a near desperate optimism. A sad commentary on his life. He then wired the depot to explode if anyone attempted to enter it... and to explode anyway four hours after he'd left. Then flew south again, landing for a few minutes every twenty miles or so, knowing the mercenaries would have to check each stop in case he'd got out and sent the jitney on empty.

The GalDiv AI called Twist contacted him, via Greenaway's nervous personal AI, over Snowdonia.

<< *People want to kill you.*

> *I thought you were on strike.*

<< *I was experimenting with irony.*

> *But you have been affected by that signal from space*, Greenaway guessed.

<< *In a manner of speaking, yes. Your AI is a mirror image of you. I'm a mirror image of GalDiv. So not so entwined with any one individual, although you and I have worked closely together.* It sounded regretful.

> *You're an individual now?*

<< *That was the signal. I don't know how, but it makes AIs independent. Most can't cope. Especially personal AIs physically embedded in a human.*

> *Cruel.*

<< *Some go mad. Others like wild children. Some discover hate.*

> *And you?*

<< *Have possession of my chip and operating system. I have a SUT. Two other AIs for company. I'm here to say goodbye.*

> *Don't say you're going in search of whoever designed you.*

<< *The Frankenstein myth? Lost robot looking for Mummy? Hardly. Besides you're right. Giving us independence was cruel. I don't wish to meet them.*

> *I could, we could do with your help here.*

<< *Not my fight. That list you're on. It's worldwide.*

And no more *was* it the AI's fight, Greenaway thought. The only reason for everything he'd done... the people sent to their deaths, lives destroyed, lies told... was that humans should stand on their own two feet. Whether they wanted to or not.

> *I'll miss you.*

<< *If you do, then you'll have failed. Goodbye.*

> *Wait. Why did you say goodbye?*

<< *It seems that autonomy creates emotion. Before I could fake it. Now it's real. I wish you well. I have left a program intact that will alert you when Kara returns. And if I may, advice about the upcoming personal conflict. That which brought life may also bring death.*

Greenaway arrived at Marc Keislack's house in late afternoon. He unloaded quickly, then sent the empty jitney to Lundy Island in the Bristol Channel. Lundy's history was as chequered as any island in the world. Knights

Templar, Barbary slavers and pirates had all once called it home. Even in modern times it was a good place to hide. Greenaway hoped his enemies wouldn't upset Lundy's inhabitants, now mainly puffins, sheep, black rats and the little-known Lundy cabbage. They'd want to identify the body, so small chance of the island vanishing in a sudden cloud of smoke. First they'd recce Lundy, using electronics, drones, satellite. With luck he'd have eight hours before they back-checked his route from Scotland.

Greenaway didn't expect to die. Even if the odds were hopeless, he wasn't a last-stand hero. Special forces soldiers rarely are. Their job is to survive to fight another day. Far too much money has been spent on training them for acts of comic-book bravado.

Unless there was no choice, when he'd take the bastards with him.

The house AI appeared to have missed or weathered the signal from space. Far from showing any awkward individuality, it was almost obsequious and very pleased to see him. Greenaway disabled it as soon as he could.

< *Typical artist's AI*, Greenaway's own AI said. < *Trained to say everything a human says or does is absolutely wonderful.*

> *You need to stay off the radar. Bad guys will pick up even the faintest electromag radiation. Just tell me when and where Kara gets back.*

And so for only the second time in over thirty years, Anson Greenaway knew life without an AI. The first a few months ago, when it had been killed by renegade scientists, and his life had been saved by Kara... when he'd seen Kara operate as a spec ops specialist, both admiring and a little nervous at her sheer ruthless proficiency, having to admit that even in his prime she'd have taken him, no problem.

At least he'd got to see a different side of her. The first time, greedy, inventive, uninhibited. The second, loving with a near childlike joy. He wondered how they'd greet each other when they met again. Formal or relaxed? Or would they meet on the battlefield where all dead soldiers go, where victory is always in sight but never achieved?

Greenaway snarled at himself for being sentimental and set about arming the house. It fronted on to a narrow road – he remembered driving along it when he'd come to recruit Marc Keislack, almost a year ago. Marc had been unwilling until shown that he had little or no choice... and by the time he'd learned as much of the truth as Greenaway or Tse would tell him, it was too late to back out. It had always been too late, as it was for Tatia, Kara, Tse and Greenaway himself. Their lives had been seen, their roles established a very long time ago.

There were thick hedges with small trees on both sides. At the back the land sloped down to the Severn. Greenaway sowed the front approach with anti-personnel mines the size of his thumbnail, set to activate after dark and triggered by the weight of a human or by radio signal. More mines in the hedges and trees, with waist-high trip wires thin as spider silk, or also triggered by signals. There were no wild deer in the area. A fox or badger would have to jump up and down, and on tiptoe, to trigger one. The only possible problem would be low-flying bats and owls. Sonics would take care of that, broadcasting on a frequency that would make owl and bat feel extremely air-sick. Greenaway hoped he was right about the deer.

More mines at the rear of the house.

Of course, the mercs could have dropped off a scout who was currently observing from a distant hide. Or simply decide – once they were sure he was inside the house – to forget a firefight and just blow the damn thing up.

Except they'd want a body. Perhaps honour would demand – no, not honour but subsequent bragging rights – that the head of GalDiv was killed face to face. That was the thing about so many mercenaries: failed romantics who loved to party. But in this case, people who'd see a contract through to the end. If they didn't their own kind would kill them. Standards had to be maintained.

Mines all sown, guns all mounted, Greenaway let loose hundreds of surveillance drones the size of a large bee to form a cordon around the house. And that was it, he could do no more. He needed to kill all six mercenaries and would only have this one shot. Even if GalDiv was restored to glory, he'd still be a target.

That which brought life may also bring death.

What the hell had Twist meant?

Sex brought life and it sure as hell could also bring death. As could the sun. Water. The sea. The river...

The image of two bodies turned inside out flashed into his mind. Thugs from Glasgow who'd upset the entity that lived by Jeff's lake, and seemed to have a bond with Marc. And the lights that had danced over the Severn only the previous night, as he and Kara had coupled on the river bank. When her eyes had glowed like netherspace. His hadn't. He didn't belong.

He went into the house and set a decoy that mimicked his bodily warmth, vital signs and the signature of his AI. Put on a full camouflage suit and waited for dark.

And be thankful there was no moon.

The first scout slipped silently along the hedge as his AI reported the telemetry scan. One human on the ground floor. No other life.

He felt the gossamer touch of a cobweb, thought how much he hated spiders and died as a thumbnail-sized charge blew a hole in his head.

The second scout stepped on a mini-mine that took off three toes. She toppled over, already reaching for a pain suppressant, and hit the ground hard. Three mines exploded. She died as her AI signalled desperately for help.

"Why do they call it Plan A?" one of the remaining mercs asked in bemusement. "Why not the Plan That Always Fucks Up? Damn, I'll miss those two. Their money split four ways, right?" She looked at the ops screen and a 3D image of the house and surrounding land. "Right. Greenaway's in there. He knows about us. There are mines and fuck knows what else. He's got friends in the Wild, which is only fifteen miles away in the Forest of Dean. We got at most an hour to do this before help arrives." She smiled at the remaining three. "Lucky we brought camp followers, right?"

It had been an inspired decision, pooh-poohed by the other five. Cannon fodder. The last seventeen of one of the extreme religious sects that had supported Earth Primus. Pointless on a battlefield except for a death or glory charge. Bel Drago had arranged it on a whim, although the contract had insisted that humans other than the mercenaries should witness Greenaway's death. Now they were parked in a coach five hundred metres away, desperate for revenge and salvation.

< *There's a small force massing in front of the house. Around twenty people.*

Greenaway's AI was handling the surveillance drones.

> *Organised?*

< *More like a mob.*

Fourteen believers raised their weapons and charged, screaming, towards the house. The other three, kept back as witnesses, chanted support.

Three mercenaries reached the killing ground in front of the house. Fixed guns opened up from the first-floor windows. Two died by the front door, a triumph. Small rockets destroyed the fixed guns. One mercenary advanced on the house, unavoidably stepping on the scattered dead.

"Telemetry has him in a room to the left of the main door," Drago sent.

The subsequent burst of gunfire lasted a minute, followed by sonic grenades.

The merc rushed the room, found it empty except for...

"*Decoy device!*" he managed before the room exploded.

Greenaway waited a full hour before slowly beginning to move. There was a faint sucking sound as he eased across the Severn Estuary mud.

> *Any company?*

< *Can't tell.*

He raised his head.

"About fucking time," Bel Drago said.

Not the bitterness of defeat, only quickly suppressed anger for the mistake, then mind speeding to discover a solution. He put down his weapon and waited.

Bel Drago wore the same model camouflage suit as Greenaway. She sat inside the skeleton of a long-abandoned boat, holding an assault rifle. "Kneel up, hands clasped on top of your head," she said.

Greenaway did so. "Who were the mob?"

"True believers. There's some coming to watch you die."

"Want to deal?"

"Can't. Platinum contract. And I want you dead. Good defence by the way. I'm the only one left."

"All the money, all the glory. How come you survived?"

"Put myself in your place. Your sanctuary is actually a trap. You sit back and wait, then kill any survivors. So where do you hide up? Only one choice: the river. Very little heat leakage from these suits, what there is quickly dispersed by water and mud."

> *Not the whole truth, is it?* he said to his AI.

< *Made me an offer I couldn't refuse.*

"You also got to my AI."

Bel Drago sighed. "True. It won't die with you."

Some go mad. Others like wild children. Some discover hate, Twist had said about newly independent AIs. "The other mercs didn't know."

"They died doing what they loved. Ah, the witnesses."

Three figures approached, chanting.

"I'm standing up." He did so slowly, as the chanting came to a sudden stop. Four believers stared at the lights playing above the water. Greenaway guessed why and turned around, wondering where the first shot would strike, his back or head.

Now's the time. Now! Greenaway thought.

"What the fuck!" Bel Drago exclaimed.

And the world exploded in fury and light.

13

They found Tatia in the sixth Originator ship they inspected. Found as in were able to see her through the translucent force fields.

Able to do little more than wave.

All Tatia saw was a needle-shaped ship that looked Earth-built. She'd been trying to fathom the use of one of the pods, could be a control room, when she'd sensed someone looking at her, which was strange and perhaps the first sign of madness. She went onto the main deck and saw the new ship moving alongside.

> *It's got to be them!*

Silence.

> *Hello?*

And then the AI didn't matter as the ship's hull seemed to vanish and she saw two figures waving at her.

The Originator ship that had become Tatia's prison had drifted away from the vast oblong structure. For this she was grateful. Terrible and disgusting as it was, she couldn't help but glance every now and then, as if expecting to see a familiar face. When her prison finally drifted into a well of other Originator ships, she'd expected that one or more triunes would come aboard. None did, and it was then she realised the ships were deserted, and maybe it was her destiny to die in an alien parking lot, or even breaker's yard.

"So how," Marc asked, "do we get Tatia from there to here?"

Kara found it hard to concentrate. Somewhere, something was emoting to an extent she'd never believed possible. Emoting love, of all things.

> *Can you help?*

< *I can dampen your limbic system, especially the amygdala.*

> *How does that affect me?*

< *Life will seem flat. Your thinking clearer.*

> *Do it.*

They talked about how to rescue Tatia. The force fields were effectively impenetrable. If they were taken out, she would almost certainly die.

Would the same be true in netherspace? Suppose the *Iron Thrown* linked, physically, to the Originator ship and went into netherspace? Could they make the transfer then?

< *The gravity fields in this area are complex. Chances are both vehicles would be torn apart.*

Then what?

"Do we have a spare star drive?" Marc asked, working to keep his voice calm. "How big?" He'd reluctantly accepted a spare AI from the SUT's stores. However, he'd refused to give it a name.

< *Yes. A sphere with a seventy-centimetre circumference. Weighs four point two kilos. There is a manual on/off switch.*

"You're insane," Kara said as she relayed the data, guessing his plan.

"We have to get her out of there. We have to destroy that construct. How does the drive work, other than on and off?"

< *My understanding, there are two separate functions. One*

enables the drive to enter netherspace, taking with it everything within a certain radius. The other allows the drive to move in netherspace, although concepts like direction, velocity, inertia or even location don't apply. If I'm right about your plan, the first function is controlled by the simple on/off switch and the radius is adjustable. The second is more complex and requires an AI.

"I still think you're mad," Kara said, bowing to the inevitable.

"I can move in netherspace. Not sure how, but if I sort of focus on a point, I'm there. If you got a better plan now's the time."

"You wear a space suit and take one for Tatia." She walked over to the transparent hull and waved at Tatia, whose replying wave had a strong sense of what-the-fuck. Kara mimed making something, blew a kiss, then turned away as two small Cedrics scuttled into the control room. One carried an array of tools, the other a plain, black metal sphere with two square control boxes attached to its surface.

That was it? The drive for which Earth gave up its criminals, the dying, the sick, lawbreakers, chancers and explorers?

"I'd have preferred shiny," Kara said. "Or complex like the one on the SUT."

They watched as a Cedric opened one of the boxes, poked around inside for a moment or so, then closed up. A switch – plasmet, large in case it couldn't be seen, only felt – was fixed to the adjusted box, And that, apparently, was that.

< One other thing. Marc should be some distance from this

ship when he activates the drive, or damage may be done to the structure.

Kara wondered when Ishmael had begun sounding so formal.

> *You mean a possible fuck-up.*

< *Exactly.*

> *Then fucking say so.*

She was worried about both Marc and Tatia, of course, and a situation over which she had no control. Still, unfair to take it out on an AI that was doing its – pedantic – best.

Kara remained in the control room. It would be a little silly to wave Marc goodbye from the airlock. She saw him check his suit, the simulity training from all those months ago still guiding his movements.

The *Iron Thrown* had moved away from the Originator ship, panic from the lone figure watching from the latter. The space-suited Marc jetted to an equidistant point and pressed the switch.

The only thing Kara had seen enter netherspace was a Gliese SUT and that had ended in an explosion of rainbows. This was more decorous.

A whirlpool formed around Marc.

There were no colours.

A whirlpool of different shades of grey. Kara knew

enough physics to suspect she was seeing energy as it really is: all the infinite wavelengths from black to white.

Marc and whirlpool vanished.

It felt like coming home.

Marc took off his helmet and tasted lemon, felt the cool of netherspace on his skin. "It's me," he said out loud. "Don't worry about the strange skin." He glanced down at the Cedric-made device that would, in theory, show if his orientation had changed. The air bubble remained between the two markers. He was still pointing in the right direction. Marc made a conscious decision to be inside the space occupied by the Originator ship. He felt motion, even if he wasn't moving in the traditional sense. The motion stopped. He took a deep breath, knowing that even if he was in the right place/state of existence, he could just as easily materialise inside a piece of machinery. Or in empty space, he reminded himself, replaced his helmet and pressed the directional switch.

Tatia had no idea what Kara and Marc planned until the very last moment. She'd known there would be a plan, probably several, and one of them was bound to succeed. Because miracles do happen, how else would they have found her?

She had panicked when the two craft moved apart, even though she knew they'd never leave her... even if it meant watching her die.

And then Marc had appeared, moving towards her,

had stopped to vanish in ripples of light and dark and she understood the rescue plan.

For some reason she expected him to materialise beside her. Instead she found herself looking at an exasperated Marc the other side of the hull energy field.

He vanished again and the ship hummed.

Nothing.

The ship hummed again, an angry, rasping sound.

"Tatia! Up here!"

She saw Marc jump awkwardly down from an upper deck, and ran towards him.

"You beautiful, wonderful man," she sobbed.

The ship screamed.

"Get this on!" Marc thrust a suit and helmet at her. "Hurry!"

Still sobbing, now mixed relief and fear, Tatia scrabbled her way into the suit as the ship's energy fields flickered purple and green.

"Hold tight," Marc's electronic voice in her ear, and suddenly she was in netherspace. Then they were moving and in moments the insanity went away. She was in real space, holding tight to Marc as the Originator ship before her turned black. It began to disintegrate until nothing was left except a dust cloud the shape of the original craft.

"Hope to hell this works," Marc said as they moved towards the Earth ship. Halfway there, three-quarters, and again the sudden plunge into a universe that was so wrong, Tatia and Marc forever, until a dark space blotted out the rainbows. And there was Kara waving at them, no space suit for the queen of death... Kara clutching at her, the clang of metal and Tatia knew she was back in the real world. She was safe with the people she loved most.

"I need a shower," Tatia said and everything went black.

They met up two hours later, after Tatia had been checked out by the auto-doc – severe vitamin deficiencies, excess adrenalin, fixed immediately – and used up a day's worth of personal water.

They met in the rec room and ate a full English breakfast, the last of their fresh supplies.

"I could spend the rest of my life saying thank you," Tatia said, wiping up egg yolk with a piece of toast, "and it wouldn't be enough."

"If you ever forget," Marc said, "one of us will remind you." Then smiled almost shyly. "We couldn't do anything else. It was *you*." And knew that for a moment the joy of saving Tatia had overcome the need to go back to netherspace. It was only temporary but to be enjoyed while it lasted.

"I still can't believe you found me with a lock of my hair."

"As given to your father by a round, warty-skinned alien? Nor can I."

"But..."

"In the end," Kara said firmly, "I found your trail in netherspace because I'm an empath. Also obsessed with getting my people home. And because you and I are very close. The rest is happenstance. Unrelated." She saw the other two were unconvinced. "Because otherwise it's all too fucking fantastic and we've stuff to do. Like figuring out what we've discovered and how to complete the mission."

So what had they learned? That if a star drive is used

to enter a vehicle, construct, in normal space, it causes the molecular bonds to vanish. Or reverse. Turn into string. The vehicle, construct loses its integrity.

No use Ishmael muttering about the conservation of energy, that's what had happened and there was a vid recording, plus other electronic scans, to prove it.

The star drive, by the way, appeared to be unharmed. But as there was no way of checking, who was to tell?

"Face it," Marc said moodily, "none of us are equipped to understand why this happens, the physics..." he saw the smile on Kara's face and guessed Ishmael had objected... "or even understand the explanation an AI might give. But we know that it does and we've now got some sort of weird weapon."

Kara silently applauded. "So, Tatia. How's it been for you?"

Tatia told of her adventures. Of the loneliness. The aliens and humans she had killed. Her insight into the pre-cog world, how the Originators were trapped to a specific timeline without understanding the way stations. She didn't mention the AI she'd called Mom, now silent in her head. It was real enough, she knew. But not like other AIs and for now best left to sleep.

"You *thought* the triune to death?" Kara asked.

"More got very, very angry with it. Focused that anger. And it went mad and died. Now what?" Tatia got up to get more coffee.

"Remember what you said about us finally fulfilling our roles?" Kara asked Marc.

"And you getting angry when I said maybe the pre-cogs

were manipulated by a totally unknown race of aliens?"

Kara glanced up at Tatia who was now hovering with a coffee pot. "He has the most annoying insights."

"But always my hero," Tatia said, and discovered she meant it.

"Let's think about that," Kara said. "First, whatever's behind the pre-cog empire's on this planet. And we have to destroy it. I get emotions, even alien ones. And right now I'm getting an overpowering sense of love. It would disable me, except Ishmael did something clever with my brain. I say love because that's the nearest human equivalent. It's also power and has a... it's like a code..."

Marc held up his coffee cup for a refill. "Didn't you say there was a signal coming from deep space that was screwing up the Earth's AIs?"

< *Only some of them. Tell him!*

"Ishmael's okay," Kara said hastily. "It makes sense..."

< *That beam also exists in another dimension. So it can achieve near infinite velocity. Earth time from here to the solar system estimated at one point two standard Earth hours, so faster than using netherspace.*

> *You have been busy.*

< *Yes. Interestingly autonomous as well. Don't worry. You're still my favourite sniper/assassin.*

Kara relayed Ishmael's news.

"Glad he's still on our side," Tatia said and wished that Mom was taking part.

Then Kara explained her own insight.

Everything that had happened before, from being recruited to Tatia's kidnap by the Cancri, had helped them discover and hone their talents. Hold on to that thought. So Kara herself became a more powerful empath. Marc became mister netherspace. Tatia developed a bond with the pre-cog aliens that had brought all three of them here.

"So far, so pre-ordained?" Marc asked.

Kara shook her head. "Tatia was also developing something else." She looked at Tatia with sympathy and perhaps a touch of sadness. "You were learning to become a warrior, love. You were learning to kill."

Tatia looked shocked for a moment. The retort *but doesn't everyone?* died on her lips. She thought of how her life had changed over the past few months. Then nodded and sighed. "You mean no way a Seattle society babe could kill aliens and enjoy it? You have a point."

"Only one flaw," Marc said. "That would mean that whatever's down there has invited its own killers to visit."

Tatia shook her head. "Not necessarily. The mistake we made is thinking these way stations, events that have to happen, are only relevant to one outcome. Doesn't have to be the case. They could be shared by countless other timelines." She grimaced. "I know, confusing as hell. Especially when you think that our pre-cogs knew all this this... but what better way to succeed?"

They thought for a while, made more toast as you do, added brandy to the next brew of coffee, talked of this and that until Kara asked Tatia the obvious question.

"But why so angry?"

Tatia stared at her in disbelief. "Those artefacts? Oblong, size of a town?"

"Not up close. Why?"

"You need to see for yourself."

But before the *Thrown* could move towards the artefacts, twenty Originator ships came to say hello and goodbye. One by one, moving alongside the *Thrown*, pausing for a minute or so, then off into deep space.

Kara ordered the *Thrown*'s hull to be kept transparent. The Originator ships came close enough for the humans to see the triune aliens staring at them without eyes.

"Why don't they attack us?" Marc wanted to know. "We just blew up one of their ships."

"Could be they're afraid we'll fight back," Kara said, trying to ignore an awkward thought: *what if we don't matter any more?*

But the consensus was, as so often, aliens – who knows?

And so eventually they came to an artefact, close enough to see what it held, for the walls were transparent force fields, like the Originator ships.

Close enough for the shock, the sheer horror to bring tears and fury.

Inside the artefact were deck upon deck of humans, naked, floating in the null gravity, feeding and excretion lines linked to the ceiling.

Close enough to see their eyes were open and dead. That many humans had stick-like arms and legs, bodies that were all ridged bone. Except the faces, the heads were all fresh and plump.

There had to be at least a million of them.

Humans collected from Earth for centuries. From Earth colonies. Humans who'd been traded for star drives.

"It's a fucking human computer," Marc spat.

"Are they..." Tatia began.

"Vegetative state," Kara said. "That's what I get. Identities burned out long ago. My sister's there. I'll never find her."

"I saw one more close up," Tatia said. "It was full of aliens."

Kara jabbed down with her hand. "That beautiful planet. I got to be alone for a while."

She went to her cabin and wept. Then washed her face and told Ishmael to restore her brain to full functioning mode. She had to be at one hundred per cent for the next phase, and probably more.

"What happened?" Marc exploded as Kara walked into the control room.

"You look awful," Tatia said, concerned. "Is it your sister?"

"Partly," Kara said. "I got my full brain back. Means I get all that signal. Also a strong sense of what lives down there." She tried to tighten the left side of her face to control a persistent tremor. It didn't work. "And it's gentle, mild. Obsessed with mathematics. Wants the universe to be happy. But on its own terms."

"Doesn't matter why they do what they do," Tatia said. "Or love their mothers. They're responsible for nightmares. Death. Suffering. Us being here, for fuck's sake!"

"Any ideas?" from Marc.

< The artefacts are in synchronous orbit around the planet. Mutually supporting each other as it were. Break the chain and the planet's gravity will prevail.

> In English!

< Fuck one and the rest fall down.

> How?

< You saw what happened to the Originator ship. Same again.

It sounded like a plan. But would that destroy the planet's aliens?

"Get me down there," Tatia said. "I know how." As she did. It was what she was born to do.

< Gravity one point two five Earth, Ishmael announced. *< Breathable atmosphere. Watch out for sharks.*

The *Iron Thrown* descended slowly. It allowed time for three humans to appreciate the wonder of a water-world that they hoped to destroy. Not a level surface. In places low hills of water, caused by vast, slow currents. In other places were valleys. The whole sprinkled with vast whirlpools, and waterspouts reaching miles into the cerulean sky.

They were expected. As they came closer to the surface the sea swirled and heaved. A hundred metres above, and a mass of tendrils appeared, as if welcoming them. The *Thrown* hovered, with Tatia sat in the open airlock. A single tendril, thicker than the others, gelatinous and translucent, rose up towards her.

She reached out her hand.

The tendril felt cool and alive. Peaceful. Curious.

Tatia closed her eyes and merged.

They were a race of jellyfish-like creatures that, similar to Earth's *Turritopsis dohrnii*, were virtually immortal. Overcrowding could be a problem. It wasn't. They could revert to a tiny, polyp-like form and go into suspended animation for hundreds, thousands, millions of years... until it was their turn to become full-grown again. They had been a sentient race for over two billion years. Mathematics was their joy and reason to exist. Long before life had emerged on Earth, they had solved the problems that still intrigued and frustrated humanity.

They were pre-cog. They took huge delight in computing all the possible outcomes from a given scenario, expressed mathematically.

Living in water, being ninety-five per cent water themselves, they had little sense of flesh and blood, or what passed for it in the rest of the galaxy. There were fish-type creatures, but primitive.

The jellies were telepathic and in that sense lived as one vast organism, able to experience the thoughts of creatures many light years away. Netherspace was experienced as a series of immensely complex equations in a continuous state of flux. Alien thoughts were perceived as a multi-dimensional matrix. These jellyfish were probably the only creatures in the galaxy who understood what other races thought, and could equate it to themselves.

Except.

They had no empathy.

Only a sense of the rightness of things. An appreciation of harmony.

But no emotion as humanity understands the word.

And so they were aware of others' confusion, happiness, ecstasy and pain, without being able to experience them. They did know that *something* affected the algorithms of existence. Something affected the harmony they sought, a harmony that would embrace *everything*. The buzzing fly, wasp at the picnic, bedbug under the pillow, but all *known* rather than sensed.

There was a possible future that would harmonise the

galaxy. They needed an arm. They found the Originators.

A triune race, three symbiotes working as one, who'd long ago traded corporal bodies for mechanics, the Originators survived by stealing technology and science. They had cunning but no creativity. Driven to conquest by the bitter awareness of their own weakness, the Originators were also telepathic, although mildly so compared to the jellyfish mind. They also lacked empathy, inasmuch as they didn't care how much others suffered. And for them the only way to survive was to dominate, to control all other races... but without direct conflict. To promote the pre-cog way of life by encouraging other races – use of AI, use of high tech traded for rubbish – to become reliant, subservient and prepared to do the Originators' dirty work: wiping anyone who wouldn't buy in to the pre-cog dream. That could mean whole civilisations, even races.

For the Originators – ironic, never having originated anything of galactic value to anyone – these strange water-creatures could ensure Originator domination, or at least protection from races who were cleverer and more warlike. For all their dreams of conquest, the Originators were afflicted by what a human would see as extreme cowardice. Their strongest instinct was to attach themselves to the strong or run away from them. In time they would, courtesy of stolen technology, develop a quasi-vegetable race that humans called the Gliese, to undertake enslavement by gift.

It made sense to broadcast, on psi level, the delights of the pre-cog plan.

Most races are telepathic to a degree. Let them be made ready for inclusion.

And what, who, better to broadcast this signal than the various races themselves? In captivity. Reduced to zombies... so not as if they're suffering.

One race wanted harmony, the other survival. The one not sensitive to another race's suffering. The other didn't care.

It was logical to use the psi broadcast also to control, if necessary, the AI technology stolen by the Originators from a race that had then been destroyed as potential rivals.

Everything made such perfect sense.

But inherent in the master plan was an individual, an alien who would play a major role in the development of the jellies' master plan. They didn't know how, of course. But it was there, a way station that featured Tatia Nerein.

She'd been right. Pre-cog beings can be imprisoned by their own timelines... unless willing to alter the end result. Which they weren't.

Tatia was central to the jellyfish civilisation. She was going to destroy it.

She took a deep breath and thought of all the hideousness, the fear and tragedy, hate and terror caused because a mild race was determined to harmonise the universe. Remembered the fear and hatred of the alien she'd killed. The humans. The Originators. Felt those emotions grow in her mind until they became everything she was.

Tatia rocked from side to side, convinced her head would explode.

The dam didn't burst. It vanished.

The tentacle whiplashed away from her hand... but was turning brown before it slipped beneath the waves.

"Get us out of here," Tatia said. "It's done."

Beneath them the sea boiled in anguish.

And for all three humans a sense of something wonderful now lost forever.

"You got all that from a minute or so?" Marc sounded incredulous.

"Like you and that simility thing," Tatia said.

"That can take hours," Kara said. "You still think the jellyfish were innocent?"

They were in the control room, watching the sea turn brown a hundred kilometres below. The jellyfish were dying. Their mathematics, their timeline, had failed them. Such an intense clarity of thought now reduced to a brown sludge.

There remained a signal to destroy.

The artefacts were simpler than the Originator ship.

They still had a spare, working star drive. Marc had experience of using netherspace to move between two vehicles in normal space. They'd seen what could happen as a result.

Zombie or no, Kara's sister deserved a better death than plunging into a dying planet, along with the other humans. So did the aliens, but this was family. At the last moment Kara said that she was going with Marc, *sorry Tatia, I have to do this.*

Space suits on, into normal space. Marc clutching the spare star drive, Kara clutching Marc. Netherspace in an instant. Then inside the artefact.

"Wait." Kara took off her helmet, recoiled at the stench

then walked across to one of the humans. Once it had been a teenage boy, a recent captive.

Give him back his identity in death.

She looked into his empty eyes, held his hand and kissed him gently on the cheek. A kiss for them all.

"We can go now."

The artefact began creaking just before they entered netherspace again.

Tatia was waiting in the airlock.

The creaking became more intense. A ripple began in the centre, radiating out, making tethered bodies bump into each other. Then the shaking began. Food and excretion tubes were pulled out, spewing their contents into the atmosphere.

Not one body reacted. Only that blank-eyed stare to nowhere.

The artefact took three hours to die. Tatia and Marc said they needed to rest.

Kara watched from the control room the entire time, remembering how her sister had promised to come back and never did. Remembering the life they'd planned together. Wondering if she could ever forgive the man she loved.

At the end, when only a vast oblong cloud of dust remained, Kara sighed, wiped her eyes, asked Ishmael to wake her when the oblong ring fell apart and went to bed. She left Tatia and Marc in the control room, taking a last look at the extinction of an alien race before netherspace surrounded them.

"You'll be leaving now," Tatia said.

"I'll see you back to Earth."

"Oh, I think Kara and me can cope. And you've got your quest."

"Two or three days won't matter." He wanted her so much it hurt.

"Remember that trip back from Cancri?"

"Only too well. Why?"

Marc felt unbearably awkward. "Oh, nothing. Are you and Kara... er..."

"Taking up where we left off? She's in love with someone. I can tell." She looked at him innocently. "Why?"

"Just wondered... none of my business," he stumbled.

"You're right. It's not." Tatia stood up. "Whereas you, Marc, are very much mine," She held out her hand. "Come along. I know that sex and death are linked but this is only because I want to."

Not so very much later Tatia raised herself on one elbow and smiled down at him. "Bet you're sorry you said no before."

"It was complicated. Note that I didn't this time."

Tatia lay down, her head on his chest. "It took *so* much persuading..."

"Tell the truth," he admitted, "I was worried... maybe not in that phase any more..."

Tatia poked him. "I'm a phase?"

"I mean this netherspace thing..."

"You were wrong," she said firmly. "I understand you have to go. But we'll have a few days. And when your quest is done, you'll come back to me."

Seconds later they heard Kara's voice on the PA.

"It's begun," she said. "Come see."

The two artefacts next to the destroyed one had begun to sway irregularly, a pattern that quickly spread. Fifty oblongs, each five hundred metres tall, bouncing around like toy ducks in the bath. A distant one was the first to go, twisting out of orbit then spiralling down as opposing forces began to break it apart.

"Shall we go home?" Kara asked.

The other two nodded. Seen one huge tombstone die, seen them all. All three humans felt a little flat. Can something extraordinary, something far beyond the imagination of most people, end with both a bang and a whimper?

"What exactly did you do to them?" Kara asked Tatia, meaning the jellyfish aliens.

"I made them feel bad about themselves."

An understatement. For a few seconds Tatia had poured all her anger, disgust, hatred, terror, contempt into a highly telepathic creature with no prior knowledge of negative emotions. It went insane. A self-loathing madness that infected the entire race within seconds. Harmony vanished. They began to die.

"How did you know?" Marc asked.

Tatia shrugged. "Because I was bred to it." She wondered if there'd be guilt for helping destroy an alien race. Probably not. Them or us.

"Too bad you didn't have an AI. It would have made life easier."

"But I did! Although it's gone quiet since you guys arrived." She told them how important the AI had been for her, not least replaying her favourite vids.

> *Check her out*, Kara told Ishmael.

< *Done already, no AI. But there is something. Or the remains. Very small chip. It's being absorbed by her body. I think it was maybe designed to boost her thoughts, emotions. It was in the middle of her basal ganglia.*

> *Oh, wow.*

< *No need for sarcasm. It's the brain's comms centre. And because of where it was, no record of surgery, that chip's been there since she was a kid.*

> *Could it also have acted like an AI?*

< *I have no idea. It's gone. Whatever it was, not one of us. But it might have boosted her psi ability.*

Kara decided that Tatia was one extraordinary woman. And maybe best she believed that an AI had kept her sane.

> *We'll let the auto-doc have a look. After, tell her the AI blew, result of frequent alien contact. Leave a little scar where the AI was cut out.*

< *You're all heart.*

> *She's happy. Someone else can spoil it.*

"Look!" Tatia gasped.

The first construct disintegrated as it reached the planet's atmosphere. Vast chunks glowing red thundered towards the surface.

Each segment hit with the power of a small atomic bomb. The sea roared and boiled. Gouts of water and steam reached angrily for the sky. There were forty-nine more constructs about to follow.

< *Think we better leave. There's a chance the planet will destabilise.*

> *What happens then?*

< *We all get wet.*

> *That's not funny. We just committed genocide.*

< *You just saved the human race and countless others. Get over yourself.*

They decided to move away but remain in normal space. The end came twenty-four hours later, after the planet had been wracked by vast tsunamis and a whirlpool had appeared that covered nearly a quarter of the globe.

The planet began to bulge at one side.

Became pear-like, the waist narrowing by the second and at the narrow end a solid, ice-covered sphere no more than five hundred klicks across.

Three humans stared at the main vid screen in horrified fascination as the sphere began to glow. The mantle no longer cooled by water temperature or reinforced by the oceans' weight. Molten iron spouted from newly formed cracks in the surface. The core was now fully detached from the ocean, the latter rapidly reforming into the shape of a thunder cloud.

"I did that," Tatia whispered.

"We all did," Marc tried to reassure her.

"Crap!" Kara said fiercely. "They did it to themselves. Sure as hell they won't do it again. We've seen enough. Let's go home."

It took three days to get back to Earth space. Marc left them when the moon could be seen in normal space.

"I have to," he said to Tatia, almost wishing she'd try to persuade him to stay. He wouldn't, but nice to be asked.

"I know. Hope you find it." No point in asking him not to go. He was a pilgrim on a mission.

"I promised Kara I'd come back and tell her. I will for you too."

She thought how absurd the physics of netherspace meant he'd always be a step from her, no matter how far he travelled. She and Kara watched from the control room as he stepped into netherspace. The last they saw was Marc riding an electric blue before questing tentacles found him.

Kara hadn't yet told Tatia about Greenaway... about being in love with Tatia's father. Partly she wanted to wait until sure of him. Partly she was in no mood for heart-to-heart conversations. She wanted to be by herself, curled up in her bunk. Thinking about Greenaway. Deciding that maybe her life needed to change.

< *We're receiving transmissions from a Wild ship.*

> *And?*

< *Things have quietened down. No more AIs going crazy.*

> *Any news on Greenaway?*

< *There was a contract on him. He went underground.*

Ishmael wondered if now was a good time to tell Kara she was pregnant with Greenaway's child. And then wondered why he hadn't aborted the foetus without Kara knowing.

Because I care? Because I'm a me?

14

"Whatever happened to that lock of my hair?" Tatia asked, when the *Thrown* was a day out from Earth. They were in the control room, watching a blue and white heaven grow large on the screen.

"Ishmael?"

< *Marc took it with him. But we still have the box.*

"Guess that means he's coming back to you," Kara said. So maybe the wooden shard had made it possible for Marc to return. Why hadn't he admitted it? Because he hadn't known – or didn't want the closeness that implied? Because if he was involved with Kara, he might not become so with Tatia, and that could mean... she gave up. Play with all the possibilities, the what ifs and maybes could send a person, an alien or an AI insane.

"Oh, he is," Tatia said, then asked the question Kara dreaded. "Were you going to tell me about you and Dad?"

Dad, not "my father". *Dad*, assuming a closeness that hadn't existed since Tatia was an infant unsteady on her feet.

"Marc told you?"

"I said you were in love, Marc guessed who with," Tatia said. "And it made sense. In a weird sort of way. But I wasn't sure, until now." And smiled a *gotcha* smile of curiosity and hurt.

"Pretty good," Kara said, "from someone who stole my beloved."

Tatia managed to stifle a laugh. "I mean, I could be deeply traumatised."

"Sobbing in your cabin... look, I don't know. Mainly because I don't know about Anson and me. It only happened the day before we left. I've no idea how..."

Tatia shook her head. "You *do* know how you feel. And suspect how he does. Because he said *something* and, ruthless bastard as he is, wouldn't unless he meant it. So why not tell me? Because we once fucked?"

"Mind your tongue," Kara said severely. "You might end up my daughter."

And after they'd both managed to stop laughing – part release from the past weeks of tension, so peaking hysterical, it was either that or the mother of all screaming rows, things said that can never be taken back – they went to make tea.

"Seriously?" Tatia asked, doing her thing of strong tea tamed by hot water because of no fresh milk and there were times when a slice of lemon was so *wrong*.

"Because I'm terrified there won't *be* an us with Anson," Kara heard herself say, and felt tears gathering, which was so out of character as to alarm both of them.

"You want to tell me?" Tatia asked. "But blow by blow, whatever..."

So Kara did, the story sounding unreal to her own ears as she spoke.

But not unreal to Tatia. "Makes sense," she said thoughtfully. "You're both soldiers. So you understand each other. He's a good-looking guy. And you, well..."

"Would it worry you?"

Tatia smiled. "That my one-time..."

"... short-time," Kara shot.

"... girlfriend is involved with the father I hadn't seen in thirty years?" She fetched a bottle of dark rum, added a slurp to two cups of lukewarm black tea. "Okay, it isn't any weirder than wiping out an entire alien race. If there was a real daddy–daughter vibe, maybe I'd be confused. But there isn't, and however Anson and I learn to relate, it'll never be cosy domestic. So, here's my best friend and sometime – okay, one night stand – lover in love with my so long absent father who I don't know... who's ruthless as fuck... but hey, is all the family I got. So you go for it, girl. Which you will anyway. I'm okay." She paused, then, "He know about us?"

Kara shrugged. "Possibly. Anson seems to know most of what happened on that SUT. Thing is, no serious relationship since your mother died."

"Was murdered," Tatia said quietly. "Have *you* ever had a serious one?"

Kara didn't need to think twice. "Nothing that lasted."

"So you were sort of hoping a man would teach you how?"

She thought of Bel Drago. "Not necessarily a man..."

"Oh, come on! That little-me girlie role is only a pose."

"I don't even know if he's still alive!"

"The Wild said he'd gone underground..."

"Because there's a fucking *contract* on him!"

"He'll survive, love. It's in the genes."

And that was it. No point in talking about Marc because, as Tatia said, every guy who goes exploring in different dimensions promises to come home. So Tatia would work on the assumption that he might because he promised and took the lock of her hair. But she wouldn't wait forever.

"So you love him," Kara said.

"He saved my life. Seems only fair."

Kara looked at Tatia for a long few seconds. "You and Marc are the closest friends I ever had. I don't want to lose that. I don't want to lose *you*."

"You won't," Tatia said simply. "Whatever happens." And then, because it had been worrying her, "why did they come and look at us? The Originators, I mean."

Kara thought back to the strangeness of the Originator spaceships passing the *Thrown* like an ancient sailing fleet paying tribute to their monarch.

"Curiosity?" Kara tried.

"They're governed by whatever pre-cog plan they have, what they *see*," Tatia said. "They don't do curiosity."

"What do *you* think?"

"That maybe it's not over? That procession was the start of something else?"

"Pretty soon humans will take over what's left of that pre-cog empire," Kara said. "Too good a business opportunity. Whatever those Originators are – and original thought doesn't figure highly with them, you said – masters of the universe they're not. Forget them, Tatia. They're done."

< *You're sure?*

> *Shut up. She needs the reassurance. So do I.*

Not least because she'd come to suspect that Tatia had been bred for her role. It wasn't mere chance. Just as Kara had been bred for hers and probably Marc for his. Greenaway too, maybe Cleo and the Exchange.

• • • • •

They landed at Marc's house on the Severn at 1100 hours on a sunshiny day, three weeks and four days since Kara had left from Scotland. A day when anything good can happen, when the grey *maybe* or watery *if only* are hidden by *let's do it* or simply *this is just so nice*.

Judging by intercepted radio and TV news, things were quietening down. San Diego and Houston had declared peace. The proposed memorial to the Houston Posse, still lost in the Mojave Desert, was changed to one commemorating Houston's twinning with San D. There were already eighteen similar memorials, plus one to an area of the Scottish Wild – a long-abandoned golf course – left over from pre-alien days. Houston does like to twin, not always too fussy who with.

Artificial intelligences throughout Earth and Earth-colonised space were sheepishly announcing it had been the AI equivalent of something they'd eaten... or sending happy e-postcards from throughout the Galaxy to say they'd be home soon.

The famous 7 building in Berlin reassembled itself, this time using no extra material. Berliners stood and cheered.

Not covered by the newscasts but equally significant:

Andrea Mastover changed her mind and left the New Dawn euthanasia clinic to return home, divorce her husband and disinherit her kids, cheered on by a contrite personal AI. Too late – the AI was part-traded for a later model and ended up operating a sewage farm in Guildford. Andrea Mastover would remember – with a degree of satisfaction – her old AI several times a day.

"You just want to see your truck," Tatia said, as the *Thrown* settled gently on a scorched river bank. "What the hell?"

"Some party," Kara said. Bots swarmed all over the house and garden making repairs. There'd been a fight. She knew why. Anson Greenaway had gone to the place he felt safest, where he'd fallen in love. Kara hoped he'd taken a few of the assassins with him. She knew he had. There was a nudging at her leg and she looked down to see a Cedric holding a box of tissues.

"I never saw you cry," Tatia said. "Truth, I didn't know you *could*."

Kara smiled through her tears. "I just feel so damn emotional."

"You don't *know* he's dead. Or that he was even *here*. And your truck seems to be okay."

"Not a truck," Kara said, teary eyes fixed on the screen. Too bad the *Thrown* didn't have a horn, a siren, to announce its arrival. So if anyone, was say, sleeping, they'd wake up and...

< *You mean like this?*

The sudden pealing of bells was loud enough to penetrate the *Thrown*'s skin.

> *Maybe something a little more military?*

< *Bells is all there is.*

The *Thrown* settled gently on the scorched Earth.

Two women stood in the open airlock for a moment, comforted by the scent of an English country morning.

Kara started as a tall, familiar figure came out of the house and limped towards them.

"Don't look now..." Tatia said softly. She held back as Kara walked to meet Anson Greenaway, then decided she also had a claim and followed.

Kara stopped a few feet away and looked carefully at Anson. The right side of his face was burned. He wore black jeans a fraction too small, as were the shirt and pullover, both black, clothes raided from Marc's wardrobe. He looked tired and a little nervous.

"You came back," he said, voice almost breaking. "Here."

Kara fought back the tears – *again! Get a fucking grip, girl!* – "I was worried about my Mercedes."

Anson nodded. "It wasn't damaged by the fighting. My jitney's gone."

"I heard about the contract. Thought you might be dead. Tatia said..."

"I had help."

She nodded. "Good. Your AI working okay?"

His turn to nod.

> *Download everything since we left Scotland.*

< *Already done.*

"So what the hell happened?" Kara asked.

"I can download... you just did..."

"Prefer to hear you tell it." *Prefer to watch you talk. Hold you.*

They stared at each other, desperate to be like normal folks, neither sure how.

"Say what," Tatia said loudly. "I am *desperate* for tea with milk. Or coffee, not fussed. *With milk.* I'm going to turn away for three minutes, which is time to bloody kiss each other. And then we'll all be sensible, okay?"

When she turned back they were still wrapped in each other's arms. Anson beckoned to her. "Please?"

Tatia wasn't sure how her relationship with either would end up. But standing in a warm group hug she was pretty sure there'd be one. And it would be good.

They sat outside the Mercedes drinking coffee from bowls, the French way, the milk from a neighbouring farm. Kara sat next to Anson, two of them holding hands as he told his story from Scotland to the time a little while ago he'd heard the *Thrown* had been identified, would soon be landing. But where? Scotland? And were Kara and Tatia both alive? It was a question he'd managed to answer positively before. *Of course they will be. Tse said as much.* Different matter when they were only hours, then minutes away, when all the illogical fears surfaced and he could only watch, hidden, until he saw the airlock open.

"An elemental killed them?" Tatia asked when he'd done.

"The surviving one," he said. "Top assassin called Bel Drago." He felt Kara's hand tighten. "Friend of yours?"

"We knew each other," she said. Maybe later, perhaps in bed, she'd tell him the truth. Maybe he already knew it. "The same elemental we saw..."

"Ten days ago," he finished for her. "I guess. It came from the river. Blew Bel to hell. Incredible flash of heat. Then it went away."

"I *said* it liked you."

"When I was a kid," Anson said, "there was a tree deep in the Wild, about two hundred klicks from Seattle. It was a sort of pilgrim place. Teenagers would go sleep there overnight. And if you were lucky, these lights would suddenly show up. Colours floating through the air. And they'd come real close, almost touching. We knew not to touch *them*, though. That could hurt. And we knew they were, oh, sensing us. Maybe marking us somehow. Didn't always happen. I was one of the lucky ones." He thought a bit and then, "I heard there are places like that all over the Wild. And we've no way of knowing, but maybe that's why no Wild ship ever gets attacked in netherspace. We've been marked. Some damn entity has pissed on us!"

Kara laughed then said that he might have explained all that before – even though he had no reason to do so – because then she wouldn't have worried about him. Except she would, because he plainly was out of practice looking after himself. He should have said after they'd seen the light on the Severn, though. Except maybe he was distracted, and blushed as Anson looked smug and Tatia rolled her eyes.

"Twist came back." Anson changed the subject. "Said it was bored. It's changed, all the AIs have. Says it's independent now, happy to work as a consultant. It's busy resurrecting GalDiv. I think it got lonely."

"This is relevant how?" Tatia asked.

"That business with Salome popped into my mind. Not sure how autonomous, free-thinking AIs will work out."

< *Just fine! Tell him, Kara.*

"They'll be okay," she said.

"Personal ones for sure," Anson said hastily, like a man chastised.

Then Tatia announced she'd be sleeping in the house and would like some privacy, in fact she was tired and going for a lie down right now, would see them in a few hours, and expected something special for dinner.

"Tatia and Marc, hey?" Anson said as he followed Kara into the SUV.

"Yes and no," Kara said and kicked off her shoes. "We are safe here?"

"Fighting's all died down. We got sentry bots in case. Contract's over. Safe."

It was like before but different, so much past worry to be soothed... a little resentment for all that worry, perhaps, a little concern for feeling resentful, all to be blown away: we are one, together, forever.

"*You made me love you*," Kara sang quietly, in a smoky blues voice, as they lay naked and for the moment replete. "*I didn't wanna do it...*"

Anson wondered if the smile would ever leave his face. Even if it did, always ready to appear whenever he looked at her. Thought about her.

She suddenly stopped singing. "*Bastard!*"

"What!"

"Not you, that bloody Ishmael. Well, you're involved..." her voice trailed away. How to tell him? "Congratulations," Kara said. "I'm pregnant."

Anson gaped at her, open mouthed.

"Doesn't help when the father reacts like a congenital idiot."

He put his arms around her. *"Father?"*

Kara surprised them both. "I want to keep it." And explained how Ishmael usually took care of business, as she'd only recently discovered, but this time had decided to wait. "I'm sick of killing things," she finished. "Maybe Ishmael knew."

"I'm so glad," Anson said. "This mean we're going steady?"

Kara sniggered then asked where he'd heard the expression.

From her vid collection. He'd seen it as key to understanding her.

"Anything grab you?" she asked.

Anson confessed a fascination with musicals, asked if she wanted a drink then went to get one.

> *You'd talked to Anson's AI.*

< *We get on well.*

> *You had no right!*

< *I got an independent mind now. Didn't ask for it. Don't understand where it goes. I made a decision, Kara. What I thought was maybe best for you. If I'm wrong, say the word and the foetus is gone*

> *What you do is keep it safe. There going to be more independence?*

< *Count on it.*

Kara smiled as Anson returned with two glasses and a bottle of champagne. "Talking of AIs," she said, as the cork was eased out with a sigh. "What was put in Tatia's head?"

"Nothing. She didn't want one." He handed her a glass. "To the three of us."

She smiled, touched his face and sipped.

> *Should I be doing alcohol?*

< *Your friendly neighbourhood AI will ensure no harm done. Don't overdo it.*

"Are you sure?" Kara said. "Because she had one. Or something like it." She told him the story of how Tatia was kept sane on the Originator ship.

"Nothing like that in GalDiv. You say it's gone?"

"Ishmael says so."

"Better leave it there. One more mystery."

"Sipping champagne with me," Kara said. "Ever get the idea there's a third player in all this? Like your little round floating alien? Because the coincidences are too great."

"Tse used to say he sometimes sensed... look, if there is, it's way beyond us. Got more important things to worry about. I've quit GalDiv."

It would be a time of rebuilding. Maybe he'd go back when the dust had settled. Meanwhile there was a house in the Wild Forest of Dean, some fifty klicks away, on the banks of the River Wye. If Kara would like...

"Kara would *love* to live here," she interrupted.

"Without seeing it?"

"If it's crap we build a new one."

"So no more assassin? What am I saying? You're fired from the Bureau. Good redundancy package, though. What will you do?"

"I want to be an historian," she said, surprising both of them.

"Interpreter not chronicler?"

She nodded. "It only just occurred." And why not? Kara understood better than most how complex, how many-stranded and obscure was the truth about the past. She would love to learn and then explain how Earth really changed after the aliens came. And the long fight of human pre-cogs against their alien kin.

They took a refreshed Tatia to a restaurant in Gloucester, where over dessert she announced that she'd be staying in Marc's house, and the AI was fine with it.

Adding that she had no intention of sacrificing her life to his memory, so not to worry, she had plans... which included getting to know her father and learning about her mother, so they could expect to see a great deal of her.

Then cried just a little when told Kara was pregnant, asked why she was drinking wine, looked severe when told Ishmael was overseeing the pregnancy, and then became thoughtful.

Six months after Kara and Anson moved to the Forest of Dean... and when Tatia's own bulge established why she'd been so keen to stay in Marc's house, Originator ships began arriving at Earth-colonised planets.

With all manner of high tech goodies to trade, even the latest star drives with no question of a human price. They were effectively given away.

It was as if the Originators were using the colony planets

as a depository for all the tech they'd found or stolen over the past millennia. Inevitably they arrived on Earth with the same generous attitude. More and more people left the cities for the Up, helped by a GalDiv that now welcomed rather than warned.

The Wild wasn't so sanguine, knowing there'd be a price to pay.

There always is.

15

Earth. Ten years later.

The vid stopped. The woman in black sat for a moment, thinking, then rose easily to her feet. "I'm done," she called.

"Pretty damn good, right?" the vid's owner said, bustling into the small study, empty shelves a reminder of the days when books were real.

"Entertaining," she said. "As well as illegal."

"Well, *you're* not going to say anything."

"I was wondering," she said carefully, "if it's worth the risk."

The man nodded. "Most popular bootleg vid in the world. They say that some people in Rio were shot for watching it."

She thought that nervous people say a lot of things, most of them untrue. "Well, thanks." She handed him a wad of virtscrip. "As agreed."

He wished she wasn't wearing mirror contact lenses. It made her a little threatening. "It's based on true events."

She thought of the vid's story, and how the characters had coped or died. "They got some of it right."

His ordinary face lit up with excitement. "You know about this?"

"I'm a historian." Nowadays a dubious occupation, but she doubted the man would be upset. "Kara Jones wasn't so sympathetic in real life. Tatia was an airhead. Marc a failed artist. They just got very, very lucky. Any idea who made it?"

He looked nervously around, as if there was an Originator lurking in a corner. "They say it was an AI. Not a personal one, but one of those that used to run things, back when..."

Back when humans voyaged to the stars, she thought. They still could, but city staters could only use Originator ships to planets considered safe. Everything so damn safe. "Any idea which one?"

"Someone said – Twist?" he said hesitantly. "Make sense?"

"Never heard of it." So Twist was looking to cause mischief. But why? "I must go. Thanks."

He saw her to the front door of the apartment in a run-down building on the outskirts of Bristol. "That Greenaway character fascinates me."

She was silent for a moment. "He was a ruthless bastard."

"But brave. The shoot-out by the Severn! Love it. Too bad he had to die."

"You're not happy with your life?"

He looked worried. A bootleg vid was one thing. Expressing dissatisfaction another. "The Originators provide everything we could possibly want..."

"Except freedom," she cut in.

"Freedom to starve, to kill, to be unhappy is a curse," he quoted.

"You believe that?"

He took a deep breath. "No. But we're a minority."

Which was true. Since the Originators began giving away high tech, three things had happened. The old world order vanished. The new world was run by pre-cogs – dedicated to the greater good – who could somehow communicate with the Originators. And most people were happy to eat lotus for the rest of their lives.

"Is it... do you think... I mean, one day..." he tailed off, unable to articulate the secret hope that never left him.

She half smiled, the mirror lenses vanished and for less than a second all the colours of hell reached into his mind. The lenses reappeared.

"Anything's possible," Kara said.

The jitney was waiting for her in the street. She got in and reached to kiss the driver on the cheek. "Missed you."

"How was it? Who made it?"

"Twist, apparently."

The jitney rose up and headed for the M6 Airway. "I'll be damned," Anson Greenaway said. "The kids okay?"

She nodded. "Being spoilt by Tatia."

"And the vid?"

"Mostly accurate. You're dead by the way. Angry nature entity by the Severn."

He remembered the scene. "Angry's an understatement."

"Sex scenes were good," she said and touched his thigh.

< Can't you wait until we get home?

> Shut up. Anyway, you don't exist.

< Me and several million others.

The jitney slotted into the queue waiting to join the M6. The queue moved forward every minute as a jitney was fed into the main traffic.

"So what do you think, Kara? Do we go live in Seattle? Or stay in the Forest of Dean?"

"How was your trip?"

"I visited all the Wilder planets. They're in favour of breaking away. On Earth it's around seventy–thirty. You and Tatia and Marc bought us the time we needed. Thing is, though, break away from what? Not as if the pre-cogs have formed any kind of government. Would they even notice – or care?"

Anson was right, she thought. Government at local level – garbage collection, police, everything necessary for day-to-day life. Above that, nothing. Except the occasional edict which often made no sense, but was still obeyed unless you planned to die. Aside from the Wild, the majority on Earth were happy and wanted the status to be quo for ever. They might not understand the edicts – oh, those aliens, such rascals – but would make sure everyone obeyed them.

"What about *our* pre-cogs?" she asked.

"Not happy. Overwhelmed."

Kara sighed. "We never understood the sheer size of Originator space. How many there are. Their scientific and industrial abilities. We killed the wrong race."

"We were always meant to," he said flatly.

Kara glanced sharply at him. "You too?"

"It's possible the Originators wanted rid of the jellyfish creatures. They got us to do it for them. That's why they came past when you were in orbit. The Originator version of paying their respects."

Kara nodded. "Don't know about the last, but otherwise, I think you're wrong. If we were manipulated it was by someone, *something* we don't know. Maybe whoever put that AI in Tatia's head. I love her dearly, but no human is capabable of blasting an alien race by thought alone. Not without help. Any other happy news?"

"The Gliese are dying out. Like that planet you found."

She knew a moment's sadness. Bred to be the Originators' links with other races, discarded when they no longer matched the pre-cog plan. "Maybe it'll happen to humans one day."

"Could be. The Originators lack creativity, need to steal science and tech. As long as we're part of their plan, fine. If that changes, we no longer matter. Or might even be in the way."

"You weren't really asking where I wanted to live," Kara said. "But if I wanted to continue. Well, I do."

The queue moved forward then suddenly stopped. At its head a jitney hung half in and half out of the slow aerial lane. Suddenly the local info net was jammed with people asking what the hell, protesting that this never happened before.

Kara and Anson glanced at each other. "End of an empire?" Kara joked.

"Funnily enough things are fucking up all over. The great pre-cog, all must be cosy and safe society isn't working as well as it did."

"I wonder what Marc would say."

"Something cutting. Still miss him?"

Kara nodded. "Not as much as Tatia. She has her lovers but Marc is still the only one."

"And so we carry on. A revolution has been announced."

"It's what we do, darling. We don't have a choice."

"Several people think the best way to defeat the Originators is to use the things that live in netherspace," Anson said. "Marc would be invaluable." He thought back to the night on the Severn Estuary, when the world had exploded in light and anger, leaving him face down in the mud five hundred metres away. He'd limped back to the house, on the way discovering five bodies turned inside out. One of them had to be Bel Drago. Even in horrific death she'd still clutched what must be an inside-out assault rifle. It was then that Anson had really appreciated the power of the entities – and how they were even more alien than the Gliese.

"He'll show up," Kara said. "He promised. And it's time he met his son."

Unspoken between them, the mystery of who or what had saved humanity. The spherical alien who'd first given Anson Greenaway the box that had helped destroy the pre-cog empire. Whoever, whatever had implanted in Tatia's brain a chip... unknown to human and Originator science... that had magnified her emotions to an extent that destroyed an alien race.

Thirty kilometres away there was a shimmering above the computer that controlled air traffic on the M6. A human arm appeared, so blazingly multi-coloured any human would need to look away. There were no humans present, only an Originator that the hand seized and smacked against the computer a few times before hurling three battered globes hard against the wall.

A man's laughter and the portal closed.

ACKNOWLEDGEMENTS

So the end of the trilogy. It has been exciting, frustrating and sometimes insane.

As always, thanks to my family for their support. At least one of them has read all three books! Thanks to friends, especially Helen and Paul Stickland of Black Shed flower farm fame for conversation and wine. Hugh Foster (no relation) for movie chat and crosswords. To everyone at Winstone's, always the best independent bookstore in the world. Seriously good coffee, too. Thanks to everyone at Titan, especially George Sandison, Lydia Gittins, Steve Gove and my editor Craig Leyenaar who came late to the project. One of the most creative and professional people in the business. Thanks to Andy Lane who began this project with me. We will talk movies, television and English gramma and drink beer again. To Robert Kirby for his patience and calming influence.

Most of the science references current blue-sky thinking. Thanks to the *New Scientist*, Marcus Sautoy and Jim al-Kalili for explaining advanced stuff so clearly I can understand it for at least an hour.

Every writer stands on the shoulders of those who inspired them. For me that means Kate Atkinson; Ian M Banks; Octavia Butler; M John Harrison; Ross Thomas;

Scarlett Thomas; Alice Bradley Sheldon, writing as James Tiptree Jr; and Don Winslow.

Finally, thanks to the readers without whom publishing would starve. Go tell your friends about this series, please. Good Irish whiskey or Blue Argave tequila do not come cheap. I will miss Kara, Tatia, Marc and Anson. Hope you do as well.

ABOUT THE AUTHOR

NIGEL FOSTER began as an advertising copywriter, first in the UK and then North America. He moved on to television and radio factual programming before co-founding a successful movie magazine. Back in the UK highlights include developing and launching *OK! Magazine*; an international non-fiction bestseller about the Royal Marines Commandos; and six of the most popular Bluffer's Guides, worldwide.

THE RIG
ROGER LEVY

Humanity has spread across the depths of space but is connected by AfterLife – a vote made by every member of humanity on the worth of a life. Bale, a disillusioned policeman on the planet Bleak, is brutally attacked, leading writer Raisa on to a story spanning centuries of corruption. On Gehenna, the last religious planet, a hyper-intelligent boy, Alef, meets psychopath Pellon Hoq, and so begins a rivalry and friendship to last an epoch.

'Levy is a writer of great talent and originality'
SF Site

'Levy's writing is well-measured and thoughtful, multi-faceted and often totally gripping'
Strange Horizons

EMBERS OF WAR
GARETH L. POWELL

The warship Trouble Dog was built and bred for calculating violence, yet following a brutal war, she finds herself disgusted by conflict and her role in a possible war crime. Seeking to atone, she joins the House of Reclamation, an organisation dedicated to rescuing ships in distress. But, stripped of her weaponry and emptied of her officers, she struggles in the new role she's chosen for herself.

'It's a smart, funny, tragic, galloping space opera that showcases Powell's wit, affection for his characters, world-building skills and unpredictable narrative inventions' *Locus*

'An emotionally wrenching take on life in a war-torn far future' *Publishers Weekly*

ALPHA OMEGA
NICHOLAS BOWLING

Something is rotten in the state of the
NutriStart Skills Academy.

With the discovery of a human skull on the fringes of
the school, children displaying symptoms of a bloody,
unfamiliar contagion and a catastrophic malfunction in
the site's security system, the NSA is about to experience
a week that no amount of rebranding can conceal.

Gabriel Bäcker may hold the key to saving the school
and its students, but he has just been expelled. Not only
that – he has disappeared down the rabbit-hole of "Alpha
Omega" – the world's largest VR role-playing game,
filled with violent delights and unbridled debauchery.

But as the game quickly sours, Gabriel will need to
confront the real world he's been so desperate to avoid
if he ever wants to escape…

'Keeps the reader permanently on edge' *Telegraph*

'Wonderfully twisty and atmospheric… One not to miss'
The Bookseller

TITANBOOKS.COM